Also by Ellen Hopkins

Crank

Burned

Impulse

Glass

Identical

Tricks

Fallout

Margaret K. McElderry Books

Perfect

Ellen Hopkins

Margaret K. McElderry Books
NEW YORK LONDON TORONTO SYDNEY

MARGARET K. McELDERRY BOOKS

An imprint of Simon & Schuster Children's Publishing Division

1230 Avenue of the Americas, New York, New York 10020

This book is a work of fiction. Any references to historical events, real people, or real locales are used fictitiously. Other names, characters, places, and incidents are products of the author's imagination, and any resemblance to actual events or locales or persons, living or dead, is entirely coincidental.

MARGARET K. McELDERRY BOOKS is a trademark of Simon & Schuster, Inc.

For information about special discounts for bulk purchases, please contact Simon & Schuster Special Sales at 1-866-506-1949 or business@simonandschuster.com.

The Simon & Schuster Speakers Bureau can bring authors to your live event. For more information or to book an event, contact the Simon & Schuster Speakers Bureau at 1-866-248-3049 or visit our website at www.simonspeakers.com.

Book edited by Emma D. Dryden

Book design by Mike Rosamilia

The text for this book is set in Trade Gothic Condensed No. 18.

Manufactured in the United States of America

10 9 8 7 6 5 4

Library of Congress Cataloging-in-Publication Data

Hopkins, Ellen.

Perfect / Ellen Hopkins.

p. cm.

ISBN 978-1-4169-8324-8 (hardcover)

ISBN 978-1-4424-2357-2 (eBook)

[1. Novels in verse. 2. Self-esteem—Fiction. 3. Perfectionism (Personality trait)—Fiction.
4. Interpersonal relations—Fiction. 5. Family life—Nevada—Fiction. 6. Nevada—Fiction.]
I. Title.

PZ7.5.H67Per 2011

[Fic]—dc22

2010037543

This book is dedicated to every person who has ever looked into a mirror and thought, "I'm not good enough."

With special thanks to all the people who have convinced me I am good enough. To my mom and dad, who encouraged my talents; and to the teachers who honed those gifts. To my husband, who gathered me in, and to my children, who taught me patience. To my cadre of friends who prop me up when I need it. To Ash Canyon Poets, who helped grow my poetry, and SCBWI, which showed me the way.

To my agent, Laura Rennert, and the Andrea Brown Literary Agency. To my editor and friend, Emma Dryden. To the whole crew at Simon & Schuster who help my books be the best they can be. To teachers and librarians, who share my books with their kids. And, finally, to my readers, who keep faith in me.

Acknowledgments

I must acknowledge the dozens of readers who shared personal stories about eating disorders, beauty pageant experiences, and steroid use. These stories informed the characters in this book, who wouldn't be as real as they are without them. Thank you, thank you, thank you!

Cara Sierra Sykes

Perfect?

How

      do you define a word without
      concrete meaning? To each
      his own, the saying goes, so

why

      push to attain an ideal
      state of being that no two
      random people will agree is

where

      you want to be? Faultless.
      Finished. Incomparable. People
      can never be these, and anyway,

when

      did creating a flawless facade
      become a more vital goal
      than learning to love the person

who

      lives inside your skin?
      The outside belongs to others.
      Only you should decide for you—

what

      is perfect.

Perfection

I've lived with the pretense
of perfection for seventeen
years. Give my room a cursory
inspection, you'd think I have OCD.

But it's only habit and not
obsession that keeps it all orderly.
Of course, I don't want to give
the impression that it's all up to me.

Most of the heavy labor is done by
our housekeeper, Gwen. She's an
imposing woman, not at all the type
that most men would find attractive.

Not even Conner, which is the point.
My twin has a taste for older
women. Before he got himself
locked away, he chased after more

than one. I should have told sooner
about the one he caught, the one
I happened to overhear him with,
having a little afternoon fun.

Okay, I know a psychologist
would say, strictly speaking,
he was prey, not predator.
And in a way, I can't really

blame him. Emily is simply
stunning. Conner wasn't the only
one who used to watch her go
running by our house every

morning. But, hello, she was
his *teacher*. That fact alone
should have been enough warning
that things would not turn out well.

I never would have expected
Conner to attempt the coward's way
out, though. Some consider suicide
an act of honor. I seriously don't agree.

But even if it were, you'd have to
actually die. All Conner did was
stain Mom's new white Berber
carpet. They're replacing it now.

Mom Stands There Watching

The men work, laying mint
green carpeting over clean beige
padding. Thick. Lush. Camouflage.
I sit on the top stair, unseen.

Invisible. Silent. I might as well
not even be here at all. And
that's all right. At least I don't
have to worry that she will focus

        her anger on me. Instead she blasts
        it toward the carpet guys. *Idiots!*
        You're scratching the patina!
        Her hiss is like a cobra's spit.

        I might want to expose that wood
        one day. I can't if it's marred.
        But she never will. That oak
        has been irreparably scarred

by gunpowder-tainted
blood. And even more by
the intent behind the bullet.
Sprawled on the floor,

Conner wanted to die.
Mom and Dad don't think
so. In fact, for once they agree
on something besides how bad

their stock portfolios looked
last year. Both of them believe
Conner only wanted attention.
But he was way past hoping

for that, at least the positive
kind. No, Conner was tired
of the pressure. Sick of trying
to find the equation that would

lighten the weight of expectations
not his own. Listening to Mom
tell skilled laborers how to do
their job is almost enough to make

me empathize. The more she goes
on, the more I'm sure the carpet
guys understand. There is no
possible way to satisfy our mother.

I Guess In A Way

I have to give Conner a little
credit. I mean, by putting the gun
to his chest, he made an overt,
if obscene, statement—

> *I will no longer force myself*
> *inside your prefab boxes. I'd much*
> *rather check out of here than let*
> *you decide the rest of my life.*

"You," meaning Mom and Dad.
The pressure they exert individually
is immense. As a team, it's almost
impossible to measure up

to their elevated criteria. I have done
my best, pushed myself to the limit.
To get into Stanford, I have had to
ace every test, stand out as a leader

(junior class pres, student council),
excel in sports, serve as a mentor,
take command of extracurricular
pursuits—cheerleading, honor choir,

theater. All around dating Sean.
Sometimes I just want a solo vacation.
Hanging out on a beach, submitting
to the temptation of sand, sun, salt

water, sans UV protection. Who
cares what damage they might
inflict on my skin? Nice dream.
But what would my mother say?

> I can hear her now. *Don't be*
> *ridiculous. Who in their right*
> *mind would invite melanoma*
> *and premature aging?*

When I look at her, I have
to admit her beauty regime
is working. It's as if by sheer
force of will she won't permit

wrinkles to etch her suede
complexion. But I know, deep
down, she is afraid of time. Once
in a while, I see fear in her eyes.

That Fear Isn't Something

Most people notice. Not Dad,
who's hardly ever home, and even
when he is, doesn't really look
at Mom. Or me. Not Conner,

because if he had even once seen
that chink in her fourteen-carat
armor, he'd have capitalized on it.
Not her friends. (I think the term

misrepresents the relationship,
at least if loyalty figures into
what it means to be a friend.)
Book club. Bridge club. Gym

spinners. She maintains a flock
of them. That's what they remind
me of. Beautiful, pampered birds,
plumage-proud, but blind

to what they drop their shit on.
And the scary thing is, I'm
on a fast track to that same
aviary. Unless I find my wings.

I Won't Fly Today

Too much to do, despite the snow,
which made all local schools close
their doors. What a winter! Usually,
I love watching the white stuff fall.

But after a month with only short
respites, I keep hoping for a critical
blue sky. Instead, amazing waves
of silvery clouds sweep over the crest

of the Sierra, open their obese
bellies, and release foot upon foot
of crisp new powder. The ski
resorts would be happy, except

the roads are so hard to travel
that people are staying home.
So it kind of boggles the mind
that three guys are laying carpet

in the living room. Just goes to
show the power of money. In less
than an hour, the stain Conner left
on the hardwood will be a ghost.

The Stain

That Conner left on our lives will
not vanish as easily. I don't care
about Mom and her birds.
Their estimation of my brother

doesn't bother me at all. Neither
do I worry about Dad and
what his lobbyist buddies think.
His political clout has not diminished.

As twins go, Conner and I don't share
a deep affection, but we do have
a nine-months-in-the-same-womb
connection. Not to mention

a crowd of mutual friends. God,
I'll never forget going to school
the day after that ugly scene.
The plan was to sever the gossip

grapevine from the start with
an obvious explanation—
accident. Mom's orders were
clear. Conner's reputation

was to be protected at all costs.
When I arrived, the rumors
had already started, thanks
to our neighbor, Bobby Duvall.

> *Conner Sykes got hurt.*
> *Conner Sykes was shot.*
> *Conner Sykes is in the hospital.*
> *Is Conner Sykes, like, dead?*

I fielded every single question
with the agreed fabrication.
But eventually, I was forced to
concede that, though his wounds

would heal, he was not coming
back to school right away.
Conner Sykes wasn't dead.
But he wasn't exactly "okay."

When People Ask

How he's doing now, I have
no idea what to say except for,
"Better." I don't know if that's
true, or what goes on in a place

like Aspen Springs, not that anyone knows he's there, thank God.
He has dropped off most people's
radar, although that's kind of odd.

Before he took this unbelievable
turn, Conner was top rung on our
social ladder. But with his crash
and burn no longer news of the day,

all but a gossipy few have quit
trying to fill in the blanks.
One exception is Kendra, who
for some idiotic reason still

loves him and keeps asking about
him, despite the horrible way he
dumped her. Kendra may be pretty,
but she's not especially bright.

Kendra Melody Mathieson

Pretty

That's what I am, I guess.
I mean, people have been telling
me that's what I am since
I was two. Maybe younger.

Pretty

as a picture. (Who wants
to be a cliché?) Pretty as
an angel. (Can you see them?)
Pretty as a butterfly. (But

isn't

that really just a glam bug?)
Cliché, invisible, or insectlike,
I grew up knowing I was
pretty and believing everything

good

about me had to do with how
I looked. The mirror was my best
friend. Until it started telling
me I wasn't really pretty

enough.

13

Pale Beauty

That's what my mom calls the gift
        she gave me, through genetics.

We are Scandinavian willows,
        with vanilla hair and glacier blue

eyes and bone china skin. Two
        hours in the sun turns me the color

of ripe watermelon. When I lead
        cheers at football games, it is wearing

SPF 60 sunblock. Gross. Basketball
        season is better, but I'll be glad

when it's over. Between dance lessons
        and vocal training and helping out

at the food bank (all grooming for Miss
        Teen Nevada), I barely have time for

homework, let alone fun. At least
        staying busy mostly keeps my mind

off Conner. I wish I could forget
         about him, but that's not possible.

I tumbled hard for that guy. Gave him
         all of me. I thought we had something

special. He even let me see the scared
         little boy inside him, the one not many

other people ever catch a glimpse of.
         Did he show that boy to the ambulance

drivers who took him to the hospital, or
         to the doctors and nurses who dug the bullet

out of his chest? Sewed him up. Saved
         his life. I want to see him, but Cara says Saint

Mary's won't allow visitors. Bet he doesn't
         want them—scared he might look helpless.

What He Doesn't Get

Is that everyone gets scared. I used
       to get sick to my stomach every day

before school. Reading, writing,
       and arithmetic? Not my best things.

I just knew some genius bully
       was going to make major fun of me.

Then I figured out Rule Number One
       of the Popularity Game—looks trump

brains every time. While it might be
       nice to have both, I'll settle for what

I've got. College isn't a major goal.
       Don't need it to model. Everyone says

I have what it takes to do runway.
       I don't think I do yet. But I will.

My Mom Has Groomed Me

For modeling for years, ever since
        she entered me in my very first baby

beauty pageant. I wasn't even one yet.
        Couldn't walk, but already had a killer

smile. Mom dressed me up in pink swirls
        and paraded me down that runway herself.

We went home with a tiara. Next thing
        you know, I had an impressive portfolio

and a dozen more rhinestone crowns.
        Soon, my cute cherub face was smiling

for diaper ads and shampoo commercials.
        Once I could toddle, the trend continued,

with pricey gowns and big-girl makeup
        and hair that made me look years older.

Then I did catalogue shots—wearing
        the latest JC Penney and Sears fashions.

All through grade school, weekends
          centered around pageants. And after

school, instead of homework, I studied
          ballet and tap and gymnastics. Plus

the coaching in poise, and prepping
          for interviews. Oh yes, and cozying up

to sponsors, who helped pay for outfits
          and entry fees. Mom ended up leaving

Daddy for one of them—an orthodontist
          with a client list full of beauty queen

hopefuls. Patrick is my stepdad now,
          and he's still paying our way in. I took

a year off while he straightened my teeth.
          Braces and pageants don't mix. It was

right about then that the mirror started
          showing me flaws. When you're younger,

a bump in the nose and a few extra
          pounds don't mean much. But now they do.

The Rhinoplasty

Is already scheduled for spring break.
>A week to heal the swelling and bruising

that come with nose jobs. Scared?
>Yeah. Statistically, I should be just fine.

But there are always those annoying
>what-ifs. What if it doesn't work?

What if it makes things worse? Or,
>best of all, what if I have a bad reaction

to the anesthesia and fricking die?
>The plastic surgeon comes highly

recommended—she and Patrick went
>to college together. Not sure how that

makes her better than anyone else,
>but Patrick's paying for the surgery,

so it's all good. If it turns out the doc
>rocks, I'll use her again for my boob job.

Patrick Won't Pay For That

In fact, he gave me a totally embarrassing
lecture. *First of all, for a young lady your age,*

*I'd say the good Lord gave you just enough
in that department. . . .* That, while trying not

to stare at my 34Bs. *And my guess is you
haven't finished developing yet. . . .* At that

point, Mom jumped in to agree. *I didn't
fill all the way out until my twenties.*

Not till after I had you and Jenna.
Not till after breastfeeding two babies.

But here's the deal. I don't plan on
babies or breast milk augmentation.

Doesn't matter. Once I hit eighteen,
my pageant winnings will be all mine

to spend, and I will have the D cups I need
to kick ass in the cutthroat world of fashion.

What's Irritating

Is that Jenna, who just turned sixteen,
        is well on her way to D cups already.

Of course, though she's three inches
        shorter, she's fifteen pounds heavier,

and happy to stay that way. Jenna takes
        after Daddy. Both her looks and her lack

of ambition. I watch her, tucked under
        a quilt on the window seat, reading.

She seems blissfully unaware of the snow
        crawling up the glass behind her. For some

stupid reason, that really bugs me. "Hey.
        You gonna get dressed sometime today?"

                        Jenna's eyes roll up over the rim
                of her book. *What's it to you, anyway?*

"I'm not shoveling all by myself.
        Patrick said to keep the walk clean."

She shrugs. *What's the use in doing it now? It's just going to get covered again.*

True enough. But it wouldn't hurt
      her to do it twice. "It's good exercise."

The book drops a couple of inches.
      Enough to expose Jenna's mean-edged

                  smile. *Maybe you* should *do it all,
            then. You're looking a little flabby.*

I could fast-pitch an insult back
      at her. But she's expecting that.

I'll try a slow curveball instead.
      "Really? Then I guess I'll take

my own advice. Wouldn't want
      you to have a heart attack, anyway."

Her face flares, jaw to ear tips.
      She lifts her book to cover it up.

I Didn't React Badly

Because I know she was just being
        rude. I do carry extra poundage.

But she doesn't think so, and neither
        does anyone else. Even the scale

keeps trying to tell me one hundred
        twenty-two pounds isn't too much

for my five-foot-ten-inch framework.
        But that stinking mirror doesn't lie.

                Every time I walk by, it shouts out,
Hey. Chub. When are you going to lose

           those fifteen pounds of ugly-ass flab?
Do you want to stay size four forever?

Between dance and cheer, I get plenty
        of exercise, so I know my real enemy

is food. But calories won't conquer
        me. They are one thing I can control.

And Just Maybe

If I can control them, make myself
   thin as I need to be, the rest of my life

will turn right again. Maybe, if I can make
   Daddy proud enough, he'll come see me cheer

or watch me vie for Miss Teen Nevada.
   Maybe, if I can make Mom really look

at me, she'll have something to think
   about besides Patrick. Maybe, when

I'm a size two, a talent scout will
   take an interest in me. And maybe,

when Conner gets out, he'll decide
   I'm the one he wants, after all. Maybe.

So I'll count every calorie. Train even harder.
   Fight for buff. And maybe I'll ask Sean

about that steroid I read about—
   the weight loss phenom of the stars.

Sean Terrence O'Connell
Buff

                  Don't like that word.
                  Not tough enough to describe
                  a weight-sculpted body.

"Built"

                  is better. Like a builder
                  frames a house,
                  constructing its skeleton
                  two-by-four

by

                  two-by-four, a real
                  athlete shapes himself
                  muscle group by muscle
                  group, ignoring the

pain.

                  Focused completely on
                  the gain. It can't happen
                  overnight. It takes hours
                  every single day

and

                  no one can force you to
                  do it. Becoming the best
                  takes a shitload of inborn

drive.

Drive

That's what it takes to reach
        the top, and that is where
               I've set my sights. Second
        best means you lose. Period.
I will be the best damn first

baseman *ever* in the league.
        My dad was a total baseball
               freak (weird, considering
        he coached football), and
when I was a kid, he went

on and on about McGwire
        being the first-base king.
               I grew up wanting to be
        first-base royalty. T-ball,
then years of Little League,

gave me the skills I need.
        But earning that crown
               demands more than skill.
        What it requires are arms
like Mark McGwire's.

I Play Football, Too

Kind of a tribute. (Hey, Dad.
        Hope they let you watch
                football in heaven!) But, while
                I'm an okay safety,
        my real talent is at the bat.
I'll use it to get into Stanford.

The school's got a great
        program. But even if
                it didn't, it would be
        at the top of my university
wish list because Cara will

go there, I'm sure. She says
        it isn't a lock, but that's bull.
                Her parents are both alumni,
        and her father has plenty of
pull. Money. And connections.

Uncle Jeff has connections too,
        and there will be Stanford
                scouts at some random (or
        maybe not so) game. I have
to play brilliantly every time.

Our first game is in three weeks.
Snow or no snow, we have to
practice. And on a day like
today, no school and all snow,
I'm grateful for the weight

room Uncle Jeff put together here
at home. His home. My home
since Dad died, and my kid
brother, Wade's, home too. Our
big brother, Chad, lives in Reno.

No slick roads to brave, just
steep stairs, I grab my iPod, head
first to the kitchen for a power
bar and amino drink, plus a
handy-dandy anabolic booster.

Over-the-counter for now,
just in case our preseason
pee test includes a steroid
screen. Gotta play it smart
or end up busted, à la McGwire.

All Pumped Up

And ready to lift, I'm on
               my way to our makeshift
                         gym when the doorbell
               rings. Who the hell would
be out on a day like this?

I peek through the peephole.
               Duvall, all frosted white.
                         Guess I should see what
               he wants. I crack the door.
"Hey, Bobby. What's up?"

                         The pissant pushes past me.
                    Dude. It's, like, dumping
          out there. He shakes off
               like a dog, dropping snow
                         to melt on the entrance tile.

"Uh, yeah, I can see that. . . ."
          Fricking dweeb. He just
                    stands there, and his stupid-
          ass grin is pissing me off.
"I was just about to go lift, so . . ."

29

Cool, dude. Can I watch?
Been wanting to improve
my technique. He wants
more than that, but since
he's not saying what, I don't

know how to respond
except, "Uh, yeah. I guess
so." Hope the guy isn't gay.
I don't think he is. I mean,
we've shared locker rooms

for years. Bobby plays
first-string shortstop
and second-string kicker.
I never noticed him look
funny at the other guys.

But for sure, if I even
think he's checking
me out, he'll be one
sorry fucker. My blood
pressure surges. Swells.

My Face Flushes Hot

I move quickly past
        Bobby so he doesn't see
                it and think I'm blushing,
     or hear my heart drilling
into my chest, into my ears.

It's the supplements
        and their thermogenic
                rush through my veins.
        But Bobby doesn't know
that. And he doesn't need to.

He follows me down
        the stairs, humming
                some weird-ass song.
     "What are you singing?"
And why is he singing it?

                  Zeppelin, dude. Don't
             you know "Black Dog"?
        Hey, hey, Mama, hmmm
             hmmm hmmm hmmm hm.
                  Radical. Robert Plant rocks.

If He Says So

Personally, I prefer metal,
 especially the death variety.
  I pop my iPod into a docking
  station, queue up Kataklysm,
Nile, Six Feet Under.

Turn it up. Loud. Something
 about the frantic rhythm
  encourages pumping of iron.
  Start with lighter dumbbells,
to warm up the muscles before

really working them. I can
 do a dozen easy reps while
  still conversing, so I nudge
  Bobby. "Coach Torrance
taught you this stuff, right?"

      Bobby shrugs his narrow
     shoulders. *Well, yeah, kind of.*
    But look at you, and then
     look at me. I must be doing
      something wrong, you know?

32

I choose heavier barbells
        before letting myself move
                to the weight machine.
        I love the way my muscles
start to burn. "It's not just

correct form that makes
        it happen, you know. It
                takes dedication. Hours
        and hours of hard fucking
work. Total commitment."

                Bobby shakes his head.
        Takes more than that.
Besides . . . He watches
        me fight for another rep.
                I don't want to work

                that hard. There's an easier
        way. He waits to see if
I bite. When I don't, he says,
        I was hoping you could help
                me out with some 'roids.

I Could Do That

I've got an easy source.
                I could probably even
                                make a few bucks on
                the deal. But I don't like
how the guy just assumes

it's possible, let alone that
                I will score them for him.
                                It's not like we're best
                friends or anything. If he
gets busted, I'm def going

down right along with him.
                "Uh, you know it's pretty
                                much a sure bet we'll get
                tested in the next few weeks.
The stuff you can get over

the counter works. Do
                you have a GNC gold
                                card?" Hint. Hint. Huff.
                Lift. "That's what I use,
and with the card it's not

too pricey." A hell of
a lot cheaper than
the real deal, but
I don't add that part.
If he can't figure that out

all by himself, he's even
stupider than I thought.
Barbells accomplished,
I move over to the weight
machine, waiting for him

to respond. Just about
the time I think he's been
struck mute, he says,
Guess you're right about
the piss test. But after that,

I still want the good shit.
I know you've got a line
on them. Get me some,
I'll make it worth your
trouble. How about it?

Anger Pricks

Like static, sharp and electric
           and urging me toward rage.
                      My biceps and quads already
           burn, and now my brain feels
on fire too. And just as I decide

                            to let myself blow, the door
                  at the top of the stairs opens.
           Sean! yells Aunt Mo. *Your cell*
                  is ringing. And please turn
                        down that god-awful music.

I abandon the weight bench,
           turn off my iPod. "Come on."
                  Bobby heels up the stairs.
           (Good dog.) I point toward
the front door. "See ya, dude."

I locate my now-silent phone.
           Check messages. Find a voice
                  mail from Cara, who wants
           to get together. For the first
time today, everything's bomb.

Andre Marcus Kane III

Bomb

Give most girls a way
to describe me, that's what
they'd say—that Andre
Marcus Kane the third is

                            bomb.

I struggle daily to maintain
the pretense. Why must it be
expected—no, demanded—of

                            me

to surpass my ancestors'
achievements? Why
can't I just be a regular
seventeen-year-old, trying to

                            make

sense of life? But my path
has been preordained,
without anyone even asking

                            me

what I want. Nobody seems
to care that with every push
to live up to their expectations,
my own dreams

                            vaporize.

Don't Get Me Wrong

I do understand my parents wanting only
the best for me.
Am one hundred percent tuned to the concept

that life is a hell of a lot more enjoyable
with a fast-flowing
stream of money carrying you along.

I like driving a pricey car, wearing
clothes that feel
like they want to be next to my skin.

I love not having to be a living, breathing
stereotype because
of my color. Anytime I happen to think

about it, I am grateful to my grandparents
for their vision. Grateful
to my mom for her smarts, to my dad

for his bald ambition and, yes, greed.
Not to mention
his unreal intuition. But I'm sick of being

pushed to follow in his footsteps. Real
estate speculation?
Investment banking? Neither interests me.

Too much at risk, and when you lose,
you lose major.
I much prefer winning, even if it's winning

small. I think more like my grandfather.
Andre Marcus Kane Sr.
embraced the color of his skin, refused

to let it straitjacket him. He grew up in
the urban California
nightmare called Oakland, with its rutted

asphalt and crumbling cement and frozen
dreams, all within
sight of sprawling hillside mansions.

I'd look up at those houses, he told
me more than once,
and think to myself, no reason why

that can't be me, living up there. No
reason at all, except
getting sucked down into the swamp.

Meaning welfare or the drug trade
or even the tired
belief that sports were the only way out.

I guessed I wanted a big ol' house on
the hill more than just
about anything. And I knew my brain

was the way to get it. Oh, what a brain!
My gramps started inventing
things in elementary school. Won awards

for his off-the-wall inventions in high
school, and a full
scholarship to Cal-Poly. He could have

gone on to postgrad anywhere, except
just about then he fell
hard for my grandmother, Grace, a Kriol

beauty from Belize. *Never saw any girl*
could match her, before
or since, he claims. *God sent her to me.*

Maybe. Who else would have encouraged
Gramps's crazy ideas?
Telephones that didn't need wires?

Computers, in every American home?
Ambitious goals,
especially in the sixties, when color TV

was about as technological as most people
got. But if Andre Kane
believed it would come to pass, then so did

his new wife, Grace. Gramps led the charge
into the Silicon Valley.
He got his house on the hill. And then some.

Gramps's Obese Bank Account

Came with taxes and bills. His kids—two
boys and a girl—came
with private school tuitions. Dad was oldest,

and so came programmed with the Eldest Son
Syndrome—a classic
overachiever, hell-bent on making his own

mark on the world, and a bigger one than
his father's. Andre
Marcus Kane Jr. had more than drive going

for him. He had luck, eerie foresight, and
brilliant timing. Right
out of college, Dad became an investment

banker, banking heavily on his own
investments. His stock
portfolio thrived. And somehow, he knew

to dump everything right before the last
time the market crashed.
So when things started to look iffy again,

he went looking for other investments.
Lending is too easy
these days, I heard him tell Mom. *You*

can't keep giving those loans away.
Adjustable rate mortgages
are going to bring this country down.

Which explains why we deserted the Golden
State in favor of the Silver
State some eighteen months ago. Dad keeps

pouncing on the distressed properties that
pop up regularly.
Plus, cost of living is lower here, and that

includes my tuition at Zephyr Academy,
the finest college
prep school in northern Nevada. I don't

miss California too much, except for seeing
Gramps and Grandma
Grace. That, and the street dance scene.

Dad Might Be Sympathetic

To my missing my grandparents, but
dance is not even
a small blip on his radar. I mean, it would

not jibe with *his* plans for my future.
It's an ongoing rant.
Mom, who's generally more focused on

where to nip and how to tuck her patients,
only brings it up once
in a while. Dad is more pragmatic, and

> broaches the subject regularly, especially
> with graduation in
> plain sight. *Did you decide about school?*

I've had positive responses from two
California colleges.
Either would be okay, I guess. "Not yet."

> *Stop procrastinating. Where do you see*
> *yourself next year? Because*
> *it won't be here. Time for a viable plan.*

Dorm or a homeless shelter? Nice choice.
Thanks, Dad. My plan
is art school, a frivolous career in graphic

design. I'm still waiting to hear back from
my top choice—the San
Francisco Art Institute. But when I told

                    Dad that, he freaked. Apparently, "art"
                            plus "San Francisco" can
                    only mean one thing. *You're not serious!*

                    He actually yelled, all his well-cultivated
                            self-control out the
                    window. *What are you? A homosexual?*

It might have been funny, except for
the way he looked at me—
like hinging on my answer was worthiness

of the Kane surname. I shook my head,
agreed to rethink my future,
wishing I could confess that my real dream

isn't art. It's dance. My parents have no idea.
No one does, except
my instructor, who gives me private lessons.

Ballet. Modern. Some ballroom. But I love jazz
most of all, and Liana
says I've got real talent. I don't know about

that, but I do know that dance lifts me
above the mundane.
Grounds me with the certainty that I am

good at something. Connects me to the place
inside where I find passion.
Meaning beyond possessions. Pride, divorced

from my last name. But how can I confess
that to my father?
He thinks a career in art will make me a gay

loser. If I told him I wanted to be a dancer,
it would erase any
doubt in his mind that's exactly what I am.

As For My Mom

She mostly cares about wasted tuition. *Art?*
You might as well go to
public school. What's the point of spending

all this money to insure you have a quality
education only to have you
squander it on an indulgent flight of fancy?

Funny, considering indulgent flights of fancy
bring in a good portion
of her income as a plastic surgeon. Today,

snow plummeting from the silver sky,
Dr. Kane is working in
her home office. I can hear her, purring

to a patient on the phone. *I understand and*
your concerns are justified.
Like all cosmetic surgery, liposuction can

have side effects. But you are a perfect
candidate. . . . Mom will
talk that lady into letting her suck the fat

from the woman's gut, butt, or thighs, a shortcut
to perfection. Damn
the bills. You'll be the finest woman standing

in the bankruptcy line. Your plastic surgeon
doesn't care, either.
She gets payment in full up front. Which helps

pay for her ambitionless kid's unappreciated
tuition. No classes today,
though. Today, even the snowplow drivers

are staying inside; at least I haven't heard one
go by. It's a good day
to hang out at home. But I've got other plans

and a stellar all-wheel-drive Audi Quattro.
Mom's still on the phone,
convincing. I call out anyway, "See you later."

Her voice falls quiet, so I know she must
have heard me. But
she doesn't bother to say good-bye.

Cara
Don't Bother

love

Me with promises. Vows
are cheaply manufactured,
come with no guarantees.
Don't bother to say you

me. The word is indefinable.
Joy to some, heartbreak
to others, depending on
circumstance. There

is

evidence that the emotion
can make a person live longer,
evidence it can kill you early.
I think it's akin to

a deadly

disease. Or at least some
exotic fever. Catch it, and
you'd better, quick, swallow
some medication to use as a

weapon

against the fire ravaging
body and soul.

New Running Shoes

Are the best thing in the world,
at least once you get them broken
in. The Nikes are good to go, if
only we could get a few days

of decent weather. I can run in
the gym, but inhaling sweat
fumes is so not my thing.
I can swim indoors—don't mind

that a bit. But I'm craving a long
run outside in the diamond air,
in a downpour of brittle morning
sun. Breathe in. Breathe out.

Feet drumming pavement. Leg
muscles flex, long then short.
Slip into the zone where time
disappears and no one expects

pace or performance. No one can
catch me. No one to stop me. No score
to keep. No measure but my own.
When I run, I am almost free.

But Today The Roads Are Icy

So I won't run, and I'll try not
to think about freedom. It only
frustrates me because I sincerely
doubt I'll ever know what it means

to live autonomously. I will
forever walk beneath an umbrella
of expectation. Mom and Dad
have a plan for me and won't talk

about alternatives. My teachers
have faith in me and know I'll go far.
My so-called friends mostly hang
out to see if my status will rub off

on them. Only Sean doesn't really
ask anything special of me, except
to decorate his arm like a favorite
piece of jewelry. Oh, he claims

that he's in love with me. If I knew
what love was, I might be able to
judge the depth of his feelings. But
for now, it's enough to have a stable

relationship with one of the most
popular guys at school. No matter
that he doesn't make my heart pitter-
patter faster. Maybe I'm a ventricle

short. Despite that, he's the closest
thing to a best friend I have.
Marriages have survived long
term on less. Not that I'm planning

to get married any time soon. Who
needs that kind of misery? All I have
to do is look around to know it's not
for me. Still, it's nice having a steady

someone to hang out with. Sean
is adventurous. Fun. Good-looking
in a jock kind of way. And you know,
everyone expects the perfect girl

to go out with the perfect guy.
If there's one thing I've learned
from Mom, it's that appearances are
everything. Sean and I look great together.

You Might Even Say

We look normal. Looks can deceive.
We've both had our share of emotional
trauma, though mine stems from
parents who really don't care about

me, while Sean doesn't have parents
at all. His mom died giving birth to
his little brother, Wade. His dad followed
her four years ago, fried in a fiery bus

crash. Half of his football team died
with him. He would have been forty-five
today. Sean's making his annual
pilgrimage to the cemetery, and I'm

going along. Here comes his jock-
worthy GMC pickup. It was a gift from
his uncle Jeff, who will never quite
measure up, no matter how hard he tries.

Sean idolized his father. He pulls into
the driveway, and even from here I can
see sadness in the forward tilt of his
shoulders. It's a memory-shadowed day.

The Sean Who Stops

And gets out to open the passenger
door for me is subdued. *Hey, you.*
It comes out a throaty whisper.
He kisses me, and the kiss is quiet too.

Sean helps me up into the cab. It over-
flows flowers. I haven't seen so much
color in months. "Where did you find
such a big variety this time of year?"

He gives me a tepid smile. *I had to
go to five grocery stores and Wal-Mart.
Stupid, I know. They'll freeze first
thing. It's supposed to snow tonight.*

"Well, at least it's nice right now."
Nice, meaning thirty degrees, partly
cloudy, not much wind. Some would
call that inclement. But Sean agrees

with my assessment. *Yes, it is. Let's
go before something nasty blows in.*
As we drive toward the city, I notice
there isn't one rose in these dozens

of flowers. Lilies and asters, tulips,
carnations, sunflowers and mums,
but . . . "You couldn't find roses in all
those stores?" Sean drums the steering

wheel with one hand, musing.
Finally he says, *My mom loved
roses. She grew them everywhere
in our yard, and when she died,*

*Dad went kind of crazy and
tore them all out. I can't even
look at a rose without thinking
about that day. I was so afraid*

*he'd flipped out for good and
I would lose him, too. He kept
saying he'd replant them in
her memory. Never happened.*

February Doesn't Seem

To be a big month for mourning.
Maybe it's too cold to die?
Wow. Too cold to die. Wonder
if that's why Conner's still alive.

Okay. That's dumb. I know people
die in February. But obviously,
their loved ones don't come to say
hi in dead of winter. The cemetery

is—uh—dead. No one here but
Sean and me. Which makes it
exponentially creepy, even in
daylight. The only time I've been

to a graveyard was for my grandfather's burial. Dad said the old
jerk deserved to go early. Who
knows? I had one bad experience

with him. Of course, it was the only
time I actually met him. So, yeah.
Anyway, I've never shared any
of that with Sean yet. And this

is probably not the right time
or place to mention it. He looks
scared. Flustered. Duh. The flowers.
"Let me carry some of those."

Sean leads the way, and as we walk,
a fist of clouds chokes out the sun.
Despite the overwhelming gray, our
blossoms mist the gloom with color.

Scarlet. Lilac. Tangerine. Bronze.
Evening star gold. Late morning
sun yellow. Any place but here,
it would be romantic. It isn't far

to the gravesite, on a slight rise well
away from the road. This time of year,
there's no grass, just packed layers of old
snow. Sean stops to lay his flowers

in front of an ice-rimmed headstone.
Hey, Dad. Sean's breath steams into
frozen air, and his voice pierces
the silence of death. *Happy birthday.*

No Answer

At least, not one I can hear, unless
it is the disturbing mutter of wind.
"Should we find something to hold
the flowers?" They'll soon clutter

> the cemetery if we don't, but Sean
> says, *Let them blow if they want to.*
> *That way everyone here can enjoy them.*
> It is so unlike anything I'd expect

from him, I hardly know how to
react. So I kneel to place an armful
of spring atop slick layers of winter.
Within seconds, they chase each other

across the grounds, halted here and
there by marble and granite head-
stones. I glance at the inscriptions here:
CLAIRE JENNIFER O'CONNELL, adjacent to

"COACH" BRYAN PIERCE O'CONNELL.
It hits me, electric, like lightning.
"Your mom was so young when she
died." Only twenty-eight. I wait for some

sign of sadness. But Sean responds
instead with a quick jab of anger. *Stupid
bitch.* He takes a deep breath. *If she hadn't
gone all New Agey, she wouldn't be dead.*

We've never really talked about
her, or how exactly she died.
"New Agey? What do you mean?"
He trembles, but whether from cold

or memory, I can't be sure. *She decided
to use a midwife instead of going to
the hospital. If she had been at Saint Mary's,
she wouldn't have bled to death when*

*she hemorrhaged. The paramedics
couldn't save her. And you know
the worst thing? I was standing right
there. I saw her go. I was just a little*

*kid, but I'll never forget watching her
fade away. One minute she was Mommy.
The next, she was a mannequin.
All that was left of her was Wade.*

Bitterness

Tints his voice. That, and anger.
How can he blame his mom?
I'm not sure I understand. Then
again, I have no frame of reference.

My mother is still one of the walking,
talking, breathing. But she doesn't
do a whole lot more for me than Sean's
mom does for him now. We never

spend time together. Rarely even
attempt to communicate. For all
our daily interaction, she might
as well be dead. I don't hate her.

But I'm not really sure I love her,
at least not in the classic fashion.
And if she loves me, she hides it well.
Parenting should be a passion, not

a part-time pursuit. The wind kicks
stronger, branches clatter. Or maybe
skeletons. Bones of abandonment.
Ghosts of what will never be.

Kendra
Ghosts

Take shape under moonlight,
materialize in dreams.
Shadows. Silhouettes
of what is no more. But

                              ghosts don't

bother me. The day brings
bigger things to worry about
than flimsy remains of
yesterday. No, spooks don't

                              scare me.

Gauzy apparitions might
prank your psyche or
agitate your nightmares,
but lacking

                              flesh and blood

they are powerless
to hurt you—cannot hope
to inflict the kind of damage
that real, live

                              people do.

Miss Teen Spirit Of The West

Is not the biggest pageant I've ever done.
        But as regional pageants go, the prize money

is good, especially compared to the entry fee.
        And every pageant I compete in keeps me

tuned up for heavier-weight competitions.
        This one is in Elko, a five-hour drive from

Reno. Five hours, listening to my mom remind
        me about stuff I don't need to be reminded

                about. *Remember to keep your chin tilted*
        up and your shoulders back. Act like . . .

"The royalty you pretend to be. I know,
        Mom. You've only told me that, like, eight

gazillion times. If I can't remember it by
        now, I never will." The tone was testier

than I intended. Mom looks a little stung.
        "Sorry. It's just, I've got it, you know?"

Interstate 80 is mostly flat Great Basin desert.
        Salt flats, sage, and carrion. Not much to excite

the eye or stimulate conversation. I guess
        I should be grateful to Mom for trying.

                After several very long silent minutes,
        she tries again. *Do you still enjoy them?*

                Pageants, I mean. You used to love them,
        at least I thought so. But now I'm not sure.

Does she want the truth? Do I want
        to give it to her? I decide to compromise.

"I like winning them." Like every eye on me,
        and when those eyes find me fairest of all.

What I don't like is what it sometimes
        takes to win. Backstabbing. Manipulation.

Out-and-out bribery once in a while,
        and not always the monetary kind.

Beautiful Bodies

Are ripe for the picking. It's rare. But not
       unheard of. Unless I am willing to go that far,

I'll always be at a slight disadvantage.
       I most definitely wouldn't stoop so low

to win Miss Teen Spirit of the West.
       Miss America, however, might be a whole

different tale. Not even sure Mom
       would object. Pageants are a means

       to an end, as she reminds me now.
       Winning is good. Every crown puts

       you one step closer to the runway.
       You get there, you'll never have to

       depend on anyone else. A self-reliant
       woman. That's what you'll be.

I've heard it before. She's drummed it
       into me. My looks are the key to the kingdom.

Still Two Hours West

Of Elko, the silence becomes stifling.
    At least for Mom, who digs too hard

        to come up with something. *Do you
want to talk about Conner?* She waits,

patient as one of the vultures I watch,
    circling above some vile desert-claimed

corpse. "What about Conner?" The buzzard
    wheel widens as more black wings link

        to the cog. *Well, um . . . Do you think it
had anything to do with you breaking up?*

What is she talking about? "Do I think
    what had to do with us breaking up?"

        She huffs a little, like she thinks I'm
dense. *You know. The gun. The hospital . . .*

Okay, she's the one who's dense. "Why
    would Conner shooting himself have

anything to do with 'us'? Accidents hap—
        Wait. Are you saying it wasn't an accident?"

Heat flowers at the back of my neck,
        radiates toward my skull. "Well? Mom?"

                She slows the car. *It was* not *an accident,*
        Kendra. Conner tried to kill himself.

Suicide? Conner? "No! He'd never!" Would
        he? But even if he did, "How do *you* know?"

                I was dealing with another Jenna issue
        and was in the guidance counselor's office.

                I overheard him talking about where to send
        Conner's schoolwork—Aspen Springs.

Aspen Springs. Psych hospital. Residential
        treatment center. Lockdown for druggies and . . .

I have to know for sure. I jerk my cell from
        my bag, check for a signal. Two bars. Still,

66

a text might work. IS CONNER IN ASPEN
SPRINGS? Hit the send. Wait for Cara

to answer. Mom watches me sideways,
out of the corner of her eye. *You all right?*

"No. Yes. Wait . . ." What was she saying
about Conner and me breaking up? No! No way!

"Even if Conner *did* try to kill himself,
it wasn't *my* fault! How can you think that?"

I cut off her denial. "Just drive, okay?"
I think about the last few times I saw him.

I could barely look at him through the smog
of my pain. And Conner was never easy to

read, anyway. But I only remember him
smiling. Laughing. Easygoing. All Conner.

My phone chimes suddenly. Incoming.
WHO TOLD YOU? No denial, so it must

be true. DOESN'T MATTER. DID HE TRY
        TO KILL HIMSELF? I don't expect a quick

                answer, but it comes back right away.
        NO ONE KNOWS. PLEASE DON'T TELL.

Don't tell? That's what she's worried
        about? My eyes sting and my cheeks burn.

YOU SHOULD HAVE TOLD ME. I HAD
        THE RIGHT TO KNOW. Bitch. I THOUGHT

YOU WERE MY FRIEND. Then I remember.
        The Sykes family doesn't keep friends.

                But they do keep secrets. I'M SORRY. MY MOM
        WOULD HAVE WRECKED ME IF I TOLD YOU.

Probably literally. Doesn't make it right,
        though. One last question. WHY DID HE DO IT?

We go into a tunnel. On the other side, Elko
        comes into view, along with Cara's last message:

                WHO KNOWS?

Elko Is A Mining Town

And while the surrounding countryside
        is stunning, the town itself has seen

better days. Parts of it are pretty. Others
        are shabby. Run-down. Battered by time

and circumstance. Sort of like how I feel
        right now. We were up before dawn to

hit the highway, but this soul-drooping
        weariness comes from some absurd sense

of guilt. I didn't make Conner pick up
        that gun. But was there anything I might

have done to stop him? Why didn't I see
        warning signs? Was any of his hopelessness

because of me? Ridiculous, I know. *He* broke
        up with *me*. But I still don't know why.

Mom pulls into the Thunderbird Motel.
        Checks us into a this-will-do kind of room.

"Why do we always stay here?
        The Holiday Inn isn't too far away."

                She's busy hanging my dresses in a tiny
        closet. *I don't know. Memories, I guess.*

"Memories of what?" Pretty sure Patrick
        has never been here with her. "Daddy?"

                Mom pulls her head out of the dank
        cubicle. *Weird, huh? We stayed here*

                *not too long after we met. Spent long
        days hiking Lamoille Canyon. Gorgeous*

                up there . . . She loses herself in some
        recollection. Comes back again. *Anyway,*

                *I'm starving. Let's get some lunch.
        We've got a couple of hours to kill.*

Lunch? Don't think so. "I'm more tired
        than hungry. Think I'll take a nap. You go."

Her Eyes Say The Words

Her mouth refuses to—*I'm worried*
    about you. Why don't you eat? What

        she does say is, *Are you sure? You have*
    to be hungry. You didn't eat breakfast.

I never eat breakfast. But all that does
    is prove her unspoken point. "I'm sure.

If I don't get some sleep, I'll look awful
    tonight." To make her happy, I ask her to

bring back a salad. Off she goes. I lie down
    on the plywood-and-cotton-lumps mattress.

Oh, Conner. How could you try to die?
    And why didn't you? You hardly ever fail

to get the things you really want. Did
    a switch flip inside your brain? If it did,

I think what flipped it was that little boy
    who suddenly grew tired of being scared.

I've Only Known

One other person who ended up in Aspen
        Springs. Tiffany took dance with me for

three or four years. Rumor had it her stepdad
        liked her a little too much. She coped with

his "bad, bad touch" by binge-and-puking.
        Bulimia is nasty. Hanging your head in

the toilet after every meal? Sticking your fingers
        down your throat? All that stomach acid,

carving holes in your esophagus? And even
        after all that, still wearing a size eight? Talk

about a waste of energy. Real control is
        not putting in more than you can work off.

Knowing the exact count and keeping track.
        Shaving off every extra caloric unit you can

without passing out. And the most important
        thing of all—keeping everyone else in the dark.

Sean
Everyone Else

If

Don't

plot.

I fail

Seems to stumble through
life. Fall. Get up. Go
stumbling on again.

they happen into a really
good place, do they then
make plans how to stay there?

I

don't understand how
people manage without
a well-drawn game plan.

they want some promise
of success? Every good
novel requires a considered

Should a biography not
demand as much? How do
you function without structure?

to comprehend.

Plotting

Is important to me. How
              do I manage to reach
                         Point B if I kick off
              from Point A? Logic,
that's what it takes. I hate

the illogical. And really
              despise when it actually
                         pays off for somebody.
              You know, right place,
right time, whoopee, you

win, without putting in
              one damn lick of effort?
                         Bugs the shit out of me.
              Especially considering
my life has been mostly

about wrong place, wrong
              time, too damn bad for
                         you. Lost my mom that
              way. Lost my dad that way.
Not going to lose Cara, too.

Which is why I've got
            a game plan. One I'm
                        sticking to. When you've
            only got one little shimmer
of sunshine, you capture it

best you can. I will marry
            that girl one day. Not
                        that I've asked her yet.
            That page of our memoir
isn't ready to be written.

Right now I'm working
            on the chapter that sends
                        us to college together.
            First things first, and I
always prefer to write

in chronological order.
            Mostly because it's [chrono]
                        logical. I keep hearing that
            love isn't a logical emotion.
Should I worry about that?

It Does Worry Me Some

Which is probably why, until
          Cara, I refused to give my
                    heart away. I mean, I've
          never had to work to get
a girlfriend. I have sampled

more than a few yummy
          female delicacies. But
                    they've all been appetizers.
          Cara is a main course.
I'd call her comfort food.

Just not to her face. Don't
          think she'd appreciate
                    the metaphor. Truth
          is, I've got nothing but
respect for that girl. I love

her more than anything,
          and I know this love is
                    real because, unlike
          my other relationships,
it's not all about sex.

So Far, In Fact

It isn't about sex at all. Lots
of kissing. A stolen second
base or fifty, plus a definite
leadoff toward third a time
or two. But the only home runs

I've hit lately have been at
baseball practice. I think
if love is real, and headed
toward the altar, the sex part
can—within reason—wait.

My big brother thinks I'm
crazy. *Dude,* he told me, *if
you're really thinking forever,
you'd better take a test-drive.
What if she sucks in bed?*

I've test-driven four or five.
And the thing is, there wasn't
a helluva lot of difference
in the way they handled. Tune
'em up, hit the freeway. Fly.

One of My Former
High-Horsepower Rides

Happens to be texting Cara
            right now. Kendra and I had
                        a short, sweet, ten thousand
                RPM fling before she and Conner
hooked up. Kind of incestuous,

I guess. Wonder what's going
            on. Not like she and Cara are
                        tight or anything. Lukewarm
                buddies at best. "What does
she want?" Hope that didn't

                                    sound as impatient as it felt.
                            Nothing important. If that's
                true, why do they keep going
                        back and forth for so long?
                                    She's on her way to Elko.

"Another brainless beauty
            contest?" Right up her alley.
                        She's got it all in the looks
                department. Intellect-wise,
however, she's no Cara.

Probably. I'm not sure.
Now she's sounding kind
of short. In between texts,
she stares out the window,
contemplating each answer,

it seems. Finally she sighs,
thumbs one last message,
hits send, and puts her cell
away. "You want to tell me
what that was all about?"

Not especially. That's it.
Not exactly what I'd call
communication. Sometimes Cara
reminds me of her mother.
I'll keep that to myself.

I've Talked To Her Parents

A few times. Her dad is cool.
Meaning chilled. I think it
probably takes a lot to get
the dude excited. He isn't
friendly. But he's cordial.

That probably has a lot to
do with being a lobbyist.
Totally outstanding butt
kissers, especially those
who lobby for insurance.

They might have a shitload
of "buddies," but I bet they
don't have a lot of friends,
unless you count the ones in
high places and back pockets.

Anyway, considering who
he's married to, the guy
deserves credit for being
even tepid. Especially
when holed up at home.

Because Cara's Mom

Reminds me of crystal—
        all sparkly and beautiful
                distraction while it carves
        you clear to the bone. She
is a don't-turn-your-back-

                on-her kind of woman.
        Our first encounter was
a lot like a job interview.
        We are careful about who
                our daughter is allowed

        to date, she declared, before
        basically third-degreeing me
as to my qualifications. She's
        a high-society high roller who
                steamrolled right over me.

It was almost enough to make
        me rethink things with Cara.
                Except she's just so damn
        perfect. Well, other than when
it comes to communication.

We'll Have To Work On That

But, hey, we've got plenty
            of time. *Forever* takes a while.
                        Meanwhile, I'm practicing
            how to get my way without
her noticing. Subtlety is not

my best thing, but control
            and Cara are not easily
                        juxtaposed. It's a challenge,
            but one I'm equal to. Not
that I'd say so out loud.

Staying (subtly) in control
            requires current information.
                        "So have you heard from
            Stanford yet?" She pretty
much aced her SATs. Grades

                        are outstanding. Community
            service likewise. *Not yet. Dad
says it will probably be a few
            weeks still. I did hear from
                        Loyola, though. They want me.*

"Loyola? I didn't know
        you applied there." Not in
                the game plan. Suddenly
        my gut feels scrambled.
"You're not even Catholic."

                        We don't go to church often,
                and when we do, it's usually
        to Holy Cross Lutheran. Mom
                isn't into the whole Pope thing.
                        But Dad was raised Catholic.

"So, he really believes in all
        that 'wine into blood' bullshit?"
                I bet the real reason they go
        Lutheran is so he doesn't have
to confess. Too much time,

                        trading Hail Marys for penance.
                I'm not sure. My grandmother
        did, and my grandfather
                still does, at least when his
                        Alzheimer's lets him. He doesn't

remember a whole lot most
of the time. Which is why
they invented special care
retirement communities. If I
get that way, please shoot me.

She shudders at the last two
        words, and I'm guessing
                she's thinking about Conner.
        "How's your brother doing,
anyway? All healed up yet?"

                        Not really, and what the hell
                is up with everyone today?
        Is it Dig Up Information on
                Conner Day? Because I don't
                        have anything new to tell you.

Jeez. What was that about?
        "Hey, I'm not trying to dig
                up anything, new or old.
        Just trying to communicate."
Will that always be a problem?

Andre
A Problem

Is really just a solution
in need of a reason to exist.
If you think about it,

        life

would be kind of boring
if it were completely free
of friction. Each day

        presents

choices. Turn this way, it's
a downhill coast. Turn that
way, you will stumble across

        obstacles.

Some are easily conquered.
Some require intelligence,
will, and perseverance

        to overcome.

To win is to prosper.
The game is defeating doubt.
And the fun is in the game.

Today's Game

Was faking my way through a trig
test. I probably passed,
but just barely. Trig? What for? Not

like I'll need it beyond June, except
to have it, with a C
or (unlikely) slightly better grade

on my transcript. Okay, my mom might
argue that I'll want to
know math for a future career. She uses

it all the time, calculating body fat
percentages and how
many millimeters of bone to remove

or skin to tighten to achieve the desired
effect. Not to mention
how much anesthesia per pound

of person will allow said person to wake
up from deep sleep
and walk out, covered in bandages, alive.

And Dad utilizes the ol' calculator
to figure price points
and down payments and monthly

fees, and whether or not a prospective
client's take-home
salary can cover those things, at least

on paper. But if I had to follow in either
of their footsteps,
I'd use math to calculate how fast

I'd have to drive my car over a cliff
of x feet in height
to attain the proper distance to make

sure I'd end up dead instead of paralyzed.
Wow. A real-world use
for trigonometry. Who'd have believed it?

School Behind Me

For the day, I stop by the house on
my way to Reno.
Change out of my stiff white button-up

shirt, khaki slacks. This isn't my usual day
for dance lessons, but
Liana had an opening, and I'm itching to work

off a little stress. Dad's relentless pressure
is getting to me. He caught
me on my way out the door this morning.

> *I'm off to Vegas for a few days. When I get*
> *back, we'll arrange a trip*
> *over spring break to look at those schools.*

It totally hit me wrong. "Would you please
stop micromanaging my life?
What if I have my own plans for spring break?"

> His jaw clicked audibly as it tightened, and
> he silenced me with
> two words. *Cancel them.* End of discussion.

I Have To Make A Stop

On the way to Liana's. I need two hundred
dollars for this month's
lessons. But I'll tell Mom the money is for

a haircut and some new clothes. Last year's
sweaters are dated.
If I say that, she won't even think twice.

Perception is everything to Mom, and style
is a vital component.
She wants her son to be a fashion trendsetter.

Three p.m. on Wednesday, her regular day
for pre-op consults,
her office is humming. "Hello, Simone,"

I say to her receptionist, eliciting her
smile with my own.
"Will my mother be tied up very long?"

> *She's with a patient, but should be*
> *finished soon. Take*
> *a seat. I'll let her know you're here.*

She scuttles off, and I turn toward
the plush waiting
room. A girl, seated in one of the cushy

chairs, lifts her eyes up over a magazine.
Damn! She's a spectacular
creation, the kind you'd like to paint

a portrait of, so you could hang her on
a wall and stare at her
forever. And speaking of staring, she is

staring at me, so I'm motivated to say
hello, only it comes out,
"H-he-hello." She smiles at the stupid

stutter, and I can't help but notice
the perfect shape
of her plump little pout. Delicious.

>   *Hello back at you,* she says, her voice
>   rich and sweet as
>   caramel, and all the invitation I need.

I Choose A Seat

Close to her, where I can better study
her. She's younger
than me, maybe sixteen, but the curves

of her body belong to a woman. Surely
she doesn't want more
nor less than what she's been gifted with.

I can't help but ask, "You're not here
to see my mom, are
you?" Forward, yes. But I have to know.

She smiles again, and in that smile
is something Eve-like.
Me? No way. My sister is in there

now, choosing a new nose. But I kind
of like what I've got,
you know? How could I in good faith

disagree? "You are a wise girl." One, I've just
decided, I really want
to know. I offer a straightforward, "I'm Andre."

Her Skin

Is flawless, and the color of fine ivory.
Together we are
a keyboard. Or maybe a chessboard.

My color has never been an issue for girls
before, but there's a first
time—or person—for everything and in Reno,

ghosts of Wild West prejudice still haunt
certain neighborhoods.
This girl, however, doesn't seem put off

> by my skin. *I'm Jenna. And are you,*
> *like, hitting on me?* She
> laughs at how I can't quite confess it.

> *It's okay. I don't mind.* She watches
> Simone scurry back
> to her desk. *Do you want to call me?*

Her forwardness is both a little scary
and a lot refreshing.
"You know, I really would." We exchange

appreciative smiles and cell phone
numbers, as down
the hall a door slams open, followed

by scattered voices. One of them belongs
to my mom. The others,
I'm guessing, are Jenna's mother

and her sister. Both of them look like
her, except her sister
lacks the abundant flesh that makes

Jenna so attractive. She notices where
my eyes keep roaming.
My sister is a pageant girl, she says in

a low (luscious) voice. *She also wants to*
model, which is why
she thinks she needs her nose "fixed."

"I hope it's enough for her. Some people
get addicted to
the 'fixing.'" Some are never satisfied.

Jenna, However

Appears more than satisfied with the way
she looks, every move
designed to draw the eye. My eyes,

for sure. And I can't believe other guys
wouldn't feel the same
way. There is something extremely

alluring about a girl who's completely at ease
in her own skin.
And this one loves how she's put together.

Her sister, however, for all her beauty-
focused goals, seems
to hold something in reserve. She is closer

to my age. But she is so not my type.
Not sure why I think
Jenna is, but I can't wait to research.

Her mom tells her it's time to leave. I watch
her exit, enthralled
by the performance. She is one of a kind.

She Is On My Mind

On the short drive to the All the Right
Moves dance studio.
Usually, when I meet a girl, I make her

wait a day or two before I ask her out.
For some reason,
I'm driven to skip the whole coy charade

and call Jenna right away. She answers
on the third ring. "Hey.
It's Andre. Are you free Saturday night?"

> *Wow. You're direct. I like that, and I'd*
> *like to say yes, but I*
> *kind of had tentative plans for Saturday.*

That stings. And I'm late for my lesson.
"Okay. I'll try again."
I go inside. The place is empty, except

> for Liana, who is on her own phone.
> *Warm up,* she mouths,
> nodding toward the open studio door.

I start my stretching, thinking about
the magnetic smile that
drew me immediately to the girl I can't

seem to get off my mind. Liana comes in,
and we begin a familiar
routine. I've done these steps dozens

of times, but I can't keep them in the right
order. I can hear my dad
saying how if he wants something, he won't

> let anyone tell him he can't have it. *Andre!*
> scolds Liana. *Where's your*
> *head today? Did you forget how to count?*

Focus, Andre, focus. One, two, three, four . . .
Somehow I make it
through the rest of my lesson. Pay Liana

the money I finagled from Mom. At last,
I can call Jenna again. "You
know those tentative plans? Cancel them."

Cara
At Last

It's a perfect winter day.
No wind. No Arctic freeze.
Cloudless azure sky. A day

to fly.

Snow drapes the mountain
like ermine, fabulous feather-
light powder coaxing me

to flee

the confines of my room, brave
the mostly plowed road
up to the closest ski resort.

To run

from the cloying silence
connecting Mom and Dad,
into encompassing stillness

far away

from city dirt and noise.
Far above suburban gridlock.
Far beyond the grasp of home.

First Decent Day In Weeks

Mt. Rose will be swarming by noon.
Good thing I got here early.
Nothing much better than first
tracks beneath cloud-clear skies.

Heaven must be something
like boarding on night-crisped virgin
powder. Lingering atop a cornice,
few other people in sight, I take

a deep pull of winter-spiked air, finesse
over the lip. Two sweeping turns
to safety. Here, where there are no
hypercritical eyes, I slip

past denial, into the moment.
It's all up to me. Slide down
the steeps, into belief. I am
no more, no less than this ride.

Midmorning

The crowd is starting to build.
Most people prefer the high-
speed chairs, and those lines
are long. Not sure why so few

enjoy the old-fashioned slow
lifts to the top, but I love these
unrushed minutes. Suddenly
the chair bumps to a stop.

Problems below in the loading
zone, no doubt. I look over
at the racecourse run. The pines
at its edges have grown. How long

has it been since Conner and I
raced there? Four years? Five? I was
never fast enough to earn the medal
I coveted. Conner often placed in

the top three but never cared about
winning. I've often wondered how
twins could be so different. Why did
the one with the talent lack the drive?

The Lift Starts Up Again

I survey the terrain beneath me,
find a relatively unpopulated route
down through the trees. Risky
to ride there alone, but I doubt

I'll have a whole lot of trouble.
Despite my parents' lukewarm
support, I've been skiing or boarding
for years. I might not be as fast

as Conner, but unlike him, I rarely
take a fall. I disembark the chair,
traverse the flats, brake to a stop
beside a tall sugar pine, scan

the landscape for the approximate
path I saw. There. That's it, I think.
Swoop into the woods, slalom
cedar and fir, each low branch a claw

menacing my hair and face.
I manage to avoid them all.
What I don't miss is the boulder
tip, lurking out of view, just

beneath the surface of the snow.
It scrapes my board, catching
it just enough to send me, face
forward, into a deep, wide drift.

I inhale snow. I swallow snow.
When I open my eyes, I see white.
I cartwheel my arms, but can't get
traction. I bite back panic. Think.

For some weird reason, though
I'm pretty much buried, I can
breathe. What I can't seem to do
is get myself out. I'm such an idiot!

I could die right now and who
knows when they would find me?
Silent here, in my tomb. Warm.
I could sleep. That would be easy. . . .

      Suddenly I hear, *Hang on.*
      The snow around me loosens.
      I am yanked backward. My lungs
      grab air. My eyes find color. I'm free.

My Rescuer

Rolls me onto my back. *Are you
okay? Damn, girl, it's a good
thing I happened to come this
way. You're crazy to shoot trees*

solo. She looks down at me with
black walnut eyes, and in them I
find equal parts disgust, amusement,
and awe. She offers her hand, pulls

me up on my feet. "Thanks."
I should say more, but it hits
me that this stranger might have
saved my life. All repartee deserts

me. She is close to my age. Tall.
Exotic. I don't know her, but
I want to. Our eyes lock, and I feel
something stir. Something restless.

Disquieting. A rustle of leaves.
A rattle of glass. A snarl, before
the witch wind awakens,
screeching, impossible to ignore.

And this person is to blame.
She smiles, and I like how warm
that makes me feel. I am melting.
Maybe we should buddy up?

Why not? "S-sure." The voice
is throaty, not mine at all. Oh
my God. What's wrong with me?
My face flares, dry-ice hot.

She can't help but notice. *You
sure you're okay? You look . . .
never mind.* She lowers her goggles.
I'm Danielle, by the way. Uh, Dani.

"Cara." God, could I manage
multiword sentences, maybe?
"And thanks again." There.
Three words. Blood *whooshes*

in my ears and I barely hear
her say, *No problem.* She turns,
pushes off, and I follow her down
through snow-draped trees.

This Part Of The Hill

Is steep. Unforgiving. A lot
of work. But Dani surfs it like
she was born on a board. To keep
up, I have to forget about face-

plants and possible outcomes.
Finally we exit the trees, and our
trail merges with a beginner run.
Newbies and posers fan out across

the gentle slope, some upright,
some on their butts, some flat on
their backs like sea lions sunning.
Dani cuts through them. I follow.

I hate crowds, and would call it
quits, except . . . I'm not sure.
I feel scared. Hopeful. Borderline
sick, sort of like it's my first day

at a new school. I watch Dani
hold a tight line down the side
of the run. Confident. Lithe.
Bold. Oh yes, I have to know her.

It Isn't Until

We are both seated safely on
the (slow—hurray!) chair that it hits
me. "You said I was crazy to shoot
trees solo. So what about you?"

> *What about me, what?* She scoots
> sideways, her knee touches mine.
> And for some crazy reason, I want
> her to kiss me. Wait. What?

She hasn't come on to me at all.
Oh. She's waiting for my answer.
"Why did you take that way down?
You were riding all by yourself."

> She shrugs. *Maybe I'm psychic.*
> *I saw you go that way. Figured*
> *I'd better keep an eye on you.*
> *Why* are *you alone, anyway?*

Keep an eye on me? How long was
she watching me? My turn to shrug.
"I asked my boyfriend to come,
but he had baseball practice."

Oh. She makes a point of moving
her knee away from mine. *For
some reason, I had a different idea
about you. I thought you might be . . .*

I slide my leg back against hers.
"I might be." Then I admit, "But
I'm not sure." I don't say that falling
in love with a girl doesn't fit

well in my master plan. *Love?*
What dark little recess of my brain
did that word creep out of?
This isn't fire. It's only a spark.

*Well, I definitely am. I've known
since I was, like, five and wanted
my Barbies to get married. To each
other. My friends were disgusted.*

Her Laugh Is So Freaking Sexy

Husky. Deep. And totally real.
Somehow I doubt she's fake
about much. "What about
your friends now?" But there's

no time for her to answer.
The chair swings wide at
the top of the hill. Together
we stand, move to one side

> to discuss the best way down.
> *Let's take that long beginner run*
> *around the back of the mountain.*
> *A no-brainer will be fun.* She doesn't

wait for me to say okay,
so I trail her along a wide
track, dodging snow-plowers.
She seems to take a wrong

turn into a thick stand of trees.
But when she stops, I realize
she came this way purposely.
We are curtained by pines.

When I draw even, she looks
into my eyes, sending shivers up
my spine. *Have you ever kissed
a girl?* Her boldness is a surprise,

but when I shake my head,
her reaction is no more than
I expected. And honestly, hoped
for. Dani's lips are soft, raspberry

gloss sweet. The kiss is tentative,
but only for those few moments
that can never happen again.
Desire is scratching at the door.

Terrifying. Electrifying. But I have
to know what it means. I inhale
the perfume of the forest, of the girl.
The two are intoxicating.

Dani stops. Pulls back. *So?*
The kiss was saturated with need.
I feel light-headed. Hungered.
The witch wind has been freed.

Kendra
Light

That's how I feel—
like the winter-fringed
breeze might scoop
me up into its wings,

                    fly

away with me trapped
in its feathered embrace.
I am a snowflake.
A wisp of eiderdown,

                    liberated

from gravity. My body
is light. Ephemeral.
My head is light.
I want to sway

                    beneath

the weight of air,
dizzy with thought.
Light filters through
my closed eyelids.

                    The sun,

chasing shadows,
tells me I'm not
afloat in dreams.

Dreams

Keep me in bed late this morning.
        Usually I'm up with the sun, but not

when I'm slow dancing with Conner.
        Even in sleep, the familiar scent

of his skin—clean and tinged with
        some deep woods perfume—fills

the vacant place inside me, the one
        he emptied when he left me behind.

But well beyond daybreak, he holds me
        so tightly I can barely draw breath.

        We move to the music, and his lips buzz
        against my ear. *I love you. I want you.*

Then, as dreams often do, the scene
        shifts, fast-forward, and we are floating

on a sea of soft summer grass, clothes
        strewn around us like wildflowers.

Conner traces the outline of my body,
         fingers dipping lightly into the concave

                  spaces between each rib. *Perfect.* He kisses
         the line of my jaw, down my neck,

                  to the raised ridge of collarbone. His tongue
         slides across it. *Mmm. Delicious. What else*

                  can I taste? He finds other places, each
         more intimate than the last, and I am beyond

ready to let him take me all the way
         there. But just as I think we finally

will, he sits up. Pulls far away. I don't
         know what to say except, "Don't stop."

                  I'm sorry, he answers. *I can't stay.* And
         even though I can still feel his hand

stroking the hill of my hip, he is gone.
         I wake, crying out for someone never there.

I Don't Feel Light Anymore

I feel like someone has tied bricks
        to my arms and legs. Weighted by loss,

I lie immobile for maybe twenty minutes,
        eyes closed, hoping I'll fall back into

the dream, find Conner has changed
        his mind. But I don't sleep. Don't dream.

Across the room, I hear Jenna stir.
        She always sleeps late on weekends.

If I'm still in bed, it usually means
        I'm sick. When she notices me, she gasps.

                But she doesn't bother being quiet.
            What's up with you? Got the flu?

My head never leaves the pillow.
        "Don't know." What am I going

to say? That I want to go searching
        for Conner? "Why do you care?"

I don't want to catch anything nasty.
Keep your germs all to yourself.

She goes to the closet, digs for a bit,
emerges with one of my favorite

sweaters—a cornflower angora. *Hey.*
Can I wear this? Pretty please?

Is she crazy? "Not even. Not
the way you treat my clothes."

It doesn't fit you anymore, anyway.
She slips it on. *See? Just right.*

I have to admit it looks great on her,
accentuating each and every curve.

I would probably swim in it. "Okay."
When was the last time I wore it?

Jenna Goes To Shower

And when she emerges from the bath-
        room, steam trailing her, there's something

about her that I can't attribute to the sweater,
        or the makeup, or the way she has blow-dried

her long white-gold hair. At last, I pull myself
        upright. "Um . . . got a big date or something?"

Fact is, I've never seen her with a guy.
        Didn't know she even had one on her radar.

                She smiles. *Don't know how "big"*
            it is. But I guess you could call it

                  a date. It's just lunch and a movie.
            She doesn't volunteer more, and

I know she's expecting me to want
        information. I definitely do. "With who?"

                Her grin widens. *I met him at your*
            plastic surgeon's office. He's her son.

Her Son?

Okay, wait. Process . . . process . . .
　　　"So, you mean . . ." She can't be serious.

　　　　　　　He's black? Yep. Definitely black.
　　　　　　And really cute. And smart. And rich . . .

Won't mean a thing to our father, who's a half
　　　step away from the KKK. "Uh, what about . . . ?"

　　　　　　　Her face darkens, eclipsed by thoughts
　　　　of Daddy. *I don't give a damn about Dad.*

"Well, you should. He didn't walk out
　　　on Mom, you know." We've had this

　　　　　　　argument before. Her answer will be
　　　　the same as always. *That doesn't mean*

　　　　　　　he needs to take it out on me . . . or you.
　　　　We didn't ask Mom to leave him.

She's totally right. Daddy pretty much
　　　pretends we don't even exist anymore.

We sometimes get cards on our birthdays,
        once in a while with Wal-Mart gift cards

inside. Ditto Christmas. But he never asks
        to see us. I think we remind him too much

of Mom. One thing's for sure, though.
        If he finds out Jenna's going out with

a black guy, he will most definitely take
        an interest. "Okay, well, it's all fine by me.

Just remember guys are mostly only
        after one thing." I sound like a mom.

                        Her smile returns. *Even when
                you're dreaming about them?

Oh my God. "What do you mean?"
        Now I really feel sick. Burning up.

                        Jenna laughs. *You talk in your sleep*
                sometimes. And sometimes you moan.

I Throw My Pillow

It misses her by a mile, and it comes
            to me that we haven't shared a sister

moment like this in quite a while.
            Not since we moved in with Patrick.

                        I have to get ready to go now.
                        Andre's picking me up at eleven.

Eleven? Holy crap. I slept away
            most of the morning. Not a good

way to burn calories. I'll have to
            work out an extra hour. I try not

to look at the mirror as I make my
            way to the toilet for an overdue pee.

When I come out of the bathroom,
            I glance out the window just in time

to see Jenna scoot into a hot little
            Audi. Metallic blue. Nice car. I hope

this Andre person is nice too. My sister
        pisses me off regularly, but I don't want

to see her get hurt. And a guy is the surest
        path to heartbreak that I know. I put on

sweats, pull my hair back into a ponytail.
        If I'm going to work out for two hours,

I have to eat something. Our kitchen
        is the devil's den, the cupboards filled

with carb-laden crap. The kind that
        goes straight to your thighs and belly.

The fridge is a little better. I've become
        an expert label reader and calorie counter.

One orange: thirty-five calories, eight grams
        carbs. Ten grapes: thirty calories, nine

grams carbs. One tomato: nine calories,
        two grams carbs. I choose the tomato.

One Tomato

Two thin slices of Healthy Fare
       turkey, and two glasses of water

later, I make a call. "Hello? Is Sean
       there?" Long pause while his little

               brother goes to look for him. Finally,
          Uh, no. He's got baseball practice.

"Oh. Well, this is Kendra. I was hoping
       to use your workout equipment." Why pay

for a gym when the O'Connells have
       state-of-the-art stuff in their basement?

               Wade doesn't hesitate. *You can use
          it. But only if you let me watch.* Pervert

freshman. But, hey, what do I care
       if he gets off on watching me sweat?

By The Time I Get There

Wade has rounded up a friend. They follow me
        downstairs, stare as I program the elliptical

to level five. Cardio first. Weights after.
        The guys stand there, gawking. Might as well

give 'em a good show. I strip down to a sports
        bra and Lycra pants. "Can you turn on the TV,

maybe find a music channel?" Wade obliges,
        and I climb on the machine, tune into the music,

find my zone. Breathe in. Breathe out. Lose
        track of time. Push myself harder. Forget about

freshman eyes and banter. Breathe deeper
        as sweat trickles turn to rivulets, carry away

toxins. One tomato, two turkey slices. Fat.
        Breathe. Burn fat. Forget about the taunts

of the mirror and too many hours tangled in sleep,
        deep woods perfume, and the arms of a ghost.

Sean

Arms

Worked to the max.
Pumped to capacity.
Muscles bathing in lactic
acid. Slow build to

burning.

Lift. Rest. Stretch.
Push to the edge
of "can't," knowing
the only way to leave

your mark

is sheer devotion to
the power of "can."
Focus. Empty every
negative thought

into

a box labeled "not
allowed." Embrace
the pain, now electric.
Brand your name into

the skin of history.

Bulking Up

I look in the mirror, like what
            I see—triceps building. Pecs,
                        and flexors, too. The last,
            hugely important to sending
a baseball over the fence.

But it's not just my upper
            body I work. Core muscles.
                        Leg muscles. All must sync
            to become the best I can be,
and the best hitter in Grizzlies

history. Scratch that. Nevada
            state high school history.
                        No lesser goal will do, and
            to help me attain it, I have
resorted to help-in-a-bottle.

No more over-the-counter stuff.
            No, this is the real steroidal
                        deal, brought to me courtesy
            of Thailand, through a trusted
source. It isn't cheap. I had to

dip into my savings account,
            but hey, what else is that
                        money for, if not helping
            me get into college? Might
be a warped way of looking

at it, although any seriously
            ambitious athlete would
                        probably understand.
            Yeah, I'm taking a chance,
but not a big one because,

despite what I told Bobby,
            tests for steroids are really
                        expensive. Without solid
            suspicion, most coaches
won't ask for random ones.

And my guess is that if
            a team is winning games
                        by breaking home run
            records, most coaches
will close their eyes.

Case In Point

Uncle Jeff, who is definitely
        closing his eyes, but whether
                it's on purpose or just because,
      I really don't know. Today
we are in the basement, lifting

                        together. He wants to be
                buff too. *Take it easy, son.*
        You can use the heavier weights
            for your legs, but don't risk
                injuring your arm muscles.

I know he means well, but it
        isn't the first time he's told
                me the very same thing. I'm
      not fricking stupid. But I say,
"Okay, dude." Three more reps.

                You know, push-ups are good
        for your baseball groove too.
      Did he really just say baseball
        groove? I nod and do another
                set while he starts in on squats.

The fatherly advice is really
            starting to bug me, so when
                    he asks about Cara, my face
                prickles irritation. But I say,
"I think she's mad at me."

                            Women. Give 'em an inch
                        and they'll want the whole
                    yardstick. Huff. Puff. *Did*
                        you get her something nice
                            for Valentine's Day, I hope?

"Val—Shit. Is that today?"
            I forgot all about it. Well, at
                    least it gives me the excuse
                to say, "I have to run into Reno.
Thanks for the workout, Jeff."

Showered And Dressed

I call Cara's cell, half expecting
　　　　her not to pick up. But she does.
　　　　　　　　"Hey, you. It's Friday. We're going
　　　　to get together tonight, right?
You're not mad, are you?"

　　　　　　　　　　　　She is quiet for a few seconds.
　　　　　　　　　　I'm not mad at you, Sean. But
　　　　　　　　I'm busy tonight. It's Galena's
　　　　　　　　　　last basketball game and
　　　　　　　　　　　　I have to cheer, remember?

"But it's Valentine's Day
　　　　and I have something
　　　　　　　　special for you. . . ." God,
　　　　I'm such a liar. "Please?
I know you're going to love

it." Whatever "it" ends up
　　　　being. She agrees to meet
　　　　　　　　me after the game, but her
　　　　voice is tinted with reluctance.
Why, if she's not mad at me?

My Hand

Is on the front doorknob,
just starting to turn it, when
Uncle Jeff comes down the hall
from the kitchen. *Wait. You*
might take a look at this.

He hands me a shiny ad
from Zales Jewelers.
GIFTS FOR YOUR
VALENTINE, it says
at the top. FROM $39.99.

They're at Meadowood Mall.
One word of advice, though.
If you really think she's mad
at you, I'd spend more than
thirty-nine ninety-nine.

Then he really surprises
me, handing me a crisp
C-note. *That's the minimum*
necessary to make an angry
woman not angry anymore.

I stand, hundred between
        thumb and forefinger, not
                quite grasping this sudden
        generosity. "But . . . why?"
I try to give the money back.

                        He shakes his head. *I want*
                you to have it. There's more
        to life than baseball. Before
                you and Cara started dating,
                        I was worried you'd never

                        figure that out. I want you
                to succeed at your sport,
        but not at the expense of
                your happiness. She makes
                        you happy. Make her happy too.

I Want To Make Her Happy

I really do. But I'm not
        sure jewelry is enough.
                Cara is a riddle with no
                evident clues. Sometimes
she just fills the whole space

around me with light. Other
        times, she covers me with
                shadow. And I'm not sure
                why. She's beautiful. Talented.
Brilliant. Rich. She has it all.

I think about her all the way
        to the mall. Zales is crowded
                with last-minute shoppers
                like me. Mostly men. Trying
to make their women happy.

A glitter of diamond chips
        catches my eye. The old-
                fashioned necklace is three
                hundred dollars, and worth
every dime if it makes her smile.

It Is Past Ten

By the time Cara is finished
          cheering. She exits the gym
                    with Kendra and Shantell,
          all three looking pretty hot
in their short black skirts.

Comparing the three, Shantell
          is on the short side, round,
                    big boobs. Kendra is the flip
          side of that—thin as a twig
and almost as tall as I am.

And Cara? Cara is perfect—
          all taut, muscular curves
                    wrapped in kid-leather skin,
          with hair like waves of summer
wheat and golden eyes that

remind me of autumn leaves.
          I want to eat her up, keep
                    her a part of me always.
          I wave, and she peels from
the group, heads my way.

A winter-clipped breeze
            blows through her sweat-
                        dampened hair. She shivers,
            and when I open my arms,
she leans into me gratefully.

                        Thanks for being so patient,
            she says, head against my chest.
I don't know what's wrong
            with me. She looks up, smiles,
                        and the world rights itself,

shimmers with her glow.
            "Ah, you know, we all get
                        a little crazy sometimes.
            Anyway, tonight is about
what's right." I find the red

velvet box in my pocket.
            "I knew this was you as
                        soon as I saw it. Happy
            Valentine's Day. I love you,
Cara." So much it hurts.

I Wait For Her

To tell me she loves me, too.
She doesn't, but she does
open the box, and when she
sees the heart-shaped diamond
pendant inside, she gasps.

Oh, Sean. It's beautiful, but
you shouldn't have spent so
much. . . . I mean, I love it, but . . .
But? I don't like the sound
of "but." I take the necklace

from her hands. "Turn around."
I wrap the chain gently around
her neck, fumbling the clasp
like a dork. "This isn't even close
to what I'd give you if I could."

Cara lifts onto her tiptoes,
looks deep into my eyes.
Thank you. And now she kisses
me like I want to be kissed. So why
does my body refuse to respond?

Andre
To Be Kissed

Like they do in movies—
glossy lips parting
in bold invitation,
hungry mouths

                  meeting,

igniting the blistering
passion most can only
dream of. To be kissed
like they do in books,

                  some exotic

setting beguiling two
ordinary people, bewitching
them with its subtle
perfumes until,

                  stranger

inextricably linked to
stranger, their lives
are forever changed.
I am only kissed like this

                  in dreams.

Academically

The Zephyr Academy is a fine school.
Great, engaging
teachers. All advanced placement classes,

no more than twelve students to a classroom.
You can't ask
for a better environment if you want to learn

the things you need to get into an Ivy League
college. (I gave up on
that idea years ago, though I kept that decision

to myself until I absolutely had to confess it.)
As far as a thriving social
scene goes, though . . . uh, there isn't one.

Oh, there are a couple of campus romances
happening. But
face it, two hundred sixteen kids, grades

seven through twelve, most of them much
more focused on
academics than dating, the odds of hooking

up with someone special here are slim.
Probably why so many
Zephyr students actually get into their chosen

colleges. Easy to focus on your work.
That's not to say
that there aren't any cute girls here.

There are a few, and yeah, I've had some
casual sex with one
or two. (Okay, maybe three.) But mostly

I go looking elsewhere. Never expected
to find someone
in my mom's office, waiting for her

sister to get out of a pre-op counseling
session. Jenna is a one-
of-a-kind piece of . . . art. Kind of stuck

on herself, but who isn't? And yeah,
I'm a couple of years
older. Something to keep in mind.

Still, I Don't Plan

To marry her. Don't even know about
getting in deep.
Mostly, I like how we look together.

Okay, and I like the way she smells.
And the way she feels
when she rubs up against me, purring.

Hmm. I guess I like her. We've only gone
out a couple of times.
Tonight will be the third. I'm picking her

up at four thirty. Reno, Friday night, if you
want a decent restaurant,
you get there early or wait for hours.

Almost time to go, I notice Dad is home.
I can hear his poor excuse
for music leaking out from behind his office

door. I should probably say hello. We don't
see much of each other
lately. Two knocks. "Hey, Dad. What's up?"

He pulls his eyes away from his computer.
Doing some research.
He gives me a once-over. *You going out?*

Like I always dress in a button-up shirt
and leather jacket. But
I say, "Yeah. Going to dinner and a game."

Now he looks at me as if he's seeing
a complete stranger.
Really? You have a girlfriend or what?

Or what. "She's not really my girlfriend.
We've been out a few
times. But it's not anything serious."

Why must he take such an interest in
my uninteresting life?
Oh yeah. Control. *Tell me about her.*

I shrug. Give a brief description, omitting
the age difference
thing. Mention she goes to Galena.

He absorbs the information. Blinks twice.
Finally comments, *Blond,*
huh? Which means, "So she's white?"

"Yes, Dad, she's white. But don't worry.
Like I said, it's not serious.
Not even close. We're just friends."

I know what he's going to say, and he does.
You really should date
black girls. Are you ashamed of your race?

He goes on to talk about artificial beauty
standards, European
versus African, etc. All stuff I've heard

before. And more than once. But . . . "Look,
Dad. It's not like there
are a whole lot of African Americans in Reno,

anyway. Running into the exact right
black girl won't happen
that easily. And *this is just a date.* Okay?"

He Says Okay

And we leave it there, though I could
have said a whole
lot more. Like how his own wife

(my toffee-skinned mom) skews
way toward the Anglo
ideal. Like how she has made a fair

amount of money altering the features
of her African American
sisters, all to make them more "beautiful."

Like, right, wrong, or who fucking cares,
I happen to think
Jenna is pretty and enjoy spending time

with her. Like maybe tonight I might
even kiss her, just to
try it on for size. And if that works out,

well, who knows how much further
we might go? If she
feels the same way about me, of course.

On My Way To Jenna's

The conversation with Dad replays.
If I were to be honest
with myself, the truth is I have always

been more attracted to girls who reflect
the European standard.
Not that there aren't gorgeous black women.

But the ones who I'd label beautiful are
models—Tyra Banks,
Naomi Campbell. Selita Ebanks. Tall.

Thin. Long, straight hair. Fairer skinned.
Am I wrong to feel
this way? Does it make me a stereotype?

Or does it in some weird way make me
racist? If it does, would
I be less racist if I were only attracted

to black women? It's hard enough to
find someone you want
to be with. Why worry about color at all?

It's A Little Before Five

When we reach Red Lobster. Already
the place is busy.
There's a twenty-minute wait. We sit

in the lobby, people-watching. And
I'm pretty sure we're
being people-watched too. Funny,

two hours ago, I wouldn't have felt
nearly as self-conscious
as I do right now. Jenna intuits it.

> *Are you okay? You're awfully quiet.*
> Doesn't she notice
> the way people are staring? Then again,

considering how luscious she looks,
perfect little legs peeking
out from under a way-short skirt, and

dream girl breasts gloved sweetly by
a quite tight sweater,
they are probably not seeing me at all.

Jenna reaches for my hand, reminding
me that she asked
a question. Her fingers thread mine,

a checkered weave. "Sorry. Just thinking
about some stuff my dad
said earlier. It's not important." Not

nearly as important as how her skin
feels, sea glass smooth
in the palm of my hand. Or the way

.

       her gardenia-scented hair reminds me
          of California summer.
     Nothing my dad ever says is important.

     Not that he bothers to say much to me
           anymore. She goes on about
       her parents' divorce, beauty pageants,

orthodontia—oh, and did I know her stepdad
and my parents went to
college together? News to me. Weird connection.

Maybe Fate Does Exist

I've never much believed in it before.
But now I wonder if
some things are just meant to be.

If so, I should probably quit overthinking everything.
Jenna orders lobster raviolis, Caesar

        salad, dares to ask the waiter for cabernet.
        His dubious expression
        makes her say, *Doesn't hurt to ask, does it?*

God, she is ballsy. "Do you drink much
cabernet at home?"
I expect her to answer in the negative,

        or maybe with a joke. But, no. *Probably*
        more than I ought to.
        Mom always has an open bottle around.

        She and Patrick are connoisseurs. The last
        two syllables are hissed.
        And now I know a lot more about Jenna.

After Dinner

Walking to my car beneath a sift of new snow,
I slide my arm around
her shoulder, and she tucks herself into

the warmth of my jacket, one slender arm
snaking my waist. Very good.
This feels the way it should. The Quattro

is parked out behind the building. We stop
beneath a muted streetlight,
and I turn her so she faces me, her sweater

soft and warm against my thin cotton shirt.
I look down into eager eyes.
"Have you ever kissed a black guy before?"

Who, you? You're black? I never noticed.
And are you saying
you want to kiss me? She doesn't wait,

but tilts her chin and parts her lips, a quick
flick of her tongue inviting
me in. Our first kiss isn't uncertain. It's smoking.

Cara
Not Uncertain

About the fabric of me.
My skin is unblemished,
kept that way by some
amazing dermatologist

who

discovered the secret of
"zit-free" somewhere deep
in the Amazon jungle.
I'm sure that my hair

is

enviable—a burnished
bronze waterfall. What
I'm more than a little
vague about is

the stranger

who keeps insisting
she is the real me—
and that if I would allow
her to take up residence

inside

this flawless shell,
I will finally come to terms
with who I was born to be.

I'm Not Sure Who I Am

Not sure who I want to be,
or if I have any choice at all.
Maybe I'm two people.
God, maybe I'm many.

Does that make me a freak?
Do I belong in Aspen Springs,
finger-painting scenes from
my childhood, right along with

my messed-up brother? Now
there's a great family snapshot.
Twin number one: a warped sex
addict, filled with enough self-hate

to try and end it all. Twin number
two: unclear about her sexuality.
In love (?) with a guy. In lust (!)
with a girl. I have zero doubt

about the lust. As for the love,
I believed it was real. But how
can I want to touch someone
else if love is what I truly feel

for Sean? We've been together
almost a year, have plans
to continue seeing each other
postgraduation. In fact, I know

his college plans revolve around
me. For the most part, he's kind.
Supportive. Not once has he ever
tried to force me to give him more

than hot make-out sessions. Sex
is something that, up until now,
I haven't felt ready for. But without
it, how can I possibly answer

the question grating the inside
of me—scraping till I'm raw. Lust?
Love? Are they mutually exclusive?
Absent sex, how will I know?

Maybe I'll Find Out Tonight

Sean and I are going out after
his exhibition game. I'm getting ready
to go watch him play when I hear
a familiar name spill from behind

> Mom's half-open bedroom door.
> *. . . don't care about legalities,*
> *Mrs. Sanders, and I'm certain*
> *the school board won't either.*
>
> *Not to mention the press, and if*
> *you refuse to see my side of things,*
> *that's where I'm going next. Anyway,*
> *I'm sure you could use a fresh start.*
>
> *You won't find a teaching position*
> *in this city again. I think the best*
> *option for everyone involved is for you*
> *to move on.* The smell of Mom's drink,

acrid and telltale strong for so early
in the day, hangs like incense in
the air leaking from her room. I hurry
away from it and down the hall.

Poor Emily. Against the furious
force of my mother, she is powerless—
flotsam riding a whitewater
course impossible to divert.

No wonder my father offers gauze-
thin excuses to not come home.
Lately, he's almost nonexistent.
Something to do with Conner?

Surely I'm not the only one lifting
a backbreaking load of guilt.
Or maybe they really don't care.
Me? Sometimes I think I might implode

from the pressure. But implosion
is not what's expected of me.
Everyone I know would totally
freak if they even suspected I have

splintered, alone in my room.
I never reveal that Cara. That girl—
frail and choking back secrets—
is the Cara I am determined to conceal.

Bundled Up

Against the flecks of snow,
fluttering from the sky, I sit in
the sparsely populated bleachers,
watch Sean belt a long fly

ball to center, where it sinks
into the fielder's glove. Sixth
inning. No heroics so far today.
He gives the catcher a little shove

> as he turns toward the dugout.
> The catcher springs to his feet,
> gets in Sean's face. *What the fuck?*
> Before they can beat each other

> bloody, the umpire steps in,
> issues a reprimand. Sean smiles
> and looks up at me with searching
> eyes, as if to ask, *Understand?*

I shrug. Frustration is evident
in the taut slope of his shoulders.
But there's also a copper-hot seethe
of anger I hope he never directs at me.

I Have To Admit

It's not the first time I've seen
a hint of someone . . . hateful
lurking behind nice guy Sean.
Is he flint, waiting for a flick

of steel to spark some inner
grenade? He never used to be
this way, at least never in front
of me. When did his temper surface?

I notice it now in the way
he attacks the ball, charging
grounders, slamming them home.
I see it in how he smacks base

runners, tries to intimidate them
wide. This isn't about winning.
It's about conquering, and when
he errs, there's more than pride

on the line. Bottom of the ninth,
two-all tie. One out, Sean comes
up to bat. Please let him hit!
"Come on, baby," I shout.

"Piece of cake." First pitch,
he tenses, swings way out ahead.
Easy. Easy. *Thwap!* He bloops
one over the shortstop's head,

an ugly hit, but whatever. Grant
Blakemore takes two quick strikes,
and Sean's chancy lead pays off
when he steals second. That makes

the pitcher pissy. He throws
hard and inside, nicks Grant's leg,
sends him limping on over to first.
Our coach plays a wild card,

sends Bobby Duvall up to bat.
He fouls off the first three pitches.
Perfect. Perfect loser, that is. But on
the fourth, he must see the fastball

coming. He squares, slams a solid
hit into right field. Sean scores,
he and Bobby co-heroes this time.
It will be a good night after all.

It Starts Out Great

Sean is famished, so we go out
for pizza. I pick at one piece
while he polishes off four.
Are you sick or something? he asks.

"No. I just like watching you
eat." Not really a lie. I like how
he tears each bite almost daintily,
wiping tendrils of hot, gooey cheese

with a napkin before they can drip
down the front of his clean denim
shirt. I like the way he's careful
to keep his food unseen behind

closed lips. Sexy lips. Full. Soft,
for a guy. I like how his arm muscles
flex when he reaches for another
slice. I like the charm of his smile.

I like knowing he loves me.
There's something safe in that,
and yet, beneath pepperoni and onion,
he wears a thin scent of danger.

Danger Scent
Is Somehow Attractive

I follow it to Sean's truck, its big
chrome bumper leering through
a delicate veil of snow. I climb
up inside, determined to gain

some understanding. I need
to know if this is where I belong.
At this moment, it feels very right.
I scoot close to him. "Let's go."

> He looks at me with confusion-
> clouded eyes. *Go? You mean*
> *home? I thought we'd hang out*
> *a little or something. No?*

I run my hand along the meaty
muscle of his thigh. Wow. All
that lifting paying off. "Can we
go someplace private?" I sigh,

> and implicit in the soft exhale
> is something I've never offered
> before. Sean does not fail
> to notice. *Really?* He hesitates,

then starts the truck and heads up
the highway toward Virginia City.
Thank God it has stopped snowing.
My fingers play with the pendant

Sean gave me, sliding it back
and forth along the chain, the motion
sensuous. The road snakes south,
then north, ultimately taking us east,

and I wonder if life is like that. Go
one way, then another, to end up
someplace else. Finally Sean pulls
into a turnout overlooking city lights.

"Beautiful." I lift up on my knees,
turn to face him, kiss him as if this
might be our last kiss—intention clear
in the race of my heart and the way

> my tongue tangos over his. He pulls
> back. *Wait. Are you sure?* In answer,
> I squirm free of my sweater. *Now, that's*
> *beautiful.* His lips move over me,

wet and rough and punctuated
by sharp nips of teeth. He lays me
back across the seat and his thumb
runs along the waistband of my jeans.

Danger scent envelopes me. *You
are ready, aren't you?* He fumbles
at my waistband and I hurry
the unbuttoning, desire a steady

thrumming, like rain upon
tin. Strangely, I'm not afraid.
Sean is a hot salt rub, friction
against my skin, and it all feels

good. Right. I reach for his belt,
want to touch what's below his belly
button. Except . . . it isn't how it should
be. Sean rolls away. *Goddamn it. No!*

Stunned, tears spatter my cheeks.
"What's wrong? What did I do?"
Hands shaking on the steering
wheel, Sean whispers, *It wasn't you.*

Kendra
It Wasn't Me

That's what you said—
it wasn't me who sent
you running, spinning
into someone else's arms.

                         No,

it had nothing to do with
me. So why do I think
if I had only been thin
as rays of dawning sun

                         it

all would have worked
out differently? Flawless,
you needed a girl without
imperfections, and that

                         wasn't

the troll who lives in
the room beyond
the looking glass. No,
your perfect girl wasn't

                         me.

An Ugly Rumor

Has surfaced, scum rising to stink
          up the hallways at school. I get it

                    from Bobby Duvall. *Did you hear
                about Mrs. Sanders?* His tongue, I swear,

                    lolls to one side, like a summer-tired
                dog. *She and Conner were . . . you know.*

"What are you talking about, Bobby?"
          But I see the story in his eyes, and in

how some of the other kids passing
          by stare, then quickly look away.

                    *Kali Benson told me. She was in
                the office and heard Jerkwad Taylor*

                    *talking to the superintendent. Looks like
                we'll have subs for the rest of the year.*

I want to scream that it's a lie. But
          certainty plunks into my empty stomach.

Of course it's true. Conner trashed me
          for a teacher. A woman twice his age.

                    I don't see what all the hype is about,
          you know? I mean, she didn't, like, force

                    herself on him. Ask me, he was a lucky
          son of a bitch. She's a fucking babe.

I smoke him with my eyes. "Shut up,
          Bobby. The whole thing is totally vile."

Blood whistles in my ears, and my face
          drains, cold. The mirror would tell me it's

the color of chalk. I reach one shaky hand
          inside my locker, grab a small bag of dry-roasted

almonds. I take five, chew them one
          at a time, seven calories each. Thirty-five total.

I'm starving. Haven't eaten since breakfast,
          yesterday. So why is it so hard to swallow?

Distracted

Light-headed. Irritated by the stupid
        gurgling in my stomach. Five almonds

will not get me through PE, which means
        I have to eat lunch or risk passing out. Good

thing I brought a salad. Lettuce. Red cabbage.
        Half a carrot, grated. No dressing. Forty-three

calories, all negative. Now, to find a private
        place to eat. I can't handle the swarm of voices.

                Every time I let my ears pick up conversation,
           hey hear the same snippets: *Mrs. Sanders.*

                Conner Sykes. Sex. Sex. Sex. Goddamn him.
           He told me he loved me. I loved—love—

him, too, so I said okay. Did he love me?
        Did he love her, too? Did she love him?

Love is supposed to take the "wrong"
        out of making love. Was any of "us" right?

Too Icy

To run outside, we're doing laps
        around the gym. The wood is slick

and hard, but I like how my legs feel,
        pounding against it. Some of the girls

jog slowly, doing their best not to breathe
        hard. Slugs. I sprint by them, spraying sweat.

                Comments follow me: *Ooh. Disgusting.*
        What's she trying to prove? Stupid

                cheerleaders think they're special.
        If she gets any skinnier, she'll blow

                away in a good, stiff wind. And then,
        She used to go out with Conner Sykes. . . .

I run even faster, before the rest catches
        up to me. I glance at the big clock on the wall.

Thank God. The period is almost over.
        Thank God I can leave when we're through.

Picking My Way

To my car, trying not to slip on
        the snow-frosted parking lot, I am

almost there when I spot Cara,
        working her way to Sean's truck,

parked in the row behind. "Wait!" I yell,
        picking up my pace, even if it means

falling flat on my butt—something
        I just barely avoid. "I need to talk to you."

                The scarlet flush of her face tells
            me she knows what I have to say.

                  I'm sorry, Kendra. This was a bad
              way for you to find out. Zero denial.

Not at all what I expected. Still, I have
        to know. "Why didn't you tell me?"

                She stands, a hand on each hip, little
            in the way of compassion in her eyes.

I couldn't. Her voice is sharp as new nails. *But even if I could, I wouldn't have.*

You'd been hurt enough already. I'm sorry you had to find out. That anybody did.

"Me too. How is he doing? Do you know? Have you talked to him?"

She shakes her head. *He's still not allowed phone calls. And my parents*

don't want to discuss him with me. Or each other, for that matter.

That doesn't surprise me. He never said much about them either. And what

he did say wasn't very nice. "Okay. Well, I've got to go. I have a photo shoot."

We head opposite directions—she, toward her boyfriend. Me, forever away from mine.

That Seems More And More

Like reality. Not sure why I thought
       maybe we'd get back together again.

Wishful thinking pretty much always
       comes back to slap you in the face.

I think about Conner all the way home.
       Think about him and Mrs. Sanders while

I curl my hair, and put on the kind of makeup
       that makes you look older in magazines.

My agent, Maxine, showed me how to
       do it. She is forty, trying to look twenty-

five. And she wants me to look the same
       age. Easier for me. First, concealer, to cover

those sleep-deprivation shadows. Wait. OMG.
       Close inspection reveals embryonic tendrils

at the corners of my eyes. Perfect. Wrinkles
       before I graduate high school. Oh well.

That's why they invented Botox, right?
  Mrs. Sanders has great skin. Wonder if

she's doing the Botox thing. Wow. Talk
  about irony. Wonder if she's had a boob

job, if that's why Conner chose her over
  me. Damn it. If I keep stressing over this,

I'll really get wrinkled. The irony, like
  frown lines, deepens. I need something

to take my mind off it. I'd hit the liquor
  cabinet, except alcohol is so fattening.

(One hundred calories per ounce for
  the hard stuff, and I'd want it hard.)

But here in the medicine chest, between
  the ibuprofen and the Benadryl, is a little

amber bottle, with Jenna's name on
  the prescription label. Percocet.

I Don't Know What
It Is Exactly

But I do remember that Jenna got it after
            oral surgery. Some kind of painkiller.

And I also remember it made her really
            giggly. I could use a good laugh. I read

the label. Lots of warnings. Don't drink
            alcohol with. (No problem.) Don't drive

while using. (Could be a problem.)
            Don't use for more than five days,

as dependency is a risk. (Not enough
            pills left in the bottle to worry about.)

There's a whole list of possible side
            effects, too. But I'm only going to take

one. I wash it down with a huge
            glass of water. And by the time I finish

my makeup—blush, liner, smoky eye
            shadow, mascara, lip gloss—I feel better.

By the Time

I get in my car and drive halfway to
        the studio, I'm feeling great. No worry,

no pain at all. And, in fact, my empty stomach
        doesn't bother me either. This stuff rocks,

except it does make my eyelids heavy.
        I turn up the radio, crack the window. Cool

air streams over my face, fights a sudden
        desire to let my eyes close. Just for a second.

Thut-thut-thut-thut-thut. Whoa. That's why
        they put those bumpy things in the yellow line.

Okay, I'm awake now. Lots of traffic around
        me, and this time of day, there are bound to be

cops doing speed control. I signal, pull
        into the slow lane, and somehow I manage

the last five miles without drifting off, arrive
        at the shoot all in one piece. And happy.

The Photog

Isn't quite ready for me, so I sit in a big
      comfy chair. I'm not alone in the waiting

room. The man, who is fit and tan and wears
      pricey clothes, stares without apology. "What?"

           His smile reveals perfect predatory teeth.
    Sorry. It's just that you've got a great look.

           You here to do portfolio stills? His eyes—
striking green—continue their assessment.

I shake my head. "Pre-pageant publicity.
      Miss Teen Nevada. I've got a portfolio."

           *Of course you do. I'd love to take a look
at it.* He pauses. Then, *You repped?*

"Yep. I'm with Maxine Delgado."
      The studio door opens just as he says,

           *She's good. But I'm better. Here's my
card. Call me. I think we need to talk.*

Sean
We Need To Talk

Four words. Twelve
letters that strike terror
like a hint of a slither
through tall grass.

I

know what she wants
to ask me, know how
I made her feel. But I

am

afraid to admit
there's something wrong
with me. Something
fundamental. I'm

not

sure if it's fixable.
But without it,
I am less than

a man.

How can I possibly
tell that to
the perfect woman?

Can't Stop Thinking

About the other night—Cara
             so coming on to me, and me
                          unable to give her what she
             wanted. What I wanted too.
My body's betrayal is not

acceptable. And the really bad
             thing is, nothing is making
                          it work right. Not the girl
             I've lusted after, but had to
wait for since we were freshmen.

And not the hottest Internet
             porn. Okay, probably not
                          the best thing for me to be
             looking at in my spare time,
but I figured if anything could

encourage this piece of dead
             wood attached to my groin,
                          that would be it. So far, no
             good. Not giant boobs, not
girl-on-girl action, not even

the vilest three-way romp
            I've ever been not-quite-
                        disgusted to view. The damn
            thing just lays there, like
a bored housewife. And now

Cara wants to talk to me.
            If she wants to break up
                        over this, I'll totally freak
            out. Maybe I should go
to a doctor. Except a blood

test, if he wanted one, would
            not be a good thing. Can't
                        talk to Dad. Embarrassing.
            That pretty much leaves
Chad. He's a loser, capital *L*.

But I have to trust someone.
            I've trusted him with other
                        stuff, maybe even bigger
            (so to speak) than this.
After all, he is my brother.

Chad Is A Senior

At UNR, majoring in nutrition.
       Not that he cares much about
              it. He wants to go into sports
      medicine, and nutrition
was the closest he could get

without moving too far from
      home. He'll go to Vegas
            next year, if he can get into
      their graduate program.
Grades may be a factor.

Like I said, he's not the most
      ambitious guy, which explains
            why he never became Dad's
      best hope for a professional
athlete son. Lucky me. I did.

Chad has been very helpful
      to me there. Glad he isn't
            the envious type. Then again,
      jealousy takes a certain
amount of effort. Just saying.

I Could Call

But a visit to his apartment
        is almost always an interesting
                experience. He attracts a certain
        kind of people. Partiers, mostly.
And that usually means girls.

Yeah, I'm already attached
        to one. But it doesn't hurt
                to look at other ones, especially
        hot coeds. Chad may be lazy,
but I guess he's got charisma.

I go straight to his place after
        practice, stopping to pick up
                sub sandwiches—the healthiest
        fast food I know. Chad would
probably prefer burgers and fries,

but oh well. I do let him know
        I'm on my way, so if he does
                have a female there, they won't
        be mid-dirty. Wonder if watching
it live would fix my little problem.

But Today He's Company-Free

Good thing. His place is a sty.
        I pick my way through piles
                of clothes—clean or dirty,
        I can't really tell—cereal boxes,
crumpled Keystone cans, somehow

                        make it to the kitchen, where
                Chad's actually studying.
        Hey, bro. Thanks for bringing
                dinner. Have a brewski.
                        He gulps a big swig of his own.

I go to the fridge, grab a beer,
        sit across the cluttered table
                from him, unwrap my sandwich.
        He waits for me to say something,
but I'm not sure how to start.

                        Finally he jumps in. *You look*
                like you're bulking up pretty
        well. You ready for opening
                day? Uncle Jeff said you rocked
                        during your exhibition game.

I take a giant bite, wash it down
          with bitter beer. "I did okay.
                    But I've got to do better to
          impress a Stanford scout.
I'm working my ass off."

                    Work is a good thing, hence . . .
          He points to books, stacked
tall on the table. Only one
          is actually open, however.
                    Wanna tell me why you're here?

To the point, which is probably
          good. "Well, this is kind of hard
                    to talk about. Like embarrassing."
          Like maybe it was a mistake
to come. How do I say this?

                    He looks up from his sandwich,
          studies my face, which must
be the color of pomegranates.
          What? You got an STD or
                    something? He shakes his head.

Fuck it. Just say it. "Not
              an STD. I couldn't get one
                          if I tried. See, the problem
                  is, I can't get it up. Not even
when I really want to. Not

even when my girlfriend
          takes her clothes off and
                      climbs all over me. I'm barely
              eighteen, and my dick acts
like it's eighty. What's wrong?"

                              Chad grins. *Dude, you know*
                          about 'roids and nut shrinkage,
              right? At my horrified grimace,
                      he says, *Too much artificial*
                              testosterone makes the real

                              deal go away. That's one
                  reason why you don't want
          to do too many cycles in a row.
                  Stop using, things should work
                      like they're supposed to again.

Chad, Steroid Expert

Is also my supplier. And not
        just mine. He underwrites
                his living expenses dealing
        illegal substances. Steroids
are just the tipping-off place.

I'm glad there's a sound
        explanation. Still, "So I can't
                have sex until I quit, or what?"
        What about all those pro
athletes and their hot women?

                    Well, I wouldn't say that
                exactly. Haven't you heard
            of Viagra? He's got to be
                kidding, Viagra is definitely
                    for eighty-year-old dicks, right?

I Leave Chad's

With a pretty good beer buzz,
            one more round of muscle
                        enhancers, plus a penis fixer.
            Holy crap. But it's just for
a little while. I also got a lecture

about not combining Viagra
            with other drugs. About 'roids
                        and high blood pressure. About
            probable acne, potential liver
or kidney problems, and (this is

a great one!) the remote
            possibility of growing
                        breasts. About steroids
            staying in your system for as
long as a year or more after

you quit them. Chad is quite
            the lecturer, considering
                        he's also the pusher. Guess
            he doesn't want to feel guilty
if I wind up needing a bra.

Personally, I Think

It's all hype. Well, other than
            the penis problem. And I guess
                        my skin has looked better.
            That, at least, can be fixed
without resorting to pill popping.

I have to admit I'm curious
            to see if the "little blue pill"
                        can fix me. If it can make me
            some kind of sex superstar.
None of the times I've had

sex before were what you
            might call memorable. Easy.
                        Fast. Not much in the way
            of intensive foreplay. Nothing
like what you see in movies.

I'm a total amateur. Time
            for some real practice, with
                        a little chemical assistance.
            Now if only Cara is up for
it too, like the other night.

A Little Fuzzy

(Foamy?) around the edges,
        I decide to wait until I get
                home to give her a call.
        I manage the icy drive without
incident, park mostly straight,

make my way inside. I'm pretty
        much a lightweight drinker,
                so the four beers I downed
        at Chad's have blunted my
motivation. Glad I already

                        ate, because as soon as Aunt
                Mo hears me come in, she calls
        from the kitchen, *We're all at*
                the table. Were you going to
                        grace us with your presence?

She's bitchy. I'm fuzzy.
        A deadly combination.
                "No," I yell. "I don't feel
        so hot." Not a lie. Suddenly
bed sounds like a good plan.

Andre
So Hot

Beneath her cool veneer,
she's steaming. You'd think
she was thirty, not just
sixteen, and I can't

                              help

but wonder how she learned
the dance of the cobra.
Sensuous. Dangerous.
Deadly venomous. And

                              I'm

the snake charmer who
snaps out of a trance
to find the serpent
has tricked him into

                              tumbling

under her spell. I swore
this wouldn't happen.
Never believed it was
possible to fall so

                              hard.

Wish I Could Say

I've fallen for the perfect girl,
but that would be
a lie. Or at least a gross exaggeration.

There's a lot about Jenna to love.
The way she looks,
of course, all curves and frothiness.

Cotton candy. Or cumulus clouds.
And when she turns
her focus on you, brother, you are king

and she is part lady-in-waiting, part
concubine. You want
to put her up on a pedestal, as long

as she's naked. We have gotten
naked a time or two,
and Lord help me, that girl has shown

me things most grown women
would blush at.
All that stuff goes in the plus column.

In The Minus Column

Loitering beneath the sweet fluff,
the wide-eyed faux
innocence, is something hard. Maybe

even just a little bit scary. A fallen angel,
perhaps. A creature
of the heavens, surviving in earthly shadow.

I don't see that part of her very often.
Just a bitchlike snap
at someone she might consider competition.

A misplaced remark, revealing under-
belly. But never directed
at me. At least, not yet. There's something

else, too. Something harder to define.
It has to do with the way
she can shift between demanding total

attention to turning herself off to the rest
of the world. Blanking
out everyone else completely. Even me.

It's A Small Price

To pay for spending time with her.
Because, despite
her few shortcomings, I think I'm in

love with her. It sure feels that way
when I'm with her.
I never want to let her go. She even

has me trying new things—crazy things
I'd never do on my own.
Today we're going to the Ultimate Rush

Thrill Park at the Grand Sierra Resort.
Not sure what the rush
is in miniature golf and bumper cars,

but we'll see. First Saturday in March,
the sun is out but
the air is still pre-spring crisp, so when

I pull up in front of Jenna's house, I'm not
expecting to see her
dressed the way she is. Then again,

it *is* Jenna, so why am I surprised
that she has chosen
butt-clinging shorts and a low-cut

sweater that leaves absolutely nothing
to the imagination?
At least she brought a very small, very

tight leather jacket. "Damn, girl, you
sure you're going
to be warm enough? Kind of chilly out."

She shimmies into the passenger seat.
Smiles. *Yeah, but
you know how to keep a girl warm.*

I can't help but admire what her push-up
bra is pushing up. "Not sure
who's keeping who warm, but let's go."

The Ultimate Rush

Is more than a little obvious as soon
as we pull in and park.
I've driven past the Grand Sierra a few

times, and for some reason I never really
looked at what these tall
white towers were. Namely, truly frightening

thrill rides, especially for someone like me,
who is not especially
fond of heights. "I thought we were playing

peewee golf and driving go-carts." A scream
pulls my eyes past
the windshield just as the backward

bungee jump yanks a couple in a small
cage some seventy feet
into the air. "Uh . . . that doesn't look fun."

> *Sure it does. And just in case you need*
> *some liquid courage,*
> *I brought this. It will keep us warm, too.*

She pulls a flask out of her purse, offers
it to me. *Cinnamon
schnapps. Careful. It's got a little bite.*

Alcohol and backward bungee jumping?
Sounds like a bad
combination to me. "I don't know . . ."

Come on, she purrs, taking a sip herself
before urging the flask
into my hand. *It will take the edge off.*

Slow burn the edge off is more like it.
Cinnamon schnapps is
like cinnamon cough syrup. Thick

and too sweet, despite the signature
Red Hot flavoring.
Liquid flame trickles down my throat.

"Lord, girl." It comes out a raspy whisper.
And I can feel a sticky
smolder creep into my empty stomach.

Yet I help myself to another nip before
handing back the flask.
"Your mama should have named you Delilah."

> *Huh?* She takes a long pull and doesn't
> even cough as it goes
> down. What a girl. A crazy, soon-to-be

drunk girl. "You know, as in Samson
and Delilah?" The rumble
in my belly tells me I really need to eat.

> Jenna shakes her head. *Samson is, like, in*
> *Greek mythology, right?*
> *We studied that in fifth grade.* She smiles.

"Actually, the story is in the Bible and . . .
oh, never mind. You
hungry? I am. Let's get food and then . . ."

Two people on a giant rubber band slingshot
past the window, shrieking.
It doesn't look fun either. "Then we'll see."

Jenna Knows

A good burger restaurant inside the Grand
Sierra. We have to walk
through the casino to get there. I hook

my arm around her waist, claiming her. Not
to mention keeping her
a little more steady on her feet. She rocks

slightly, exaggerating the sway of her hips.
Heads turn and every old
pervert in the place looks at me with envy.

> Jenna puffs up on the attention. *Did you*
> *see that guy? I thought*
> *his eyeballs were gonna pop out of his head.*

I should feel proud, right? So why does
my face flush, fever-hot,
and blood roar in my ears? "Do you have

to shake your ass like that? Those dudes
probably think you're
a hooker." Immediately, an apology

springs to my lips. But, schnapps or just
because it's her, Jenna
couldn't care less. *Hey, you got it, flaunt it.*

She's so cute, I don't want to argue and spoil
the day. But I really do wish
the only guy she played flirt with was me.

Instead she flaunts her way to Johnny Rockets,
exposes five-star cleavage
to get us a better table a little quicker.

If it wouldn't be too, too obvious, the host
would probably walk
backward, to better enjoy the view.

Our order is taken in record time, although
the waiter lingers, making
suggestions, awash in Jenna's sensual aura.

When we're finally sort of alone, I can't help
myself. "That kind of
attention could get a girl into trouble."

Her Smile Dissolves

And her eyes ice over. She is silent for
                            several seconds, then
            opens up. *A girl can get into trouble*

*without doing a goddamn thing. Better
                to know what you have
        and how to use it to get what you want.*

*At least then, you're in control. You
            have the power. I never
    want to be powerless again.* She doesn't

offer anything else, and though I know
there's a lot more,
I'm not really sure I want to hear the rest

anyway. She leans forward, and my eyes
are drawn to the inhale-
exhale in the deep scoop of her sweater.

That makes her smile again, and I can't
think of anything to
say. Thank God our food arrives.

Post Burgers And Fries

The day has warmed even more, and
it feels good to walk
in the sunshine, holding Jenna close.

I'm glad I brought plenty of cash. Each
attraction is a separate
cost. The big ones are major. "Holy crap.

Twenty-five dollars each to lose our lunch?
Are you sure you want
to do this? I mean, I don't mind paying. . . ."

I look up at the rubber band thingie. Jenna
laughs. *Let's start with the
go-carts, see how we feel.* She, of course,

outdrives me, and somehow I'm not amazed
when she convinces me
to spend fifty bucks to try the slingshot.

We climb into the cage, and as they strap
us in, I wonder if I am
more afraid of the ride or of my girlfriend.

Cara
Am I More Afraid

Of taking a chance and
learning I'm somebody
I don't know, or of risking
new territory,

only to find I'm the same
old me? There is comfort
in the tried and true.
Breaking ground

might uncover a sinkhole,
one impossible to climb out
of. And setting sail in
uncharted waters

might mean capsizing into
a sea monster's jaws.
Easier to turn my back on
these things

than to try them and fail.
And yet, a whisper insists
I need to know if they are or
aren't integral to me.

Status quo is a swamp.
And stagnation is slow death.

Sunday Mornings

I usually sleep in, but today
I wake from a weird dream about
trying to extricate myself from quicksand.
I can't quite shake the dread,

so I haul my butt out of bed,
force my blurry eyes to look out
the window. What a stellar day—
sun-washed, brittle blue sky.

No hint of wind. Maybe I'll go
for a run. Now that I'm finished
cheering, I need regular exercise
or I'll turn into a big tub of nerves.

I dress in sweats, a long-sleeved
tee, my favorite running shoes.
The house is quiet when I go
downstairs. Guess no one but me

had bad dreams last night. I swallow
a power bar, a glass of water.
Stretch a little, head out into the cool
brass morning. I swing onto the bike

path that snakes through
our neighborhood. The sun
slips warm fingers through
my hair, and I try to outrun

the demons nipping my heels.
Sean. Conner. Dani, who called
yesterday and asked when I was
going boarding again. She wants

to see me. I had almost convinced
myself our connection was all in
my head. That our kiss was a test.
One I failed. Then came her call

and the husky promise of her voice.
I push myself faster, engage
overdrive, tugging in air scented
with wet sage. At the three-mile

mark, I turn around, slow to catch
my breath. Jog until my muscles
start to relax. As the old song says,
"I feel like I'm a cog in something turning."

Down The Home Stretch

I approach the Sanderses' house
and slow even more. In the driveway
is a moving van, and now I notice
the FOR SALE sign staked in the lawn.

Men hustle in and out, carrying boxes
and wheeling furniture-laden dollies.
I watch for a minute, absurdly
feeling like I am somehow responsible.

No. Not me. And not Conner. This
is my mother's doing. Well, okay,
Emily Sanders has to take some
of the blame, but it bothers me

that my mom not only got her fired,
but also strong-armed her into
selling her house and moving away.
That is wrong on so many levels.

The most messed-up thing about
it is that Conner's warped need started
the whole thing. Yes, it takes two
to dance. But somebody has to lead.

I Run Home

Blow through the door, down
the hall. Mom and Dad are drinking
coffee. At the same table, even.
It's all so civilized, so domestic,

I can hardly believe it and almost
forget what upset me to start with.
Almost. "What have you done?"
I glare at Mom, and she responds

> with an amused stare. *I'm sure*
> *I don't know what you mean.*
> *And are you dripping sweat on*
> *the tile?* She is always so measured,

sometimes I wish I could make
her yell. But I can barely get her
to frown. "How did you manage
to make the Sanderses sell their house?"

> *We have a restraining order in*
> *place. I pointed out the obvious—*
> *it would be easier if she and Conner*
> *simply never came face-to-face.*

And anyway, their divorce is no
doubt imminent. It's just as well
they think about how to divide
things up when the house does sell.

God, she is smug. "Oh, so you
talked them into getting a divorce,
too? Awesome, Mother. Who
knew you could be so persuasive?"

She levels me with her eyes.
I had nothing to do with that.
It was Emily Sanders's extremely
bad judgment that got her into

this mess. No husband in his right
mind would stay with a woman
like her. Isn't that right? Directed
at Dad, who dares not say a word

unless it's the exact word Mom
wants to hear. Dad shrugs, goes
back to his paper. And all I can
do is quit dripping sweat on the tile.

I Turn The Shower Hot

I feel dirty, and not from my run.
Nothing Mom said was totally
wrong, but I just can't get it out
of my head that she has taken

the Sanderses' tattered lives and
made sure they could never be
sewn back together again. And
I think she would do the same

to me, if I ever gave her a reason.
All she cares about is being right.
Winning. And taking out anyone
who might tarnish her sterling

reputation. No wonder Conner
went to such an extreme. If you're
going to make a statement, make
it a big one, not that I'd dream

of taking on Mom. Now *that* is crazy.
I wash my hair with coconut shampoo.
Scrub my skin with lemongrass soap.
When I'm through, I am almost clean.

The Afternoon Is Looking Long

I need to get out of here. I could
call Sean. He'd probably stop
lifting long enough to do something
with me. But we haven't seen all

that much of each other since
the night I basically threw myself
at him and he left me still a virgin.
Not sure who was more embarrassed.

Instead I try Dani, who answers
right away. Almost as if expecting
my call. Was she? "I was wondering
if you had plans for today."

> *Glad you called. No plans. What*
> *did you have in mind?* In mind?
"I don't know. Just have to get out of
the house for a few." Hours, that is.

Movie? No. I want to talk, get to
know her better. "It's pretty out
today. We could take a walk."
She agrees to meet me at Rock Park.

It's A Twenty-Minute Drive

In my stomach is a tentative flutter,
moth wings against a muted light.
On the radio (some kind of sign?),
Katy Perry sings about kissing a girl.

And liking it. I take myself back
to that day in the trees. Kissing Dani.
And liking it so much it made me
turn feeble in the knees. Did kissing

Sean ever make me feel that way?
I don't think so. Don't think
kissing *any* boy ever made me feel
that way—like standing at the brink

of a very tall cliff, wind at my back
tipping me forward, the rock
beneath my feet starting to crumble,
but not afraid to go slipping into

the unknown. I could retreat
from this place. Instead I take
a deep breath, plunge into some
mysterious space. And I like it.

The River Is High

Winter-fed currents rush down-
stream, chew at the rocky banks.
Dani sits on a picnic table,
watching a few intrepid kayakers,

and even in profile, she defines
stark beauty—all steep slopes
and sharp tilts and spikes of russet
hair. I call her name, and when

she turns, her smile is like April
sun on the March snow drifted
deep inside me. Just seeing her
has lifted the morning's weight.

She senses something, or it shows
in my eyes. *You okay? What's wrong?*
I could say nothing, but why lie?
"It's a long story. Let's walk."

We start down the riverside bike
path, and I begin my lurid saga.
Cool, distant father. Frigid,
twisted mother. Sad, sick twin.

When I get to the stuff about Emily,
Dani's fingers knot into mine. *Wow.*
That's like something you see on TV.
But darlin', you're not the only one

with a messed-up family. My mom
left us for heroin when I was six.
She OD'd a couple of years ago.
In between, she was turning tricks,

and got pregnant with my little brother.
She came crawling back. Dad was great.
He took her in, and when she left us
for smack again, he raised Caleb like

his own. We were doing okay, except
when Mom died, Caleb freaked out.
Like she'd ever been his mom, you know?
Anyway, he fried his brain on ecstasy.

Stole a car and drove it the wrong way
down the freeway, head-on into a semi.
He was only fourteen. So now it's just
Dad and me. Everyone else is dead.

Her Hand Trembles In Mine

And now it's my turn to be strong.
I stop. Pull her very close to me, swim
into the glittering pools in her eyes.
"I'm sorry." She nods, parts her lips,

and when our mouths meet, it is with
urgency. Need. Lust. And understanding
that this might be only the beginning.
We feed on each other. Draw strength

from the nourishment. We are alone here,
but were we not, I wouldn't care who might
be watching as we wrap each other in
each other, caught up in a net of desire

so strong there can be no breaking
free. Her skin is softest leather.
Her tongue, butter melting on mine.
She smells of ginger. Tastes of mint

and strawberry. She is angle. I am
curve. Together, we are geometric
sculpture, and we make perfect sense.
But just how far am I willing to go?

Kendra
How Far

Down can this one drop me?
Will it plummet me into a no-
man's-land so pleasure-dense
that memory can't

follow?

How high will this one launch
me? Will I soar above this
pain-infused planet, no fear,
and no desire to ever

turn back?

Who knew so many answers
might be found inside
little amber bottles? Sad?
Pop a pill. Fat?

Run screaming for

the medicine chest.
Calorie counting becomes
obsolete when all you want
to swallow is water and

Mommy's Little Helper

makes that happen for you.

I Don't Know Why

It took me so long to find my way
        to Pharmaceuticalville. I guess I thought

pill popping was for losers. People who
        couldn't hack reality. Couldn't control

themselves or conquer their weaknesses.
        Ha. I never thought I was weak before,

not even when the mirror insisted I was
        a total wuss. It's all very clear now, though.

And I can't believe how easy it is to not
        feel hungry. To not feel sorry. To not feel

sad or worried or like the whole world
        just wants to crush me, and all I have to do

is match the messed-up mood to the proper
        chemical adjuster. If that makes me weak,

oh well. But I think it makes me smart.
        Why push uphill when you can coast?

I Was Only Going To Take

One Percocet. I needed it the day
       I found out about Conner and his skank.

His old skank. The one who just moved
       away. Thank God I don't have to see her

ever again. But even if I did, all I would
       have to do is down another Percocet.

Sheesh, if I did two, I'd probably ask her
       to prom. Except, now the pills are gone.

There were only four to start. After
       the first one, I waited a couple of days.

Then my dad decided to show up drunk
       at our spring honor choir performance.

It was the first time I'd seen him in months.
       And there he was, slobbering all over some

random woman and yelling like he was at
       a football game. And then he spotted Mom

and Patrick and, for whatever reason,
        decided to go say hello. And more.

While we were still singing. From
        where I stood on the stage, I could see

Mom trying to shush him. Which made
        him get louder. Soon everyone turned

to stare, and Patrick actually had to take
        hold of his arm, steer him out of the gym.

Then everyone was looking at me. Like
        I had anything to do with it. And here's

                the capper. Mom blamed me. *Why did
        you even tell him about the performance?*

We were all safe at home by then (well,
        not sure about Dad. Patrick handed him

off to his girlfriend.) I couldn't believe
        it. "Well, I sure as hell didn't invite him."

Which made Patrick jump in. *Don't you
dare swear at your mother, little girl.*

Anger sizzled in my head. "Don't tell
me what to do. You're not my father."

*In light of what happened tonight,
I'd say that's a darn good thing.*

"Darn? You can say 'damn,' Patrick.
I promise it won't damage us children."

*You are still a child, and it would
be good to remember that. . . .*

I was pretty much boiling by then,
and Mom sitting there, blank faced,

only made me angrier still. "Not for
long. I'll be eighteen next month."

Then he nailed me good. *Right.
You mean after your plastic surgery.*

209

It Was An Implied Threat

And the threat was, "Apologize right now
        or consider keeping your big, ugly nose as is."

Okay, he wouldn't have put it so bluntly,
        but that's what he meant. Or something close.

I backed off. De-escalated. Couldn't
        risk calling his bluff, though I was pretty

sure that's all it was. Swallowed
        my anger. "I'm sorry I swore, okay?

But I had nothing to do with Dad
        being there tonight. Cross my heart."

As apologies go, it was snippy, but
        the best I could do, and it seemed to

                appease Patrick. *Apology accepted.*
        About that time Jenna came in, messy

hair and blurred makeup indicating
        she'd had a little too much fun that night.

The attention shifted to her, so I made
        my escape, still percolating a big pot of anger.

                At my back, Patrick's voice had risen
      again, this time at my sister. *Where*

        have you been, and what have you
been doing? Buzz buzz buzz.

I headed straight for my room, and
        the little bottle of dysfunction stashed

in a sock in my dresser. And down
        went one more Percocet. Two left. Minus

one, not quite a week later, after I found
        out my dad is getting married again and wants

Jenna and me to be bridesmaids. We
        don't even know his girlfriend, something

my sister was very clear about. More
        family drama to come on that front for sure.

I Popped The Last Percocet

Three days ago, when I was passed over for
            a *Teen Vogue* fashion shoot. I had my heart

set on it. I figured they didn't pick me
            because I still can't get into a size two. Close.

But not quite. But when I asked Maxine
            if that was, in fact, the reason, she hung

                        her head and admitted, *That's not why.*
                        I'm sorry to say I dropped the ball.

                        It was a bad week—my daughter lost
                        her baby, and I had to help out with

                        her other kids. I just forgot to put things
                        in motion. But there will be other opportunities.

I almost lost it. But how could I without
            coming off as totally heartless? So I nodded

and fumed and finally dug into my wallet
            to find the business card of Xavier Winslow.

Xavier

Cool name for an awesome agent.
      We agreed to meet over Starbucks

coffee, and though I felt a tiny bit like
      a traitor, I had it in my mind from the start

that all he had to do was say the right
      things and I'd flip reps without looking back.

      He said all the right things. *You've got*
the look, that's for sure. His eyes crawled

      all up and down my body. *If you want*
to do runway, you could maybe lose

      a couple of pounds, but I can help you
with that. Then his creeping gaze stopped

      unapologetically right beneath my clavicle.
And . . . have you considered implants?

He was so straightforward, I somehow
      didn't feel the slightest embarrassment.

"As a matter of fact, I have. But my parents
        don't want me to." I went on to tell him

about my upcoming rhinoplasty, and
        even asked what he thought about Botox.

                He just kept nodding until I was through.
                You are serious about this as a career,

                then. I suspected as much. Here's the deal.
I have the connections to take you to the top.

                But you have to be willing to do things
my way. If you have an opt-out in your

                contract with Maxine, jumping agencies
won't be a problem. And I can be very

                persuasive when it comes to reticent parents.
Give me fifteen minutes with your mom,

                she'll come around. Your stepdad may
be tougher. But that's what moms are for.

Xavier Will Be Here Any Minute

I made sure his first meeting with Mom
would be when Patrick was busy adjusting

bands and wires on kids' crooked teeth.
Mom wasn't especially interested

in my changing agents. *Maxine has
been good to us, and good for you. . . .*

"Mostly true. Except she just lost a huge
contract because of personal problems.

I need someone who will always be there.
Just listen to what he has to say, okay?"

She agreed, and when the bell rings now,
I let her answer the door. First impressions

and all. She hides her stutter fairly
well. *Uh . . . oh . . . please, come in.*

In Mom's world, Xavier Winslow
is soap-opera fine. And all charm.

Not To Mention A Natural Flirt

We sit around the kitchen table, and
        though I am the topic of conversation,

                Xavier is all about Mom. *I can see*
        where your daughter gets her beauty.

             Did you ever model? No? What a shame.
        You could have gone straight to the top.

Mom blushes and smiles and flirts
        right back. This is a mother I've never

seen before, and it's all because this
        great-looking man is playing her so well.

It takes twenty minutes at least, but by
        the time Xavier is finished, Mom is beeswax,

melting into his smile, and I have a new agent.
        When I walk him to the door, he winks.

             I'll call you next week. He slips a small
        bottle into my hand. The label says Meridia.

Sean
My Hand

Has long been my dance
partner. I learned
the routine at eleven.

Early

to the game, I guess.
Fifth grade is much
too young to understand
the nature of uninvited

lust.

It didn't even take visual
stimulation, just the raw
sensation of skin against
cotton, and the memory

is just

as vivid as the real thing.
Okay, maybe not quite.
But there was something
about the innocence—

confusing

as it was—that made
those first clumsy explorations
border on magical.

Used To Be

I'd wake up every morning
          and have to spend several
                    minutes doing the hand jive.
          It's a guy thing, I know. But
not really sure if it's because

of something that went on
          in a dream, or just because
                    of the Boy rubbing nice
          against those warm sheets.
Either way, it was a great way

to start the day. But now
          I wake up limp as a worn
                    sock. I've been tempted
          to test the Viagra solo, just
to see if things will still work.

But it seems like a waste
          of a roaring boner if those
                    pills do what they promise.
          So I've been saving them up
for a little (lot!) Cara action.

I'm Tired Of Saving Up

I really want to see her, want
             to know what it's like to make
                          love to a girl who I really love.
             But lately I'm not sure what's
going on with her. For the past

couple of weeks, she's always
             had an excuse not to see me.
                          Homework. Prom committee
             meetings. Spring musical
rehearsals. Granted, she has

a lead, but still. Why should other
             stuff come before me? Yes,
                          baseball practice has come
             first for me lately, but it's all
for her in the long run. Why

can't she understand that?
             She did promise to come
                          watch me play today, so
             maybe everything's okay.
Hope so. I've got plans for later.

Great Day For Baseball

Well, it is a little cool, but
              hell, it's barely March. At least
                        the sun is out, and we're
              playing at home, thanks to
outstanding snow removal

efforts on the part of our
              grounds crew. Amazing,
                        what industrial strength
              tarps and snowblowers can
accomplish. Not to mention

shovels and brooms. I am
              stoked. Ready to kick
                        a little Reno High ass.
              On the field for warm-ups,
I notice a couple of things.

One: serious-looking guys
              in the stands with clipboards
                        and radar guns. Scouts.
              Can't know where from,
of course. But they're there.

And two: Cara made it.
                She's sitting with some
                                girl I've never seen before.
                Dark spiky hair. Cute, in
a kind of Goth way. Cara

points at me, and the strange
                girl smiles. Then they both
                                wave. Nice. I wave back,
                still wondering who's sitting
beside my girl, when Coach

                                reminds me, *O'Connell!*
                                We've got a game to play
                here. Get your mind off
                                the bleachers or go hit
                                                the showers. Some of

the guys snicker, but mostly
                because they're jealous.
                                I glance at the scouts, one
                of whom seems to be looking
my way. Get ready, dude.

First Inning

Reno High goes down,
            one-two-three, thanks
                        to outstanding pitching
            by Gary Bell. The scouts
are doing some serious

scribbling in their notebooks.
            Our first two bats retire
                        quickly too, but the third
            manages to slip one between
the short and second baseman.

Cleanup. That's me. On
            the way to the plate, I
                        peer up into the stands,
            hoping Cara will smile
for me. But my good luck

                        charm looks distracted.
            Maybe even worried. Hmm.
            Batter up! warns the ump.
            Wonder what Cara . . .
                        Steeerike! Goddamn it.

I try really hard to focus.
        Catch a piece of a curve-
                ball. Not a big enough
        piece. It's a short fly, but
thank God I run. The first

baseman misjudges, misses
        the catch, and I arrive safely
                on base on an error. Not
        exactly going to impress
the scouts like that, but

better than an easy out.
        Up comes Bobby, who's as
                average at the bat as he is
        playing shortstop. Surprise!
He smacks the first pitch

deep into center field. Triple,
        and I score the second run
                of the game for the Grizzlies.
        Rocky start. But I'll get
my bat going yet. Won't I?

Bottom Of The Eighth

Down two runs, I've yet to
            get my bat going. Fielding-
                        wise, I've made a couple
            of great plays. Just not
when we needed them.

Distracted, that's what I've
            been, and I can't quite manage
                        to stay focused on the game.
            Every time I look at Cara,
she's talking to that girl, all

attention aimed toward her.
            And the way she looks
                        at Cara . . . Damn, what
            am I thinking? Right now,
bases loaded, one out,

I really need to get my head
            back into the game. So why
                        do I turn my eyes toward
            the bleachers? Only this time,
for whatever reason, Cara smiles.

At me. Bright and sweet
and real. And that's all
the encouragement I need
to grab my bat, step up to
the plate, throw the pitcher

a "give it your best shot" look.
It's the first time today he's seen
me swell with determination.
His shoulders twitch. First
pitch hits the dirt in front

of the catcher. My turn to
grin, and he doesn't like
that at all. Second pitch,
a big, lazy curve that I let
go by. I want a fastball. Come

on. Unbelievably, that's what
he sends. Nothing for it but
to swing for the bleachers.
Clank! It's gone. Over
the fence. Grand slam.

The Reno pitcher deflates
           as the Grizzlies crowd screams.
                     I start my trot, eyes scanning
           the seats. Yep. The scouts
are taking notes. And Cara

is on her feet, clapping.
           Not sure which one means
                     the most to me right now.
           I'll call it a tie. I round
the bases, cross home plate,

suck up the back slapping
           and high fives. I barely
                     notice Bobby make our
           third out. Barely notice
the top-of-the-ninth-inning

play resulting in our win.
           What I do notice is how
                     the scouts pack up and
           leave, right after Cara exits
with the spiky-haired girl.

Being The Hero

Ain't all bad, and while part
           of me wants to go straight
                    after Cara, most of me likes
              soaking up the limelight rays.
We trade handshakes, head

for the showers, compliments
           flying left and right. Cara
                    isn't handing them out, but
           other girls are, along with
teammates and even some

                             guys from the other team.
                  I get cleaned up, and when
        I finally emerge from the locker
                  room, Uncle Jeff is waiting for me.
                    Great hit, son. Guess you saw

                      the scouts. One of 'em is an old
                  friend of mine. He's at Louisville,
           and I can tell you they're very
                 interested. I know you've got
                      your heart set on Stanford,

but I told him you'd be happy
to talk. That's right, isn't it?
I mean, just in case things don't
work out. . . . He looks at me
cautiously. Does he expect me

to get all pissed? "Sure, Jeff.
We can always talk." It won't
make any difference. Stanford
will want me too, and it's not
a bad thing to have interest from

more than one school. Uncle Jeff
looks relieved. Guess maybe I've
been a little short-tempered lately.
"Anything else? I want to call
Cara." Jeff shakes his head, says

he'll see me at home. When I try
Cara's cell, she picks up right
away. "Can we get together later?"
For some reason, I'm a little
surprised when she says okay.

Andre
For Some Reason

More and more, day
by day, my life feels
like an ultimate

           rush

thrill ride. One minute
I'm in the air, soaring
to unimaginable heights.
Close my eyes, I

           plunge

toward the earth,
breath caught within
the fear, then inches
from the crash, I

           find

my wings again.
And it's all because
of her. She is madness,
sanity. She is hell, and

           paradise.

I Can't Believe

The things I'll do for Jenna. I mean, thrill
rides are only the start.
Today I am going to watch a cheerleading

competition that her sister is in. No way
to spend a Saturday, but
Jenna is very good at getting what she wants.

Usually when I pick her up, she's outside,
waiting. Not this time.
I sit at the curb for a few minutes, finally

dial her cell phone, which goes straight
to voice mail. Guess that
leaves going up to the door, and as I make

the long walk, it comes to me that I might
actually meet her family.
Part of it, anyway. I ring the doorbell. Wait.

Finally I hear footsteps. A fortyish woman
opens the door. She is
taller than Jenna, more slender. But they share

the same platinum beauty. "Mrs. . . ." No,
Mathieson isn't right.
That would be Jenna's dad's last name.

I realize I don't know her last name. "Uh,
I'm Andre. Jenna's . . ."
God, does she even know we're going out?

Her expression says maybe not. "Uh, is Jenna
here?" I am a total clod.
Of course she's here. If not, I should run.

> Despite her obvious shock, she says,
> *Jenna will be ready*
> *in a minute. Come on in.* She moves

away from the door, and I feel like I really
need to apologize.
"I'm sorry I don't know your name. Jenna

calls you 'Mom and Patrick.' I mean, you and
your husband . . ." I need
to shut up now. Thank God she's smiling.

Before She Can Enlighten Me

Jenna stomps into the hallway, eyes
sharp with anger.
I hate him. He can't be serious, right?

The question is directed at her mother,
who answers with a shrug.
I know I shouldn't ask, but I do. "Who?"

*My poor excuse for a father. Can you
believe he's getting
married, and he wants Ken and me to*

*be in the wedding party? Bridesmaids?
I wouldn't even do
that for someone I liked. What a joke.*

Arguing with her is not a wise thing to do.
So why do I let words fall
out of my mouth? "But wouldn't you feel

bad if he got married without you there?"
At her evil expression,
I joke, "Anyway, you know you'd look amazing

in one of those beautiful bridesmaid dresses.
Maybe amethyst or fuchsia
or something?" My grin is met with bitter stares.

Both from Jenna and from her mom. I don't think
I'm making much
of an impression on Mrs. . . . whatever her name is.

"Okay, maybe not. Well then, are you ready to go?
Does your sister need a ride?"
I haven't yet met the infamous Kendra, either.

> *She* drives, *you know. And she left hours ago.*
> *They have to warm up, not*
> *to mention all that makeup and hair stuff.*

Jenna is more the natural type. She's pretty
without makeup, and all
her waist-length hair needs is brushing.

Standing here is getting uncomfortable, though.
"It was very nice to meet
you," I tell Jenna's mom. All she does is nod.

We Are Halfway There

And neither of us has said a word. I know
Jenna is stressing out
about her dad's wedding, but I'm stressed

about something totally different. "Did you
ever tell your parents about
me? I thought your mom's jaw was going to

stick in the open position when she saw me.
Didn't help things when
I didn't know her name. What *is* it, anyway?"

                    Jenna pulls herself out of the trance she's
                              been under. *What? Mom's*
                    name is Caroline. Why do you want to know?

"Not her first name. Her last name. You
never told me, and it
was rather embarrassing not to know it."

                    I did tell—I never told you? Her—
                              Patrick's—last name is
                    Carruthers. Sorry. I could have sworn . . .

Funny, no matter what she does or doesn't
do, all she has to do is say
"I'm sorry," and my anger just melts away.

"Oh well, it doesn't matter now. I was a shock,
obviously. Don't you
talk to your mom about who you're dating?"

Seriously? Of course not. We're not, like,
best friends or anything.
God, I barely talk to Kendra about stuff.

"Why not? I thought sisters told each other
everything." Not that I'd know
anything about it, except what I've seen on TV.

You don't believe everything you see on
Lifetime, right? Wait. Do
you watch Lifetime? Because that's weird.

"Lifetime? Wha . . . ?" And now we're both
laughing. Jenna has the rare
talent to be able to turn anything into a joke.

The Carson High Parking Lot

Is overflowing cars, and a steady line of people
heads toward the gym. "Wow.
How many teams compete in these things?"

> Jenna shrugs. *Pretty much every northern*
> *Nevada high school will*
> *be here. Even some from the rural counties.*

Which makes it dozens. We squirm our way
through the door, look for
a couple of empty spaces in the packed bleachers.

The competition is well under way. We watch
a team from Reno High
complete a complicated routine. I'm not a huge

sports fan, so rarely watch cheerleaders. But
after witnessing three
or four squads do their thing, I have to admit

I'm impressed. They could be really great
dancers, not to mention
gymnasts. "They're really athletic, aren't they?"

Jenna snorts and elbows me in the ribs. *Well,*
duh. What did you
think this was? Third-grade gymnastics? It takes

years of practice to reach this level. And that
takes real dedication,
which explains why you'll never see me cheer.

"Is there anything you *are* totally committed
to?" I guess I'm hoping
she'll say me. Maybe I shouldn't have asked.

Her fingers knit with mine, and my heart
tries to convince my brain
that she's going to say the words I want to hear.

My brain is not surprised when she whispers,
Commitment means
losing yourself to gain something temporary.

Nothing lasts. Not looks. Not love. I'm living
large and living for
today because there might not be a tomorrow.

237

Her Admission

Stated so matter-of-factly is like a slap
to my cheek. I suck in
breath. How did she become so world-weary?

I want to argue. But she's right about looks
not lasting. Even my mom,
who is beautiful for her age and knows every

skin care secret, is starting to look middle-aged.
Love? Well, it seems to
fade for everyone eventually. And tomorrow?

Okay, fine. I kiss her gently on the cheek, softly
exhale into her ear. "If all
you can promise me is today, I'll take it and hope

for tomorrow. And just so you know, today
I love you, Jenna." Her face
swivels toward me, and her eyes bore into mine.

> If she's looking for lies, she can't find them
> there. But though she
> blushes pleasure, all she says is, *Thank you.*

More Than Anything

I want to take her out of here, find a warm
hideaway to show her
exactly how much I love her. But just now

the announcer tells us the Grizzly Girls are making
their way to the floor.
No need to ask which one is Kendra. She's her

mother's daughter. Except she's rice-paper thin.
"Does your sister eat?" I ask,
half expecting a rebuke. Instead, Jenna answers,

>*Only when she absolutely has to. She's doing*
>*the heroin chic thing.*
>*You'd think Mom would do something, huh?*

Actually, yes. But Kendra seems to be strong
enough. She's tall, so is on
the bottom rung of all their pyramid stacks, along

with a muscular girl with toffee hair and a chubby
redhead. A girl on the middle
tier draws my eye. She is compact. Round. And black.

The Grizzly Girls

Are a formidable team, and they place well
ahead of the rest. After
they collect their trophy, Kendra waves

toward Jenna. *Guess we should go say*
hi. She gloms onto
my hand, holds tight, leads me down

the bleacher stairs like I'm a little kid who
can't handle it on his own.
But that's okay. I like the possessiveness.

All eyes are on me, and each pair seems
to hold a different
opinion. Jenna makes the introductions.

This is my sister, Kendra. The toffee-haired
girl is *Cara*; the redhead,
Aubree. And the black girl is named *Shantell.*

It is she who gives the most scathing look.
And when I say, "Pleased
to meet you," she turns around, stalks away.

Cara
Turned Around

I can't see the hurt in Sean's
eyes. Blinders on, I can pretend
he *wants* me to run from him.

I

have opened the flood-
gates, am helpless against
the furious flow. I

don't

have the strength to fight,
can barely keep my head
above water, and I don't

know

where I'll wash up if I just
let go. Does it hurt to drown?
No one teaches you

how to

walk away from someone
who you know loves you.
No one teaches you how to

say good-bye.

I Have Become An Expert

At making excuses. Manufacturing
lies. Walking the tightrope between
fact and fiction. Why can't I just
come clean? I'm such a coward.

I am afraid of hurting Sean, who
hasn't done anything wrong except
not be Dani. And maybe, just maybe,
not belong to the right gender club.

I'm also afraid of that possible truth.
Can a girl fall in love with a girl
and not be gay? Can she dream
of silken skin, perfumed with female

musk, yet joyfully submit to a man's
calloused touch? I still think I owe
it to myself to find out for sure.
So why do I keep finding reasons

to distance myself from Sean? I told
him I'd see him last night. Instead,
when he came over to get me,
we ended up in a major fight about

my leaving the game without hanging
around to say hi. Considering his home
run won the game, I probably should
have. But I wasn't in the mood

> for questions about Dani. Not that
> he hasn't asked me about her since.
> *So who was that hot chick with crazy*
> *hair? I don't see her around school.*

I could confess a couple of things.
"I met Dani boarding at Rose. She dug
me out of a drift, in fact. And she goes
to TMCC." It was enough. For the moment.

I Hope He Doesn't Ask More

About her tonight. We are going
to a movie, then maybe (maybe!)
finding a nice, quiet place for
me to get the answer I desperately

need. I watch for him out the window,
trying not to listen to my mom and dad
talking too loudly about my brother.
They haven't really fought in a while,

but they're currently having a smack-
down. Seems Conner refuses
to come home for a scheduled Easter
visit. Dad chooses to take it personally.

> *What the hell is wrong with him?*
> *Does he really prefer the company*
> *of lunatics to that of his family?*
> Mom raises her voice in answer.

> *Let him stay in that place if that's*
> *what he wants. Who needs the stress*
> *of having him here? What if he tries*
> *again? His progress is questionable.*

Dad volleys back. *What's in question*
is the ability of his so-called doctors.
We're hemorrhaging money to keep him
there, with what probability of success?

Money? That's what he's worried
about? He could hemorrhage cash
by the barrel and still not bleed
his bank accounts all the way out.

> *I don't know what you want me*
> *to say!* Mom shrieks. No wonder
> Conner flipped. It's in the genetics.
> Both of his parents are freaks.

Unfortunately, they're my parents
too. Fortunately, headlights coming
up the drive mean I can escape them.
At least for a few hours. I start past,

ignoring the heat of their mutual
glare. And out of my mouth comes,
"Hey. What happens to Stanford
if you have to sign up for welfare?"

I Half Expect Them

To be so wrapped up in grappling
with each other to worry much about
wrestling me. Which, of course, turns
out to be wishful thinking. Mom halts

> me with her forearm. *I do not*
> *appreciate your snide commentary,*
> *nor your eavesdropping. Whose*
> *side are you on here?* She waits

for my answer. I glance toward
Dad, but I'm not sure why. He
is still-frozen as winter glass.
"I may be rude, but I'm not a spy.

You weren't exactly whispering.
And anyway, it was just a joke.
Try developing a sense of humor."
Why must I poke toothpicks at snakes?

> *There is nothing funny about our*
> *current situation,* Mom declares.
> *But Conner will be fixed. And by*
> *no means is your education at stake.*

Fixed?

Like a car in need of a tune-up?
Would installing a new set of spark
plugs make Conner run like a champ?
If so, could that be true of my parents?

Or me? Maybe I should schedule
an appointment. As for Stanford,
I have zero worries. Not going there
would mean more than disappointment.

It would mean solid defeat, especially
for Dad, who has paved the way for
his children to shadow him there.
Does he still believe Conner will play

Cardinal ball? Does he still expect
me to become a lawyer? Do I still
expect that of myself? I used to think
that's what I wanted to be—a high-

> octane corporate attorney. Just like
> my father, who reminds me now that's
> exactly what he is. *Conner's status*
> *would not qualify as mitigating*

circumstances for your not attending
Stanford. Like that would be a crime.
Dad is straightforward. Curt, even.
Except when it comes to Mom. She is,

and always has been, the driving
force in this family. And sometimes
that means driving us head-on, no
possible change of course, into a wall.

Two halfhearted horn bursts outside
in the driveway remind me I've got
something better to do than this.
"There's Sean. May I please go?"

Whether it's the "please," or the desire
to resume their spat where they left
off, Dad nods and Mom (who looks
like she'd really rather not) says, *Okay.*

The Exchange

Was not so very long, and yet long
enough to taint my mouth with acid
spit, like I just bit into lemon flesh.
The night I step into is polar dry.

Spring, in winter's stranglehold.
By the time I reach Sean's truck,
I am shaking. And though it's warm
in the cab, my teeth chatter for a full

> minute after I'm inside. *Cold? I can
> fix that.* Sean pulls me into overbuilt
> arms. *God, I've missed you.* His mouth
> covers mine. I should wilt. Instead,

> I feel stiff as cardboard. Sean doesn't
> seem to notice, or attributes it to
> the cold. *I've got a little surprise
> for you.* His voice is odd. Quivery.

And his hands tremble slightly
as he starts the engine, backs onto
the moonlit street, and heads toward
Reno, driving just a little too fast.

"Hey, slow down. The cops hang
out up here on Saturday night, you
know. And what's my surprise?"
He just grins and drives right past

the entrance to Summit Sierra, home
to our regular theater. "Where are you
going? I thought we were seeing a movie."
Sean whips right past a pokey car,

merges onto the freeway. *We are
seeing a movie. Just not at the theater.
That's your surprise.* Ten minutes
later, we pull into a private parking spot

at an apartment house near UNR.
*Chad is out of town. He said we could
hang at his place. It's probably a mess.*
He winks. *But as long as the bed is clean . . .*

This Is The Opportunity

I wanted. Right? So why do I feel
like someone just dumped mercury
into my gut? Sean leads me to his
brother's lair. Clutter and dust are

> everywhere, but at least it doesn't
> smell like garbage or dirty socks.
> *Make yourself at home. I'll get us*
> *something to drink.* Strike one.

I think he means alcohol. I'm not
big on liquor. Still, when he returns
with two brimming glasses, I go ahead
and take a swig. Maybe liquid fire

> will incinerate the moths fluttering
> in my belly. Sean turns on the TV.
> *Chad has every movie channel.* He stops
> flipping at *Good Girls Gone Bad.*

> Sean gulps down half his drink.
> *This one should be good. Have*
> *you ever watched one of these?*
> Cable porn? Hardly. Strike two.

"Sean . . ." But before I can say anything
else, my eyes stray to the screen. Two
women are kissing. One, a pretty blonde,
unbuttons her blue silk blouse, spilling

flesh like fruit from a bowl. The other,
dark-haired like Dani, is quick to sample
the offering. I can't stop watching.
Now this is what I call a chick flick,

says Sean, and when he opens my blouse,
moves his hands over my skin, I let him.
And when he kisses down the front
of me, I lie back on the couch, invite

more. Next thing I know, we're both
out of our jeans. Sean surprises me,
hesitating long enough to say, *Christ,
you're beautiful.* He means it, and I know

it, and I know he loves me. His lips,
sultry and full, feel right, in all the right
places. Sean lifts over me. I close my eyes.
And now we are skin against skin. . . .

Kendra
Skin

That's what everyone wants
to see. Skin. flawless, stretched
over perfectly sculpted flesh.
Men are easy, in their hunt for

skin.

Flash just enough, they'll go
sniffing for more, and when
they're on the sniff, nothing

is

too much to ask. They'll give
up careers, sacrifice families.
Buy a new car, hand over

the key

to the one who wears skin
they want to lose themselves
in. And the funny thing
is, they don't seem

to

care who knows it. Not
friends. Not colleagues.
Not even the people they

treasure.

Size Two Skin

That's what I'm currently wearing.
 Fifteen-milligram Meridia is one magic

little pill. You don't even want to look
 at food. The only problem is dry mouth.

Gack. Like sucking on cotton. At least
 I'm drinking lots of water. Flushing

out pockets of poison. And fat. Fat. Fat.
 Pretty soon my body will be totally

fat free, thanks completely to Xavier.
 Thank God I met him. Everything

has fallen into perfect place. He's setting
 me up with runway gigs, and because

of that I can quit worrying about Miss
 Teen Nevada. Yeah, it would be nice

  to own that crown, but like Xavier says,
 If you want to go back to pageants, there's

always Miss Nevada next year. Or even
the year after. I don't really need that kind

of stress right now. As Xavier says, *You*
know what makes worry lines? Worry.

You leave the worry to me. I'm allowed
a few lines at my age. He does have some

at the corners of his eyes, but I think
they make him even cuter. Mom thinks

so too. In fact, he's got Mom eating right
out of his hand, and that's a very good thing

because I've decided not to go to college
next year, and Xavier will convince her

it's okay. *College will always be there.*
But you've only got a few short years

to work runway. College is better
with money in the bank. You know?

Beyond Runway

Xavier has connections at all the big
    'zines. He says once the plastic surgeon

does her thing, high-fashion shoots
    are a sure bet. The nose job is only

        a couple of weeks away. The day after
    Easter. *Once you heal up nice and pretty,*

        I'll talk your mom into the implants, Xavier
promised. *Everyone will want you then.*

Everyone will want me. And I want
    that. If the price tag is going hungry,

or making a few alterations, it's all good.
    When everyone wants me, those stupid

girls at school will be sorry they made fun
    of me. When everyone wants me, Patrick

will have to shut his mouth. When everyone
    wants me, maybe Conner will want me too.

My Heart Still Cries

For Conner. But I have to admit
        I don't think about him every waking

minute anymore. And I dream about
        him less and less. Is this always what happens

when someone you love leaves? They
        fade away, blur into memory like childhood

fantasies? Part of it, of course, is focusing
        on my career, fine-tuning my goals, near

and distant. I can thank Xavier for that.
        Plus, having a man around to stroke

your ego takes the edge off not having
        one around to stroke the rest of you.

I suppose that would be nice too.
        And the longer Conner is out of my life,

the more I'm starting to realize someone
        else might want to make me part of theirs.

Not That I Have

A whole lot of time for dating right now,
        but if someone asked me out, I just might

say okay. Especially if he looked like
        the guy sitting two tables away. Yummy.

Almost yummy enough to distract me
        from the reason I'm here. Namely, lunch

with Dad and Shiloh, who have just arrived.
        Rose's is a small place, so I couldn't hide

                even if I wanted to. Dad spots me right
        away. *There's my girl. Where's your sister?*

I'm not exactly sure Jenna is planning
        to join us. But I say, "Late, as usual."

        He sits across the table, putting Shiloh
        next to me. *You must be Kendra,* she says.

        Your dad talks about you and Jenna
        all the time. I'm glad to meet for real.

Up close, she's younger than I thought.
        Way to go, Dad. "Uh, yeah. Me too."

Also on closer view, Dad's mustache has
        silvered and he has gained a pound or ten.

                What's good here? he asks, scanning
                the upscale soup, salad, and sandwich menu.

Does he not remember our pre-theater family
        meals at Rose's? "Pretty much everything."

I look up from my own menu just in
        time to catch Shiloh checking me out.

                She blushes, but doesn't look away. *So,
        what are you getting?* Maybe she wants

diet tips? She could use a few. "A half
        spinach salad." Hold the bacon, egg, and

dressing. One cup spinach, seven calories.
        A few bites of avocado. A skinny lunch.

We Debate

Waiting for Jenna. After ten minutes,
       Dad decides to go ahead and order.

Meanwhile, unfortunately, it seems it's
       time for small talk. I mention Xavier,

and (just loudly enough so Mr. Yummy
       can hear) tell them about my fast-tracked

runway career. "Xavier says I'll make over
       fifty grand next year. And that's just to start."

               Shiloh (who named her *that*?) sits, shaking her
       head. *Unlikely. And modeling is tough work.*

Anger spatters like hot oil in cool water.
       "Really? What would *you* know about it?"

               Dad intervenes. *Don't get your back up.*
               Shiloh is in the business. Sort of, anyway.

               I design costumes for showroom shows,
       she says. *I know the business inside out.*

I Wouldn't Exactly

Equate the two, but I guess I'll keep
       my mouth shut. Or change the subject.

                  Dad, however, beats me to it. *What*
           about college? Won't it be hard to keep up?

"I'm going to take a couple of semesters
       off. Put some money away. You know."

                  The tips of Dad's ears flare. I haven't
          seen that in a while. *Have you discussed*

                  this with your mother? I don't think
          she's going to be very happy about it.

"Mom doesn't care what I do," I fire
       back, not that the assessment is even close

to accurate. "And why do you suddenly
       give half a damn?" Our eyes interlock.

                  I never stopped being your father,
          Kendra. I never stopped caring.

He Excuses Himself

And goes off to the restroom about
        thirty seconds before lunch arrives.

Shiloh and I stare at our plates for
        a long minute or two. Finally she says,

        You really have no clue how much
he misses you, or how proud he is

        of your accomplishments. Did you
know he keeps a scrapbook of newspaper

        clippings about you? Photos of your
pageants and cheerleading?

I shake my head. Don't want to listen.
        Anger is easier than forgiveness.

        We are strangers. But I hope that will
change. Your father and I want you

        and your sister to be part of our family.
And here's the thing. I'm worried about

*you. Are you aware of the damage
an eating disorder can do to your body?*

*I know you want to be thin so you can
model. . . .* What is she talking about?

"I don't have an eating disorder!"
I'm practically shouting, something

that becomes obvious when Yummy
Guy's head snaps in my direction.

I lower my voice. "I am in perfect
control and know exactly what I'm doing."

She starts to say something, changes
her mind. *Here comes your dad.*

*But, honey, you are way too skinny.
You definitely have a problem,*

*and when you're ready to ask for
help, I will be here for you.*

263

Who the Hell

Does she think she is? *I have*
       a problem? She's the one who

is marrying some loser guy ten
       years her senior. He settles in again

across the table, head swiveling
       back and forth between Shiloh and me,

nothing but love for either of us reflected
       in his eyes, and I feel like a total bitch.

              You two didn't have to wait for me.
          Dig in, girls! He takes a giant bite

of a very big turkey sandwich, and
       is trying to manage chewing it when

I hear the door open behind me.
       Suddenly, food flies out of his mouth.

              Who the fuck is that with your sister?
         Guess it's time for Dad to meet Andre.

Sean
It's Time

Time

isn't

Always

on your

side

To quit overthinking.
Quit plotting. Planning.
Worrying about outcomes.

for action. Reaction.
Putting things into motion.
Emotion, something it

easy for me to communicate.
But there's more. Lust.
This snarling inner animal.

in the past I have controlled.
it. For her. But pleasing a girl
is confusing. You can be

best behavior and still not
make her happy. And she won't
tell you what's going on in-

her head. You generally find
out the hard way. So I'm taking
a risk. But it's definitely time.

I Have Never Insisted

On Cara having sex with me.
         She didn't seem ready for
                          the longest time, and being
                 in love with her meant more
than getting off with her.

It was enough to hold her.
         Kiss her. Inhale the "her"
                          of her. Enough to gather
                 in the heat of her skin,
knowing that she was mine.

Then something changed.
         That night in the truck,
                          something had opened
                 inside her—some sudden
bloom of womanhood I didn't

expect. She was a wildcat,
         come into season—enough
                          to drive any man crazy,
                 and that's what I became
when I couldn't give her

what she wanted. Practically
        begged for. Betrayed by
                my own body! Thank God
        she didn't think I was gay
or something. She gave me

another chance, and tonight
        we will make serious love
                right here, right now, on
        Chad's sweat-reeking, not
real comfortable couch.

Those girls on the TV are
        beautiful. But I've got
                the real deal, stripped
        down to nothing but skin,
beneath me. She moves like

an eel. Sinuous. Cautious.
        My kiss is a question.
                Her tongue answers.
        Now she pushes my head
lower, asking for much more.

She tastes of soap and salt.
       A knockout combination.
              It makes me high. Makes
       me thirsty. Makes me hungry
for even more. This could

easily become addiction.
       Tonight my body hints
              zero treachery. Tonight
       it wants to go for hours.
"I love you," I promise,

though she can't doubt it.
       I prove it with my mouth.
              My fingers. My tongue.
       This is her first time,
so I want her to be ready,

and I think she has to be.
       "I don't want to hurt
              you," I tell her. "Ever."
       She is flushed, her skin
hot as summer sand.

I'm crazy again, this time
            with the need to make
                        this all real. I lift myself
            over her, working forearms.
Biceps. She closes her eyes,

moans as I move into place
            right up against her sweet
                        spot. Pause at the resistance.
            "I need you," I say, before
kissing her. Before going all

the way with her. One push
            and we will be joined in
                        the most amazing way.
            Connected by love. Now.
I have to have her now.

                        But just as I test the barrier,
                  everything screaming yes,
            go, she opens her eyes.
                  And out of her mouth
                        comes a single word: *No.*

I Heard Her Wrong

I know I did, and even if
　　　I didn't, I know she means
　　　　　　now, not no, so I go ahead
　　　and push. Hard. Oh. Oh.
And her eyes pop wide

　　　　　　and she screams, *Stop. I said*
　　　　　no. Stop, goddamn it. And
　　　her little fists try to pound
　　　　　against my chest, which
　　　　　　　only feels good and I can't

stop, even if I wanted to,
　　　and I so don't, so I won't.
　　　　　And she starts to cry and
　　　I don't understand so I tell
her, over and over again,

"I love you. I love you.
　　　I love you." Rhythmic.
　　　　　In perfect time with my
　　　body's rhythmic beat.
"I love you. I love you . . ."

There's A Strange Buzzing

In my ears. With a final
        thrust, there's a brilliant
                flash and the emptying
        is syncopated. My head
clears as the mist slowly lifts.

                      And I see what I have done.
              Cara lies, stiff as old toast,
        tear-glossed eyes staring
           up at me. *I told you no,*
                she whispers. *Why . . . ?*

Fuck. Fuck. Fuck. What
        the hell just happened?
           "You wanted this! You
        told me so. In fact, you
practically raped me. . . ."

              She sobs, and her entire
            body shakes with the force
        of it. *No. You raped me.*
           Her voice slices, tempered
              steel. *I told you to stop.*

DNA Evidence

Soaks into Chad's lumpy
        sofa in sticky, red ropes.
                But I didn't rape her.
        "Cara. We both wanted
this. I love you so much.

Please don't say I raped
        you. I've waited for this
                for months and months,
        until I was sure you were
ready. And I was more than

sure tonight." Cable TV moans
        and groans remind us both
                of how this little episode
        went down. I nod toward
the noise. "You even liked . . ."

                    She strong-arms me aside,
            jumps up, stalks over to
        turn off the tube, blood
            trickling down her legs.
                Bastard. You set me up.

I have no idea what she means.
  Sudden anger is a tornado,
    hurtling through my veins.
  "Look. I'm not sure exactly
what happened here, but you

are everything to me. Even
  if you weren't, you have
    to realize you can't get
  a guy all worked up, then
tell him to stop. It's not fair."

     Cara snatches her clothes
    from the floor, stomps off
  to find the bathroom.
    Rule one of the Rapist's
     Handbook. *Blame the victim.*

I run to catch her, grab
  her shoulders, swing her
    around, pinch her cheeks.
  "You shut the fuck up, hear
me? I. Did. Not. Rape. You."

When I Let Go

Of her face, crimson finger-
        shaped marks remain. Jesus.
                "I'm sorry, Cara. Really,
        I am." I reach for her, but
she slaps my hand away.

                        Don't touch me. Ever again.
                        I can't believe I trusted you
                enough to be here like this with
                        you. Can't believe I thought
                                I was in love with you. Stupid!

"Cara, please. I didn't mean
        to hurt you. I wanted to
                make you feel special.
        You are in love with me.
You have to be. I—I . . ."

                        Her lips curl in a feral snarl.
                        May I go now? I'd like to get
                rid of the . . . residue. She
                        doesn't wait for an answer,
                                but leaves me to consider

what all this means. Have I lost
                her? No way, right? She'll think
                        things over, and understand
                that this was a mutual fuckup.
Of course she will. And I'll figure

out a way to make it all up to her.
                Losing Cara would mean losing
                        pretty much everything good
                about me. I've programmed
my entire existence around

constructing a life with her.
                College. Career. Marriage.
                        Family. Together. With Cara.
                Because what good are
any of those things alone?

She Emerges

From the bathroom, ghostlike.
      Pale. Silent. A colorless shadow.
            "Give me a few and I'll take
      you home." I really need to pee.
And it would probably be good

not to have any residue on me,
      either. I run the water hot,
            wash traces of blood from
      me. Chase them all the way
down the drain. I want to puke.

Instead I get dressed. Comb
      my hair. Pull myself together.
            She will forgive me. I'm sure
      she will. But even before
I open the scarred white door,

I know she is gone. Amplified
      by the empty room, the *whoosh*
            in my ears is deafening. I could
      run after her, try to find her.
But what good would it do?

Andre
What Good

Can come of one-sidedness?
A house with a single side
is nothing more than a wall.
Not much in the way of shelter.

What good

is there in chasing rainbows?
Even if you found yourself
haloed with prismatic light,

would it

promise a happy ending?
Could an ending do anything
but break your heart? And
yet, what good would it

do to

shutter your windows, never
dream of rainbows or find hope
in promises? Why choose to

walk away

rather than hold your ground
and fight for love?

Fight For Love?

Would I? Could I? Should I? If it came
down to fighting
someone else for Jenna's love, I might.

But fighting to hold on to her love
is something else.
Especially considering I'm not sure

she loves me, or if she's even capable
of loving someone.
Hiding somewhere in that girl is a soul

defined by pain. I don't know what sort
of hurt left her fragile,
and she would argue that she's strong

as brick. But beneath her wall of bluster
is uneven ground.
A good hard shake could bring it all

crashing down. The question I keep asking
myself is, do I want
to be standing there when it happens?

I Really Have No Option

Any crumbs of choice blew away
the first time
she kissed me. And she knew it too.

> *Now I've got you right where I want*
> *you,* she said. Of
> course "where she wants me" seems

to change, practically from day to day.
And where she wants
me today is having lunch with her father

and his fiancée. The one she's pissed
about. My gut tells me
this may not go well. We arrive at Rose's

a full half hour late. Jenna is always late.
But this was, I'm
pretty sure, a deliberate grand entrance.

She never ever talks about her dad.
And I'm really
very sure he has no idea about me.

That Theory Is Confirmed

The second we walk through the door.
Who the fuck is that
with your sister? The words slap the air,

accompanied by chunks of sandwich.
Way to break it
to him, Jenna. At least her mother

didn't yell. I consider making a sharp
U-turn and running
like hell. But Jenna tightens her grip

on my hand. *Come on*, she says. *He*
won't hurt you. I
won't let him. And she drags me across

the short distance to the food-sprayed
table. *Sorry we're*
late. I had to change my tampon. Man!

If looks could kill, I'd be embalmed
already. Jenna's dad
is seriously disturbed. By us? Me? Both?

Kendra says nothing. Just sits, staring
at us with a mixture
of amusement and—relief?—in her eyes.

The fiancée keeps one hand on Jenna's
father's arm, as if
that could keep him safely anchored.

                    Jenna pushes me into an empty chair.
                         I am starving. She checks
                    out Kendra's plate. *Not for spinach,*

                         though. We're all transfixed, even her
                              father, who clearly
                    can't quite process what he's seeing.

                    Finally Jenna notices our blank-eyed
                              gawk. *What? Oh.*
           Introductions. This is my boyfriend, Andre.

                    That's my dad. And that . . . She points,
                              quite rudely. *Uh, not*
           sure what her name is. Back to the menu.

Part of Me

Wants to break the spell Jenna has put
us under. Another
part knows I really need to keep my mouth

shut. And there is still that little voice that
keeps insisting, "Run!"
I look at Kendra, eyes begging for help.

> But it is the fiancée who finally speaks up.
> *I'm Shiloh. Glad to*
> *meet you, Jenna. And you, too, Andre.*

Jenna ignores her, but my manners kick
in immediately. "Thanks
so much, and very pleased to meet you, too.

And you as well, Mr. Mathieson. Oh, and
congratulations on
your engagement." I extend my right hand.

> What was anger just seconds ago swells
> into palpable fury.
> *Listen here, boy. I don't know who you*

are, and I don't want to know, but if
I were you, I'd get
the fuck out of here right damn now.

"Excuse me, sir, but I don't understand
what I did to make
you so angry. Is it dating Jenna? Because

I'm not the first guy she's gone out with."
I glance at Jenna, who
for some inane reason seems to be enjoying

the whole thing. *Chill out, Dad,* she says.
I don't choose who you
date. Let alone who you get engaged to.

The room has fallen morgue silent. All
activity has ceased.
"Uh, Jenna, maybe we should just go."

Mr. Mathieson starts to stand, only to
be braked by Shiloh.
You go, he says. *Jenna is staying here.*

This Is Insane

I have no idea what my next move should
be, other than to do
exactly as he has suggested. Every eye

in the restaurant is looking at us—me—
and that makes me
extremely uncomfortable. I can't meet

Jenna's father's gaze, so I speak directly
to Shiloh. "Very sorry
about—" Wait. What am I sorry about?

"Scratch that. I'm not sorry. I didn't do
anything except walk
through the door with your daughter."

Directed in a straight line at Mr. Mathieson.
"I don't know what your
problem is, but I'm not going to make it mine.

I'm leaving, Jenna. You can come with
me, or you can stay.
It doesn't really matter either way."

I Turn My Back

On the whole ugly scene, walk away
without a backward
glance. Behind me, things escalate

> into a regular shouting match. Jenna:
> *You had no right to do*
> *that, Dad. Andre is really good to me.*

> Dad: *Listen to me, little girl. I'd better*
> *never see you with*
> *someone like . . . that . . . again. Never.*

Someone like . . . that? I am almost
through the door
when Jenna confirms the reference.

> *You mean someone who's black? God,*
> *Dad. What century do*
> *you live in? Anyway, we're just going*

> *out. It's not like we're getting married*
> *and making babies*
> *together or something. Andre! Wait up.*

I keep on walking. Last thing I need
is for some racist jerk
to come gunning for me. And that seems

a likely possibility. *Jenna! Get your ass
back here right now!*
The door closes behind me, and I don't

have the stomach to turn around and
see which one of them
prevailed. Jenna is strong-willed, but

her father is a regular ogre. Can't believe
a nice lady like Shiloh
wants to hook up long term with the man.

Can't believe girls as pretty as Jenna
and Kendra could be
so closely related to someone as ugly as that.

I Reach My Car

Without taking a bullet in the back.
Thank God for small
miracles. As I unlock the door, footsteps

come slapping up the street. Not sure
I'm all that happy
to see Jenna, but whatever. A quick scan

of the sidewalk behind her tells me we've
got all of thirty seconds
to make a clear getaway. "Hurry up, okay?"

> As I pull away from the curb, Jenna sighs.
> *Wow. I didn't know he'd*
> *get* that *mad. Not that I really care. Sorry.*

I'm pretty sure she's not sorry at all.
But when I look at
her, all wide-eyed and beautiful, I'm not

sure how to be angry. "Damn it, Jenna.
You had to know how
he'd feel about you showing up with me.

I mean, it's not like he just woke up one
day and decided to
hate black people. It's programmed."

My grandparents aren't the most open-
minded people in
the world, she says. *He definitely learned*

it from them. Her hand skips across
the seat, pounces on
my leg. *But, hey, aren't you glad I chose*

to break the cycle of hate? She says it with
a completely straight
face, then breaks out in a lunatic grin.

I can't help but laugh. "Girl, you make
me totally crazy.
And just so you know, I'm still mad at you."

Yeah, but you'll forgive me. Her fingers
dance up along my inner
thigh. *That's what love is all about, right?*

Cara

What Is Love All About?

I

                    The question is asked time
                    and again in books. Movies.
                    Television. Songs. Sadly,

                    have to admit I'm clueless,
                    and the theories I've seen
                    presented seem to

have no

                    solid footing on terra firma.
                    They are spores, floating
                    in imagination, oblivious of

real experience.

                    From what I've seen, love
                    isn't about mutual respect.
                    It's more concerned

with

                    control than sacrifice.
                    And I wonder whether
                    it's better or worse when

love

                    finally walks away.

Three Days

Since the night Sean had sex
with me. Three long days, trying
to make sense of the disgusting
scene that replays over and over

in my head—the worst-ever dirty
movie, stuck in an endless loop.
In retrospect, it wasn't all Sean's
fault. It's a thin line between

outright assault and temporary
insanity. And I was as crazy as
he was, at least for a few intense
moments. What's hazy is when,

not to mention why, I changed
my mind. My head said okay.
My body said hurry. But my heart
said I'd be sorry. And I am. I am.

I Am Also Incredibly Angry

At him. At me. At us. At there
ever having been an us. I guess
I got the answer I needed. But
it was never the one I wanted.

It destroys the impeccable order
of my life.
                    Ruins the rhyme.
            Makes the meter out of sync.

I'm afraid it will never be perfect
again.   I am indelibly stained.
            Forever redefined, but
                        blurred around the edges.

Because the clearer it becomes
that this other Cara really is me,
the less I'm sure that she's the person
I want to be. I'm scared there's no

turning back. I loathe labels,
especially those I can't free myself
of. So how do I hang out a "lesbian"
shingle? How can I expose myself

(so to speak) in such a blatant
manner? God, it's hard enough
waving around the "Stanford-
bound Cheerleader" banner.

Yes, I made it. The acceptance
letter came today. I should be
celebrating. But I have no one
to celebrate with, except maybe

Dani. And I'm afraid to call her.
Because I'd have a lot more to tell
her than just about Stanford. If
I open that door, let the bad air

out, who knows if I could close
it again once the sweet breeze
came wafting in? My cell phone
rings, and I freeze. I know it's Sean.

I've lost track of how many times
he's called in the past three days.
I know I have to talk to him.
What I don't know is where to begin.

If He Really Loves Me

He should understand that I am
not the princess he so desires.
Not a princess at all. If he really
loves me, he will want me to stay

true to who I am. The person I was
born to be. What I'm trying to say
is, if he loves me, he will let me go.
How frigging cliché. But I mean it.

> His messages have been predictable:
> *Please forgive me. I'll make it up*
> *to you. Tell me what you want me*
> *to do. Get down on my knees? I will.*

> This one is different. *Cara, you are*
> *my world. I've planned my future*
> *around being with you. I need you*
> *to understand what that means.*

> *I signed my letter of intent to play*
> *ball for Stanford. Because of you.*
> *I thought we would be together. Live*
> *together. Maybe even . . . Please call.*

Maybe Even What?

That sounded serious. No, more
like ominous. Surely he wasn't
hinting at marriage? Okay, that's
purely speculation on my part,

but if that's what he meant, better
to sever this relationship right away.
Because while I might have thought
I loved him once, I never considered

marrying him. Or anyone. When
I was little, my friends would gush
over wedding gowns and honeymoons.
But I saw too many people flush decades

together right down the toilet over
money or kids or meaningless flings.
My own parents chose to stay married,
which I think is rather funny, since

they show about as much affection
for each other as pit bulls in a ring.
Tying the knot means slipping a noose
around love and choking it to death.

So Now Or Never

I dial Sean's number. He answers
before it rings, as if waiting, phone
in hand, for me to call. *Oh, thank
God. I swore if I didn't hear from*

*you, I was coming over there and
camping in your driveway. Did you
get my last message? I got in! And
I'm going to play for Stanford.*

I can picture his face, all lit up
with pride and excitement. I have
to hurry, or I'll lose my nerve.
"Sean, listen. I'm not sure why

you thought we would be together
after this year. I never promised
that. And what happened the other
night made it clear to me that I can

never be what you need. You deserve
someone who will love you with all
her heart. That isn't me. I'm sorry."
I knew he would take it hard, but

did not expect the rabid way he comes
back at me now. *What the fuck are
you saying? That it's over? Because
we finally had sex? You can't be serious!*

"Not just because we finally had sex."
Damn it. I'm crying. "Because it
didn't mean anything. I should
be dying to have it again. I'm not."

He is quiet for several very long
seconds. Finally he says, *Cara,
I love you and that wouldn't change
even if we never had sex again.*

*I'll jack off forever, if that's what
you want.* His voice slices the ether
between us. *But I will never let you
go.* He gives me no choice but to

say, "We're over, Sean. I'm sorry,
but the longer we try to hold on to
each other, the more it will hurt when
we finally fall apart. This is good-bye."

I Think I Hear Him Sob

As I hit the off button. That so did
not go well. It was the right thing
to do. So why do I feel empty? Why
must I make things black and white?

Okay, I know the answer. Like it or
not, I take after my parents. Neither
acknowledges hues of gray. Really,
though, it's my choice. Either deal

the cards faceup on the table or
withdraw from the game. I'm sick
of bluffing. This is where most girls
would pick up the phone, call

their best friend, seek sympathy.
Not me. Oh, I've got more than a few
so-called friends, but none I'm close
to. Something else I inherited—lack

of trust. I wish I had someone to talk
to. Only one person comes to mind.
Guess it's time to let out the bad air.
Straight to voice mail. "Hey, you.

I've been thinking about you. . . ."
Screw that. Try the truth for once.
"Uh, some stuff happened and it
would be really great to talk to you.

Call me when you can. Oh, this is
Cara." Stupid. She would know who.
Wouldn't she? Oh my freaking God.
What's wrong with me? I dump

Sean and *my* ego suffers? Freud
would no doubt have something
deep to say about that. I can't just
sit here stressing, so I fire up

my laptop, check my e-mail. There
are a dozen from Sean, all sent before
we talked. Delete. Without. Opening.
The usual junk mail. Nothing more.

I head on over to Facebook. No
new wall posts on my profile page.
On my home page, more messages
from you-know-who. Delete.

One from my cousin, Tiffany,
asking about summer plans. Looks
like she's getting married. You go,
girl. A shout-out from Shantell,

reminding me about her graduation
party. How could I forget? It's all
she's talked about for weeks. And
now it looks like I'm going solo.

Messages read, I return to my home
page, where status alerts announce
all the news that's fit to know. I'm just
about out of there when an update

pops into view. What the . . . ? Sean
is cyber-screaming to our mutual crowd:
*CAN'T BELIEVE THE BITCH BROKE
UP WITH ME!!!* I knew he was upset,

but I didn't think he'd go public, at least
not so soon. Comments start to appear.
Most paint me a villain. A whore, lacking
a heart. Some are written by "friends."

Enough Already

I can understand vitriol from his teammates. Guys stick together, and those
particular guys have muscles beneath
the double-thick plates of their skulls,

where brain matter really should be.
But the nastiest remarks come from
girls. A couple are on the cheer squad.
The one who comments, *CARA'S A SLUT*

would know what that word means
from experience. But I would never
post that on Facebook. Not even now.
I want to respond. React. Deny.

But that would only stoke the coals
of gossip, churn them into a raging
firestorm. Better to keep quiet,
let the coals burn down into ash.

I turn off my computer. Lie on my
bed, hoping for sleep to toss me
somewhere else for a while.
Somewhere deep. Dark. Empty.

Kendra
Empty

Is the perfect state of being.
Nothing inside to anchor
you. Nothing inside
to chain you down, keep

                              you

from living your dreams.
Empty, almost weightless,
you are an eyelash afloat
on a blink of breeze. You

                              can

rise above tension and worry,
loosed from the grip of gravity.
Adrift in thermal lift, you
ride the wing of freedom and

                              soar.

Empty, you are Eve in Eden.
Empty, you are what
you were meant to be.

Thank God For Jenna

My messed-up little sister always
                 manages to take the glare off of me.

I mean, here I am, in the red-hot seat,
                 getting the fifth degree from my loser dad

and his wife-to-be (like she has any place
                 talking all "mom" to me), when in sambas

Jenna with her boyfriend. I have to admit
                 I felt sorry for the guy. He had no idea

that Dad is stuck in the pre–civil rights
                 era. Racism is alive and well and hanging

'em high in the Rudolph Mathieson home.
                 Downright nasty of Jenna to bring Andre

to lunch. She knew Dad would make
                 a miserable scene. That way, she didn't have

to make her own scene about the wedding.
                 Wait. Okay, that was brilliant. Damn her.

Something Obvious

To me, though I'm pretty sure Dad
            missed it completely—Andre is flat

crazy in love with Jenna. It was in his eyes,
            how he couldn't pry them off of her.

It was in the way his fingers played
            music along the keyboard of her hand.

In the way he kept his mouth shut
            just as long as he could. Even when

Dad got right up spit-close in his face,
            Andre kept hold of his temper. Some

people might have interpreted it as not
            having a spine, but I could tell it was for

Jenna. And despite the awful way she set
            him up, he offered her the out. To go

or stay, her choice. Yep, he's definitely
            got a major thing for her. Poor guy.

One Thing I Have To Respect

About Jenna is she does not apologize
        for who she is or the things she does.

In that way, she takes after our father.
        I am more like Mom, saying I'm sorry

for everything, even when I don't mean
        it. The one thing I refuse to apologize

        for is my weight. *Do you know what
kind of damage an eating disorder can*

        do to your body? Bitch. I do not have
an eating disorder. I know exactly what

I eat and exactly how to burn it off. That
        sounds like order to me, not disorder.

        You're too thin. Says who? Not Xavier.
Not the big photogs. Not even my mom.

        My *real* mom. Not some phony wannabe.
I will be here for you. Yeah, right.

Not like I want her to be. Definitely not
        like I asked her to be. She means nothing

to me. Why should I mean anything to her?
        Glad I didn't mention the rhinoplasty.

I'm sure she would have had something
        to say about that, too. It's scheduled

for Monday. I'm getting a little nervous.
        Andre's mom has been very sweet.

                Don't worry. I've performed hundreds,
        with very few complications. You'll be

                just fine. You don't smoke, do you?
        Didn't think so, but needed to make

                sure. Smoking increases the risk of
        bleeding. Alcohol, too. I can tell you

                don't drink. You're much too slender.
        Slender. Not thin or skinny. Or anorexic.

I'm Online

Reading real-life nose job stories
     when I get an instant message from

         Bobby. *HEY. ARE YOU ON FACEBOOK? GET*
THAT WAY. CHECK OUT SEAN'S PAGE.

         Bobby hardly ever IMs me. *RIGHT NOW!*
Something's definitely up. Oh, wow.

I can't believe Cara broke up with Sean.
     Neither can half the senior class. Glad

I'm not her. They're chopping her into
     little pieces: *. . . IS A SLUT ANYWAY*

         . . . ALWAYS WAS FULL OF IT
         . . . NOT GOOD ENOUGH FOR YOU

And now: *. . . SERIOUS COMMITMENT ISSUES*
     YEAH, MUST RUN IN THE FAMILY.

That last one from Aubree. Obviously
     referring to Conner and me. People

really should mind their own business.
Except, of course, Sean made it pretty

much everyone's business. Before I
become an obvious topic of conversation,

however, I think I'll speak up and let
them know I'm lurking here. HEY, SEAN,

I type. SORRY TO HEAR ABOUT YOU AND
CARA. CALL ME IF YOU NEED TO TALK, OKAY?

I sign off. Get the heck out of there
before I see any more comments I can't

stomach. For some stupid reason, now
I feel hungry. Freaking stress. A small

shot of sugar should do the trick. One
Jolly Rancher. Watermelon. Twenty-three

point three calories. If I go for a bike ride,
I can treat myself to three. Game on.

Closing In

On April, less than a week away, winter
        wants to hang on this year. Late afternoon,

it will be cold once the sun nose-dives
        behind the mountain. Glad I wore sweats,

even though they make me look like Blimp
        Girl. I'll ride back roads. Tires pumped up,

I start on flat ground. Have to warm up a little
        before heading uphill. It's been a while since

I pedaled anything, and even in high gear,
        my legs start to burn fairly quickly. I like

the burn, like the way my muscles feel
        when they contract. I should do this more.

The last time I went bike riding was with
        Conner. It was summer, and his tanned legs

were sensational to watch, pumping pedals.
        The morning was hot, and once in a while

he would pour water over his head. His long
        hair dripped, catching sun, creating a halo.

God, I loved him so much, and the memory
        is a new razor blade. Too sharp to feel its slice.

Flat streets segue to a mild incline. I bear
        down on the pedals. My breathing shallows.

Pant. Pant. I think of Conner again, how
        we stopped our bikes beneath the big trees

at the park. Walked them into the heart
        of the woods, rested them against old pines,

nestled ourselves into the thick needle bed.
        The breeze stirred gently, scenting the air

with superheated evergreen. Conner pushed
        me back into the cushioned earth, and when

he kissed me, it stole my breath away. Like
        now. *Pant. Pant.* We panted then. Together.

The Hill Grows Steeper

And the memory grows deeper with
            every breath I pull into my lungs.

                  For the first time ever, the love we
           made was unhurried. *It's good slow,*

                  he said. *Do you like it this way?* I did
           but wondered just when he'd decided

that, and how. Still, I didn't dare ask
            him. Instead I just let him. And when

he finished, he stayed very close to me,
            tracing one finger in circles on my skin.

                  Don't lose any more weight, he said.
           Don't you want to look like a woman?

That surprised me too. "I thought
            you'd like me better this way."

                  He shook his head, rustling the needles.
           Don't believe the hype. Curves are hot.

To The West

The sun hides behind shadowed granite
        cliffs. But despite the noticeable drop

in temperature, sweat soaks into the fleece
        beneath my arms, and my hair dampens.

Suddenly I am starving, every calorie
        taken in today completely expended.

My heart quakes, stuttering in my chest.
        Time to turn around. Head home. Downhill.

As I swing the bike across the yellow line,
        I feel my face go white, as if the saw-slice

of memory has opened my head, let blood.
        My stomach, empty, heaves nothingness.

I begin to shiver. My arms start to shake
        and I lose control of the handlebars.

Buzzing. Horrible buzzing. My hands
        grab for the brakes. Too late. I'm falling . . .

Through The Fog

Fog? Where did that come from? No
        matter, it's here, and the only thing

that makes it lift is pain. Jolts of pain.
        In my right arm. Right leg. Right side

of my head. I try to move—have to.
        I'm in the street. I think. Must move.

                But some strange weight holds me
        in place. *Don't move.* Hands test

my body. Conner? No. That was last
        summer. My eyes work hard to focus.

                The hands belong to a lady. Don't know
        her. *I don't feel any broken bones, but*

                you could have a concussion. Stay right
        there. I'll call 9-1-1. But as soon as she lets

go, I manage a sitting position. "I'm okay.
        Please. Can you just take me home?"

Sean
I'm Okay

I'm

           Everything I've believed
           in, smashed into the mud.
           All I've worked toward,
           pulverized into dust. But

           okay. Who wanted all that,
           anyway? Who needed
           an unobstructed road to
           a tidy little future, when

really

           the fun is in breaking trail
           toward some unknown
           destination? Any sane person
           would say you should

not

           put every shred of hope
           in one human being, especially
           not a girl. The perfect girl,
           no longer mine. But, hey, I'm

okay.

Wounded

And I don't even know what
        the fuck happened. Everything
                was going perfectly. Graduating
        with a high B average? Check.
Playing top-flight baseball?

Check. Offered a scholarship
        to play Cardinal ball? Check.
                Accepted into Stanford, an
        almost impossible goal
to realize? Check. Best of

all, after waiting for a year,
        after finding a way to make
                sure performance would
        not be an issue, being right
there with Cara, both of us

naked and hot and ready
        to go, finally having sex
                with the girl I love more
        than life, only to be accused
of rape? Check. And check!!

I Thought She Was Over It

When she finally called.
        Believed she'd forgiven
                me. How could I have
        been so wrong? About
everything. I thought she

loved me, too. How could
        I have given my heart to
                someone still-frozen?
        Looking back, I see that she
never felt about me the way

I felt about her. Talk about
        one-sided affection. What in
                God's name do I do now?
        Turn down Stanford? I could
have gone east to school.

Some place far, far away
        from Cara. No, damn it.
                After all I went through
        to get in there, I'm going to
Stanford. With or without Cara.

At Least She Didn't

Publicly accuse me of rape.
            Tomorrow will be a week
                        since that night, and not
            one word has surfaced.
All things considered,

I figured she might, if only
            to save face. Reputation
                        is pretty much everything
            to Cara Sykes. And her
standing with the in crowd

has plummeted. Bitch isn't
            the only one who has friends
                        in high places. In fact, as
            of today, she doesn't have
much in the way of friends.

Period. Maybe I went a little
            crazy, posting on Facebook
                        and stuff. I kind of thought
            she might jump in and defend
herself. But no. Not a word.

That pisses me off more than
                anything. The fucking silence.
                        The least she could do is tell
                me what the hell happened.
She owes me that much.

The worst thing is, she's all
                I can think about. School?
                        What's that? Oh yeah, that
                place I used to go where
I actually became *somebody*

once I started dating Cara.
                Homework? Whatever.
                        I'll do enough to graduate,
                but why work harder than
I have to? Baseball? Now,

that's a problem of sorts.
                I've accomplished what
                        I set out to do, for sure.
                But it bothers me that my bat
has grown as cold as Cara.

On One Hand

It doesn't really matter.
              On the other hand, there
                            are records at stake. I should
              be number one in the league.
And if I get it back together,

I can still grab that title.
              I have to kick this butt-
                            rod pitcher's ass. I need
              to remember just who
the hell Sean O'Connell

                            is, with or without his girl.
              I watch the windup, try
to read the signals. Think
              about Cara, throwing off
                            her shirt that night. *Strike!*

What? Wait. I didn't even
              see the ball. Goddamn
                            it. No! The pitcher leers—
              leers! Screw you, dude.
I've got your ticket. I wait

for it . . . mind wandering
to Chad's sofa, and smooth
skin perfumed with desire.
And she's saying yes, touch
me there, all wet. . . . *Strike two.*

Damn it all, O'Connell,
concentrate. That fricking
pitcher is a goon. I swear
if I don't hit him this time . . .
he pulls back from his windup.

Trying to make me lose it
again. No effing way, jerk.
He comes set, draws back.
It's a sinker for sure. A fastball is too big of a risk. He

lets go of the ball. Here it
comes. Fast. And straight.
And I swing right through.
And the goddamn umpire
dares, *Strike three. You're out.*

And I Know I'm Out

I am so fucking out. And
        I know the umpire is totally
                right, but at this particular
        moment, I couldn't give
a damn about right or wrong.

I want to feel better. So I wheel
        to my right, catch hold of
                his mask, pull his ugly face
        right up into mine, and
I say, "You got it wrong."

                    Behind his face guard,
          his eyes go wide. *Are you*
questioning my call? Because
        I don't think that's a good idea.
                Let go of me, son. I mean now.

And I know I really need
        to stop myself, but I can't
                seem to manage it. "I'm not
        your fucking son, you piece
of . . ." And now all I can see

is Cara, telling me I have
                just raped her. And all
                                I want to do is shake
                her. And a scarlet haze
lifts over my eyes. I hate

                                her. I love her. *O'Connell!*
                        Stop! It's Coach Torrance.
                And I shake my head, and
                                the red veil falls, and I am
                                        horrified to see I've been

shaking the ump, like I
                wanted to shake Cara.
                                Oh my God. "What's
                wrong with me?" I say it
aloud, with a cracked black

pepper voice. And I'm sorry.
                Oh, yes, I'm sorry. But it's
                                too late for sorry. I am out
                of the game. No hits. No
runs. Just another strikeout.

I Hit The Locker Room

Strip down. Shower. Realize
        suddenly that this stupid stunt
                could very well end my baseball
        career. Not many coaches
want to deal with players

who go off the deep end and
        try to kill the umpire over
                a called third strike. Or anything
        else, for that matter. What
came over me? I turn the water

cool, let it flow over my head,
        chill my brain. A phrase floats
                up from some subconscious
        sea. "'Roid rage." Maybe it
fits, but I don't think so. No,

this was all about Cara. Why
        can't I just let her go? And
                now—fuck, fuck, fuck—
        I'm crying. Tears spill,
mixing with shower splash.

My legs start to shake,
         and I let them slip out
                  from under me. I scoot
         back against the cool tile,
let the waterfall rush over

                  me. And this is how Uncle
         Jeff finds me. *Are you okay?*
Obviously not. *Kind of blew*
         it out there, huh? Do you want
                  to talk about what's going on?

I do. But I can't. I look up
         at him through the streaming
                  water. "Just a lot of pressure
         lately is all." I get up, turn
off the shower. Reach for

                  a towel. *Not sure that excuse*
         is good enough to fix what
just happened. Beyond
         your likely league suspension,
                  that ump could press charges.

I Know All That

But though my first instinct
        is to say so, I also know
                that Uncle Jeff wants to
        help. "I'm sorry. Really, I am.
Do you think it's fixable?"

                        He shrugs. *I could maybe*
                  pull some strings. But I need
           to know what's happening
               with you. Anything else you
                    can tell me? He turns his head

as I start to dress. Anger
        flares again, but only for
                a second. He isn't my dad.
        But he's the closest thing
I've got. "There's some stuff

with Cara." True. "We're
        trying to work through
                it. . . ." Not exactly true. Yet.
        "It's been a rough week."
And looking to get rougher.

Andre
Not Exactly True

That skin hate is dead.
There will never be color
blindness in a culture of

            fear.

But when you live afraid
of your neighbor, the monster
you should most walk
in terror of

            thrives.

It starts as a little thing,
small enough to burrow
into your pores, take up
excruciating residence

            in

the dark recesses of your brain.
Its name is paranoia,
and it spreads like an oil
spill, there in

            the shadows,

chokes your humanity.
Threatens your soul.

I Don't usually Think

A whole lot about the color of my skin.
Most of the time it's not
an issue at all. Sometimes, I think, it can

be an advantage. Which is, of course,
a brand of reverse racism.
I mean, if you're helping some school

fulfill their diversity quota, you might
actually get a boost
up over a Caucasian male with the same

GPA. If we didn't live in one of Reno's
pricier neighborhoods,
things would doubtless be different.

But it's hard to argue with millionaires,
white, black, brown,
yellow, or any shade in between.

When you rub elbows with rich kids,
no one's especially
worried about what might rub off.

I Have Heard

That in Deep South states like Alabama—hotbeds
of racial unrest in
the sixties—even today, they have segregated

schools. Probably not officially sanctioned
as such, but according to
Jenna, on a trip to visit family down "theya,"

her cousins made it clear that they attended
the "white high school."
The one across town was "the colored school."

I was something close to stunned. "You can't
be serious! This is
the twenty-first century, for cripes' sake!"

> *Visiting down there is definitely like*
> *stepping back in*
> *time. Not everything about that is*
>
> *bad, though. Communities are safe.*
> *Families are tight.*
> *People are polite, respectful. . . .*

"Except when it comes to people of color.
Not to mention gay
people. Muslims. Jews. God, Jenna."

She slid her little hand into mine.
But that's not me.
Sometimes I'm not even sure how I can

be related to them. I know my great-
great grandpa moved
down there during the Depression.

Somehow, he found work, when other
people couldn't.
The South was good to him, and he

stayed a loyal Southerner. So did most
of his family, including
Dad. But someone had to break the cycle.

I'm sort of a cycle breaker, in case you
somehow haven't
noticed. And no one speaks for me.

Just Like That

Everything was great between us
again. She has this way
of making me forgive her instantly

for any indiscretion, tiny or unimaginably
gigantic. Good thing loving
someone doesn't require caring about

their parents. Jenna's mom just kind of
ignores the fact that
I'm still dating her daughter. She's so hung

up on Kendra and building her career that she
barely notices Jenna anyway.
Her father, I'm sure, hasn't even come

close to accepting us. Not that it matters.
Jenna does as she pleases.
I definitely do not desire a confrontation,

however. In fact, I want to steer way beyond
clear of Rudolph
Mathieson. I kind of like being alive.

I Especially Like

Being alive when I'm dancing. It's like
the best part of me
chassés out of the shadows, into the spotlight.

I usually have lessons on Saturday morning.
But Liana is taking
tomorrow off to drive to San Francisco

so she can spend Easter with her family.
So I am ball-changing
and pivot-stepping this afternoon instead.

> Liana is working me hard. *Posture!*
> *Keep your shoulders*
> *back. That's it! Beautiful, Andre.*

> *Okay, let's practice some isolations now.*
> *Left rib cage. Right rib*
> *cage.* Cooling me down after a couple

of very hard routines. She is evil. Good evil.
When we finish, every
muscle, tendon, and joint in my body sings.

I grab a towel, dry a little sweat, exit
the studio. Outside the door,
in the waiting room, is that cheerleader

on the Galena team. The one who stalked
off at the competition
that day. What was her name? Shan . . . tell.

Yeah, that's it. Head bent toward her lap,
where she is busily
texting someone, she doesn't notice me

at first. I think about backing away,
so she won't know
about what I do on my free afternoons.

God, what if she tells everyone? Yeah, Andre,
right. Like who? And
there's nowhere to back away to, anyway.

So I Take The Direct Approach

"Hello, Shantell." Her head rolls up
from her texting.
It takes a few seconds for recognition.

> Then her eyes go wide with surprise,
> and her jaw drops
> practically to her neck. *You . . . dance?*

"What? Did the leotard give it away?"
I smile. "Yes, in fact, I do
dance. You train with Liana too, I guess?"

> *Since I was little. But I've never seen*
> you *here before.*
> Her voice is acid. Sharp. Caustic.

"I take private lessons. On Saturdays,
usually." At the word
"private," she starts to nod. "What?"

> *Nothing. It just figures that you'd take*
> *private lessons.* She
> looks away as some other girls arrive

for their group lesson. "You don't like
me very much, that's
obvious. What I don't get is why not."

> She turns to face me. Points toward
> the mountain. *I don't*
> *live up there.* She means in a mansion

on the hill. And that pisses me off.
"Do you want me
to apologize because my parents worked

their asses off to become successful?
You could live up there
if you want. All it takes is determination."

> *Baby, I've got plenty of that. Talent,*
> *too. I'll get there on*
> *talent. Because I do not have connections.*

I'm Not Sure If That Means

She likes me after all. Or if it means
she has forgiven me
for living up there. Or if it means one

damn thing, or why I even care. "So are
we friends now?" I smile
my warmest smile, expect her to melt.

> She snorts. *Yeah, right. Even if I thought*
> *I could maybe like you,*
> *I wouldn't because you have crappy taste*
>
> *in girlfriends. I mean, Kendra's cool and*
> *all, but her sister is just*
> *a regular bee-otch. What you see in her . . .*

She would doubtless say more, but
Liana pokes her head
through the door and calls the girls to class.

I don't need to explain my love for Jenna.
So I say, "Whatever you think
about Jenna—or me—I like you, Shantell."

As I Say It

I realize I really do like her, despite her open
contempt for me.
Not that it matters. "Have a great weekend."

Yeah. You too. She tosses her head,
haughty and pretty
as some extravagant bird of prey.

And I watch her walk away, all rich cocoa
skin and sleek raven
hair and a dancer's well-muscled body.

She is no Jenna, but she does have
something special
going on. Wait. Jenna. I forgot to call

and let her know I'd be late. Bet she's mad.
I locate my cell, check
for messages. Uh-huh. Damn. Three of them.

Where are you? At least it's a whine,
not a roar. *And why
aren't you picking up? Are you okay?*

That's it. Play the guilt card. She's great
at that. But I should
have called. So I do now. "Hey. Sorry

I didn't call sooner. . . ." She goes off
on me about how
worried she's been. "I'm really sorry,

sweetheart. I . . . uh . . ." What do I tell
her? The truth? No way.
". . . got hung up, filling out college applications

with my dad. He's been pushing me to
do them for weeks now.
Let me get cleaned up and I'll be right there."

Don't think she'd want me sweaty.
Then again, maybe
she'd like it. I get in my car and drive

home, wondering why I don't feel like
I can share my private
dreams with the girl I'm so in love with.

Cara
Private Dreams

Snare you. Swallow you.
Make you feel
like you're all

alone,

like you don't want
to sleep and fall
into them. What good are

dreams

if you can't share
them? How sad
to think there

are

people who must
move forward into
some hollow future,

empty

of hope. Destined
to travel an avenue
potholed with broken

promises.

Spring Break

Thank God. I need some time away
from school. Away from friends who
stopped being friends because of Sean.
What's up with that, anyway?

But more, I need some time to spend
getting to know Dani better. And, if
I can find the courage, to let her get
to know me. Looking back, it's clear

that I never opened all the way up
to Sean. Not even when I thought
I was in love with him. It's genetic.
I am more like my mother than I ever

believed possible. In fact, I would
have sworn we were nothing alike,
that I have fought to be any person
other than her. I failed miserably.

I Haven't Even Seen

Dani in a couple of weeks. Not
since before the whole Sean mess.
It's not like I've purposely tried
to ignore her. Our schedules have

kept us apart. We have talked on
the phone, the sound of her voice
solace. I tried to tell her about Sean.
Couldn't. Couldn't tell anyone.

All I want is to forget the ugly
scene. But don't think I ever can.
So I'll use it to make me stronger.
Fuel myself with it, an energy drink.

Because now that I know who
I'm not, I can claim the person
I really am. Take ownership of her.
That's my plan, and it's starting

with Dani. Tonight. We're going
to a party. "A Queer Spring Break
Bash" is how it's been billed. Booze.
Beer. Drugs (?). And gay people.

Going With Dani

Means it will be my "coming out"
party, so to speak. Good? Bad?
Not sure. Am I ready to admit
so publicly who I've only just

decided I am? Answer, to come.
Now, what to wear? Jeans, of course.
Sweatshirt? (Sloppy.) Sweater?
(Girly.) Will anyone care, including

Dani? Girly is better than sloppy.
I own a dozen sweaters, all folded
in perfect colored squares on a closet
shelf. Jade. Turquoise. Ruby. Bone.

I choose the amethyst. It's soft,
warm, and clings to my body like oil
on skin. Uggs? No. Black leather
boots with tall spike heels. Overall,

the look is dominatrix girly. Kind
of cool, kind of weird. Which
sums up how I feel right now.
Half amazing. Half out of my mind.

I Do My Best

To make sure Dani will only
see the amazing half. We meet
at Summit Sierra. No need to
chance parental third degree.

I park at the far perimeter
of the lot, anticipation nibbling.
I feel like a kid, waiting for some
indication of a sleigh on my rooftop.

An aging Subaru pulls in next
to my almost new Nissan. Behind
the windshield, Dani smiles, waves
me over. "Hey. So great to see you.

Love your hair." The dark quills
are tipped with a striking blue.
          Hey yourself. And damn, girl.
          Do you know how hot you are?

The reindeer have arrived.
What I need now is for Santa
to come slipping down my chimney.
I try coy, not my best thing. "Me?"

Come on. You look totally edible.
She stretches across the console,
brings her face close to mine. *Can
I have a little taste before we go?*

For one nanosecond, I see Sean,
leaning over me. But Dani is not
Sean, and I accept her kiss easily.
It is hungry, but not demanding.

Rather, it convinces me that this
is, indeed, the place I am destined
to be. She leaves me breathless.
And freed of the weight of regret.

I leave her searching for breath,
too. *Well, then.* She inhales deeply.
*I think I'll need another snack later.
This should be an interesting night.*

I Have No Clue

What she means. But I guess I'll
find out. The party is at a little house
near the UNR campus. The narrow
street is lined on both sides with

cars. We have to park several blocks
away, on a patch of dirt by the rail-
road tracks. As I get out of the car,
I catch my right heel, but manage

to save both it and me. "That was
close. Guess I should have worn
the Uggs." Dani slides an arm
around my waist, and I press tight

> against her. *No way,* she says, *no
> Uggs for you. You're too freaking
> sexy in those boots. No worries.
> I'll keep you upright. For now.*

We start down the time-gnawed
sidewalk, linked hip to hip.
In the shadows, we hit a slick
strip of ice, but Dani is true

to her word. *Okay, those are definitely not great winter boots.* Her grip around me tightens. *In fact, I would rate them abysmal. And totally hot.*

They do make me taller than her,
so the top of her head is nose level.
Shampoo, gel, hair dye, or all three,
the soft, fruity scent of her grows

as we walk, and by the time we reach
our destination, I must smell as if I
belong to her. And I like it. How primal.
Just as Dani starts to knock, the door

opens. Laughter spills out, along
with a quite inebriated girl. *Careful
of those Jell-O shots,* she warns.
They might get you all fucked up.

And she definitely knows from
experience. She stumbles toward
a leafless hedge, hurls something
thick and red. Dani and I go inside.

I Expect Her to Let Go

Of me. She doesn't, at least not
right away. Her hold is protective,
possessive. The front room is packed
tightly with people. We work our way

through the human mesh, drawing
more than a few direct stares. Can't be
because we're together. I've never
seen so many same-sex couples before.

Not all in one place, laughing, downing
drinks, making out in plain view.
Other than the girl-girl, boy-boy thing,
it's like any party I've ever been to.

I wish I could say I feel comfortable.
I put my mouth against Dani's ear.
"What's everyone looking at?"
At first, I think she can't hear me.

> She doesn't answer immediately.
> Finally we push our way through
> the thick knot of people, into a semi-
> quiet corner. *They're looking at you.*

I know quite a few of these people.
They've never seen me with you
before, or with anyone remotely
like you. We are a topic of interest.

Sure enough, when I glance
around, I see people checking us
out. Evaluating. "What do you mean,
not even remotely like me?"

> Dani waves to a girl across the room.
> She is tiny. Cute, in a boyish way.
> *That's Bianca, my old girlfriend.*
> *See what I mean? Nothing like you.*

This is all such new ground.
Every spark of self-confidence
flickers. Did we have to run into
her ex? "Were you in love with her?"

> *I guess I thought so at the time.*
> *But love is a fragile thing. Easily*
> *broken. And what does it matter,*
> *anyway? I want to be with you now.*

346

She Proves It

With a kiss. Awkward at first,
because I rarely kiss with people
watching me. Yet I can't stop.
I want this. Want her. Don't care

who knows. I thread myself
into her arms, invite her tongue
into my mouth. Oh God, it all
feels so right, I don't want to stop.

I want to go further. Set no limits.
Dive deeper. Explore unknown
territory. Find secret places. Climb
steeper cliffs. Higher and higher.

My heart sunbursts in my chest
and my eyes quiver open. Surely
everyone is staring right now.
But I find only one. "Bianca."

> I didn't mean to say it out loud.
> Dani smiles. *Don't worry. Better*
> *she knows about us. Now how*
> *'bout we find something to drink?*

I'm Not Much Of A Drinker

In fact, I don't drink at all. But
I don't need to say so. We start
toward the breakfast bar, where
a few people are filling their cups.

Dani asks what I want. I shrug.
"Surprise me." She reaches for
a tall bottle of rum, manages
to pour some over ice, when

> a voice sharp as snipped tin
> slices into us from behind.
> *Well, hello, Dani. I never knew*
> *you had a thing for femmes.*

> Dani turns to face Bianca. *Good*
> *to see you, Bee. You know I'm*
> *not much into stereotypes.*
> *Guess she is femme. Pretty, too.*

Wait. Stereotype? What? "Don't
talk about me like I'm not here,
okay?" Anger flares, and as I start
to walk away, Bianca mouths,   *Fake.*

Kendra
Fake

Is that what you are
if you choose to improve
the basic not perfect you?

Add

a cup size or two.
Puff up your lips.
Reshape your nose.

Subtract

an inch or two from
your belly, butt, and thighs.
Tighten your skin until

what's left

behind is blotch free.
Unlined. Then, quick,
take a picture or two

of you

before it all falls apart
again and you have
to start over.

Two Days

Until my surgery. Can't wait. Wish
        I had to wait much longer. I'm nervous.

Excited. Looking forward to fixing
        something wrong with me. Why couldn't

I just be born with a perfect nose?
        One thing for sure. I can't sit here all

weekend thinking about Monday.
        It being the first day of spring break,

there isn't a lot going on to distract
        me. No lessons. No competitions. Nothing.

And anyway, I'm afraid to do anything
        too physical. If I got hurt, I'd have to wait

even longer for the rhinoplasty.
        But if I sit here at home, there will be

a battle going on, with me at the center—
        fridge (which Mom just filled) vs. mirror.

The Mirror Always Wins

But I'm sick and tired of the war.
　　　　Doesn't help when Mom brings home

ice cream sandwiches ("light" ones,
　　　　but still . . .) and (reduced fat, whatever

that actually means) peanut butter.
　　　　Really, truly doesn't help when Jenna pigs

out with one or both right in front
　　　　of me. She does it to be spiteful. Likes

watching my mouth water. Which
　　　　pisses me off, so then we fight, too.

Not up for any of that today.
　　　　There's a new *Scary Movie* playing

at the Summit. I want to go. But not
　　　　alone. Jenna's got something going on,

and even if she didn't, she'd want to
　　　　yack down candy and fake butter popcorn.

351

Aubree's at her grandparents',
　　　　Shantell has been really weird and distant

lately. And anyway, a movie date
　　　　should be with a guy, except not someone

who will put the moves on me.
　　　　Someone like . . . I pick up the phone.

"Sean? I was wondering if you had
　　　　plans today. No? Well, I want to see

Scary Movie 666. . . ." Silence
　　　　on the other end. Then a stupid question.

"Of course I'm not setting you up.
　　　　Why would I want to do that? Look, no

strings. I just don't want to go by
　　　　myself. Really? Awesome. There's a two

fifteen matinee. Do you want to meet
　　　　in the lobby, say around two? Exceptional."

In A Way

I'm surprised he said yes. Maybe
        he's sick of moping around. It hasn't been

all that long, but Sean is used to
        having someone on his arm. Wow. We do

have kind of a lot in common, don't
        we? Chill, Kendra. Remember that you

are good on your own. (Lonely.)
        Strong. (When people are looking.) In control.

(Hungry. Even though my stomach
        has almost forgotten how it feels to hold

food.) Size two. (Fat. Fat. Fat. Just ask
        the mirror. It doesn't know how to lie.)

Perfect. (Come on. Not surgery, not
        losing ten necessary pounds, not even

implants can make me that. "Just about
        perfect" will have to be good enough.)

Regardless

I dress to impress, in a very short skirt
　　　　plus leggings to keep my thighs thawed,

and a too-tight sweater that defines
　　　　my need for bigger boobs. I could maybe

go baggy on top, keep 'em guessing.
　　　　But that would make me look fat. Can't

have that. Better to go for skinny, with
　　　　a boost from a well-padded push-up bra.

I grab my jacket, start for the door,
　　　　only for Patrick to whistle me to a stop.

　　　　　　　Wait up. Are you going out? (Well, duh.)
　　　　　Were you going to let anyone know?

Obviously not. "Sorry. Just don't want
　　　　to be late. I'm headed out to a movie."

　　　　　　　Alone? What time will you be home?
　　　　　It's generally polite to ask first, you know.

"Um, Patrick. Is something going
          on?" Not like he very often takes

an interest in what I'm up to. "Because
          if everything's okay, I really need to go."

He comes closer, studies my eyes
          as if he needs to find something there.

                    Okay, look. I'm just going to ask.
          straight out. Have you been in our

                    medicine cabinet? Your mother is
          missing some of her prescription pills.

I could get snotty, but what good
          would that do? I won't even mention

that I know they're Xanax, and that
          he was the one who did the prescribing.

"Not me," I say, and that's the whole
          truth. "If I were you, I'd talk to Jenna."

He Is Not The Type

To confront, or want to play parent.
Still, he has more to say, if he can

just figure out how to say it. *I will
definitely be talking to your sister.*

*I also think it's time to call a family
meeting. Things seem to be spinning*

*out of control, in totally the wrong
direction. Prescriptions disappearing,*

*kids who take off without telling their
parents where they're going or when*

they'll be back. And then, there's you.
He tries to stop himself, but

he's on a roll. *Have you eaten anything
today? I'm worried about you. . . .*

"Oh my God. Not you, too. I eat
plenty! Worry about Jenna. I'm fine!"

Anger sizzles at the base of my skull.
I try for the front door, but Patrick

stops me with a hand on my forearm.
You haven't answered my question.

Have you had anything to eat today?
I will do an intervention if I must.

Don't blow it. Don't blow it. Lower
the blood pressure before you speak.

"I had some oatmeal." It's a flat-
out lie, but he seems to believe it.

Wants to believe it. *Okay, then. But*
you really should have some protein.

"I will." Another lie. "And I promise
to eat all my veggies, too. May I go now?"

He smiles. *I guess so. But I meant it about*
the family meeting. Over dinner. Tonight.

I Say Fine

And he lets me out the door. I hurry
        to my car before he changes his mind.

My hands shake against the steering
        wheel, from lingering anger and also

because Patrick happened to be
        right. I haven't eaten anything today.

I reach into the glove box. Grab
        a diet protein bar, take two bites. Three.

Half the bar should satisfy my
        stomach growl and keep me thinking

straight. I put the rest in my pocket
        to nosh on while everyone else is eating

Skittles and sucking on Slurpees.
        By the time I reach the theater, the shakes

have stopped too. I park. Buy a ticket.
        Go inside to wait for Sean, feeling great.

Unbelievably

In through the door walks Conner,
            surrounded by a group of people

I've never seen before. He's with
            a kind of cute guy, a rude-looking girl,

a twentysomething woman, and one
            who is older than that, all dressed up in

business-type clothes. They head
            straight for the bathrooms. Conner, who

hasn't seen me, waits outside the doors
            for the rest of them. My heart tumbles

into my mostly empty stomach. I have
            to say something. Like what? That I hate

him for what he did? That I still
            love him, and always will? Oh God.

I go over, wanting to touch him, but
            afraid if I do he'll disappear. And out of

my mouth spills, "Hey, Conner.
        I heard you tried to die. That right?"

                Hello, Kendra. He turns on one heel
        to face me. Stiff as a fresh corpse—

                and why did I have to think that? *Guess
        I did. Next time I'll have to try harder.*

I can feel my face turn white.
        "Don't say that! Believe it or not,

a few people care about you.
        One or two of us even love you."

                His eyes cloud with . . . disbelief?
        I'm sorry. I didn't mean it.

"There's Sean. Gotta go. Hope to see
        you again soon, Conner. Give me a call,

if you want to. I'm a good listener."
        I turn my back as he joins his friends.

Sean

Back Turned

You

       don't have to look at
       what you've left behind.
       And the person who first
       turned their back on you

can't

       watch you break down
       and cry. Never allow
       an enemy to

see

       weakness in you.
       Go for the throat.
       Shoot for the groin.
       Don't let your loss

yesterday

       redefine who you are.
       Fight the good fight.
       Today is your day to win.

Fighting Depression

Is hard when you have no
        real reason to fight it. Why
                pretend everything is fine
        when everything pretty
much sucks? Two weeks

since the blowup with Cara,
        you'd think I'd accept it.
                Move on. But all I do when
        I'm alone is think about
the good times with her.

I've tried to talk to her. Tried
        to figure out exactly when
                everything went to hell. It
        wasn't the night we had sex.
It started before. I can see

that now. But what started
        it? The more I try to figure
                that out, the more frustrated
        I become. I work out, to keep
my frustration in check.

But once I'm done, anger
      beaten down by reps upon
            reps, I am muscle sore
      and heart-emptied. I have
no one to talk to about it.

Okay, I did a fair amount
      of screaming on Facebook.
            Heat of the moment is all.
      What good did it do, except
to make me feel validated

for a little while? One thing
      I learned. Cara's so-called
            friends aren't really friends
      at all. The only one who
had nothing awful to say

about her was Kendra. Not
      that she exactly stood up
            for her, but at least she
      didn't trash her. I've got
to respect her for that.

Her Call Surprised Me

But, hey, I was just sitting
               here, alone in the vacuum
                            that is my room. Getting
               out for a while sounds
good. Anyway, Kendra

is pretty cute, if a little on
               the skinny side. Going to
                            the movies with her, no
               strings attached, might
Band-Aid my injured ego.

And maybe word will get
               back to Cara. Wouldn't
                            that be fun? She *would*
               be upset, wouldn't she?
'Cause if I found out she's

been seeing some guy behind
               my back, I would have to take
                            matters into my own hands.
               And it definitely wouldn't be
pretty for that guy. Or for her.

I Get To The Theater

A few minutes after two.
        Through the big glass
                doors, I can see Kendra,
        talking to some guy. . . .
Holy shit. It's Conner.

By the time I get my ticket
        and go inside, he has hooked
                up with some strange people,
        including one majorly hot
lady, who looks to be about

thirty-five. Damn that Conner.
        Not only does he have a thing
                for older women, they seem
        to have a thing for him. At least,
that one does. She takes his arm,

leads him away. Whispers
        something into his ear that
                makes him laugh. But I have
        to say, he looks uncomfortable.
Maybe because of Kendra.

She wanders up, all weird and
shaky. *Hey. Thanks for coming.*
Guess you saw who I was
talking to. He looks better,
right? She sways a little, and

I think I might have to catch
her. "I suppose. But since
he was, like, bleeding out
when he went to the hospital,
he'd almost *have* to look

better. Come to think of it,
though, he looked well
enough to be back in school.
Why isn't he? And who were
those people he was with?"

I don't know. She sighs. But
I'm not sure which question
she doesn't have the answer
to. *The movie's going to start.*
Do you want some popcorn?

Does That Mean She's Buying?

I'm kind of afraid to joke
        with her, so I won't ask.
                She's sad, seeing Conner.
        I guess I understand.
I would be sad, seeing Cara

right now. Especially if
        she was having fun with
                other people. Unfamiliar
        people. Especially a new
guy. God, I've got to stop

beating myself up inside
        my head. And I don't
                suppose I should mention
        the older woman thing.
Conner wouldn't be out

in public with one he was
        doing, anyway. Would he?
                Maybe she was the girl's
        mom. But then, who was
the girl? And the guy?

And Why Do I Care?

I get a Coke and Kendra goes
           for diet. No surprise. I spring
                       for a big tub of popcorn.
           "Butter?" Kendra shakes
her head, but when she isn't

paying attention, I ask for
           it anyway. Hey, I'm buying.
                       Kendra keeps looking toward
           the corridor Conner disappeared
into. Hoping he'll materialize.

The attendant points us
           down the opposite hallway.
                       Kendra goes first. I watch
           her walk, all spindly like
an aspen sapling wobbling

in the wind. She is model
           pretty. And death-camp thin.
                       Don't guess she'd appreciate
           me telling her that. None
of my business anyway.

The previews have already
          started by the time we get
                    inside. We find our seats
          in the semi-dark, stumbling
up the stairs to the very back,

tripping over purses and feet.
          Scary Movie 666 is pretty
                    much like all the other
          *Scary Movie*s, except with
more devil stuff. Entertaining

enough, for crap. Kendra,
          who wanted to see this
                    dumb movie, might be
          staring at the screen, but
she doesn't react to the funny

parts, doesn't jump when
          she should. And she hasn't
                    touched the popcorn. Glad
          I got butter. And I'm also
glad this isn't a real date.

We Sit Watching

The credits roll. People filter
        past us, down the stairs, out
                the doors. And still we sit
        here. The popcorn bucket
is less than half full, thanks

completely to me. "You sure
        you don't want a little? Hate
                for good popcorn to go to
        waste." Not that it was really
that good. Kind of stale, in fact.

                        Kendra shakes her head. *No*
                thanks. I'm not really hungry.
        Anyway, we're supposed to
                have a family dinner tonight.
                      That usually means lots of carbs.

I can't help myself. "You could
        probably use a few carbs. But
                I know what you mean. Aunt
        Mo is big on the pasta, and
I'm a protein kind of guy."

She lets the carbs remark go
on by. *You look great. Beefed
up a lot. Which reminds me,
do you know anything about
Clen?* She's talking Clenbuterol.

"Uh. It's a steroid, right? Why
would I know anything about
that, other than the stuff I've
read about people using it for
weight loss? You're not thinking

about using it, right? Because
if you lost any more weight,
you'd flat not even be here.
Jesus, Kendra." I'm not sure
her body could handle Clen.

She ignores everything I just
said. *It would help me gain
muscle, though, right? Then
maybe I could eat more
without putting on poundage.*

Point Taken

I tell her I'll look into it for
        her. I've got to visit Chad
                for a refill myself. I probably
        should take some time off,
but what the hell? I need

something to get my bat hot
        again. One more cycle and
                I can lay off for a while.
        When the lights come up,
we get to our feet. Kendra

moves about like a tortoise.
        I bet a little food could
                help her walk faster.
        But when we start down
the hall, she keeps looking

around, and I realize she's
        being deliberately slow,
                hoping for another glimpse
        of Conner. Damn, she's got
it bad for him. Stupid girl.

Andre
A Glimpse

Of greatness should inspire
the desire to attain greatness
too. So why, then, do

              I

mostly feel intimidated
by my father, whose success
I covet? Is it because I

              am afraid

to attempt, and fail?
Or do I somehow find
comfort in failure?

              To

face a competitor and lose
is expected sometimes.
No shame. But if I

              take

a shot at a personal best
and come up short, it means
maybe I'm delusional to take

              a chance

on myself.

Breakfast This Morning

Was unusual. Dad, Mom, and me, all
at the same table.
It was orchestrated, the two of them

double-teaming me. *You graduate in nine*
weeks, said Mom. *What*
course have you decided to embark upon?

Okay, just semantically, the sentence
irritated me. "Are you talking
'course,' as in course of study, or 'course,'

as in a river's course, or the course of my life?"
I wasn't trying to be
snotty. Well, not *really* snotty. But go figure,

she took it that way. And Dad was already
mad at me for refusing
to plan the trip to California to look at schools.

I do not understand your attitude, he said.
Don't you realize your
entire future is at stake? Stupid questions

don't really demand answers. I didn't
say anything, which
made every inch of skin above his too-

               tight collar turn the color of a boiled
                     lobster. *Are you being*
              deliberately obnoxious? That made

me laugh. "Not deliberately, Dad. I can't
help it. I was born
this way. I think it must be genetic."

Mom scowled. I figured I probably
shouldn't mention
the web of facial lines that created.

              Would you please be serious? she said.
                 Have you even thought
         about what you'll do after graduation?

"Of course I've thought about it. How
could I not? Dad's been
on me for months. I told him what I want

to do, but he says art won't pay the bills.
In fact, he thinks it
makes me gay. . . ." Mom flinched.

"Okay, I'm not gay. And to tell you the truth,
design is a compromise.
I . . ." I had said too much. I backpedaled

quickly. "Gramps always said if you do what
you love, the money will
follow. Worked for him. It will work for me.

I don't want to spend the rest of my life doing
something that makes me
miserable. Not even if it means drowning

in money." Suddenly it got very difficult
to choke down my
soggy cereal. "Look. I promise I'll be okay,

no matter what. Cheer up. Maybe I'm just a late
bloomer, and there's a mercenary
lurking somewhere deep inside me after all."

It Wasn't That Funny

But it did make both of them smile long
enough for me to
escape. What I didn't tell them, and have

no idea how I will, is that I'm thinking about
taking a semester or two off
school. There's a theater conservatory

I might look into. Or maybe I'll get a job,
an apartment. Chill
for a year or so, until I figure out exactly

what it is I want to do. Become. God,
the harder they push me
to "become" something, the more I want to

dig in my heels and just be whatever it is
I am. And what I am right
now is once again running late. I've got tickets

for the ballet tonight. Thought I'd surprise
Jenna. I told her to dress
up. Hope she listened. And I hope she's ready.

She Isn't, Of Course

I call her as I pull into the driveway.
More and more, I try to
avoid relating to either one of her parents.

"Hey. Ready to go? You wore a nice
dress, right?" I hear
muffled voices in the near background.

> *I'll be out in a minute,* she huffs. Then,
> to the muffled voices,
> *Can I* please *go now? Andre is waiting*

> *for me!* Garbled responses. *I promise.*
> *I don't know . . . Wait . . .*
> And to me, *What time will I be home?*

The performance starts at eight. Two hours
makes ten o'clock. "Around
eleven, I guess." Suddenly they care?

It is another several minutes before she exits
the house, teetering down
the walk in some extremely tall—and hot—heels.

She shimmies into the car, pushes down
into the cush leather.
God. Unbelievable. Let's go, before Patrick

changes his mind and makes me stay home.
I back out of the driveway,
noticing the length of her almost nonexistent

skirt. "Wow. Short dress." Hope her top
is covered better. Can't tell
because of her jacket, but my guess is, no.

I'm afraid she'll draw more attention than
the ballerinas. That's my girl.
I'm almost used to it. "So, what's going on?"

She pulls a familiar flask from her pocket.
Takes a long drink. *I love
peppermint schnapps.* Her voice is husky,

slow. *Want some?* I decline, and she takes
a drink for me. *For some
asinine reason, Patrick decided he needed*

to play Daddy tonight. He called a family
meeting. First, he accused
Kendra and me of stealing Mom's Xanax.

Then he said there are new house rules
about going out, and
how they want to know who we're going

with, where we're going, and when we'll
be home. I bet he starts
checking out our rooms and stuff too.

Considering she's sitting here, sucking down
alcohol, maybe he's got
a point. "Did you take your mom's Xanax?"

Maybe a couple, she admits. *Just to get me*
through the wedding
stuff. Who knew Mom'd actually keep track?

The Girl Has No Shame

It's one of her better qualities. But it also
makes me worry about
her. And us. "Xanax is expensive. Why

wouldn't she keep track? But the bigger
question is, did you take one
tonight? Xanax and schnapps don't mix well."

> *How would you know? I kind of like*
> *the way they mix.*
> She laughs. *In fact, they mix perfectly.*

This is going to be an interesting evening.
"Jenna, please be careful.
People die every day from drug interactions. . . ."

> She flips. *Don't worry about me! I am*
> *completely in control.*
> *Anyway, why do you care what I do?*

"Because I love you, goddamn it. You're
supposed to worry
about people you love. Don't you get it?"

She Does Not Respond

For a long while. Finally she says, *I don't*
believe in love. Not sure
it really exists, but even if it does for some

people, it won't for me. She is serious.
Then she lightens up.
But, hey, if you think you love me, cool.

My turn not to know what to say. I exit
the freeway, thread
through a maze of side streets, park a few

blocks away from the theater. We get out
of the car, and I go around,
take Jenna into my arms. "I do love you.

Not always sure why. But you are unique.
Exceptional, in so many
ways. Why do you think love will never

come to you? It already has." I kiss her,
as sweetly as I know how,
hoping she will believe love has found her.

Finally She Wiggles Free

No acknowledgment. No reciprocal
declaration. Just,
Okay. Where are we going, anyway?

It's so Jenna, I can't even get mad.
"The San Francisco Ballet
is in town. Ready to soak up some culture?"

The ballet? Are you kidding? Her inflection
gives away nothing. Surprise?
Disgust? *Nothing ventured, nothing gained,*

I guess. She takes my arm, struts toward
the theater, drawing
the usual stares from passersby, and a catcall

from some derelict-looking guy. Luckily,
we don't have to walk
all that far. But then, when we get inside

and she takes off her jacket, my worst
fears are confirmed.
Her V-necked top hides nothing. She pulls

every eye, and not just the guys'. Our seats
are in the balcony, front row.
Great view. Jenna actually seems excited

to be here. It's a special performance
of *The Little Mermaid*.
I figured the story would be familiar

enough to make the dance enjoyable
for Jenna. But, not quite
forty minutes into the program, I look

over to find Jenna asleep. Xanax and
alcohol. A knockout
combination. She rouses when the lights

come up for intermission. *Guess I dozed
off. Sorry. But this stuff
is just so boring. You don't like it, do you?*

Why did I expect anything different?
"Actually, I don't like it.
I love it. Sorry you don't feel the same way."

Cara

Did I Expect

To

learn something new,
walking the same old
avenues? Did I believe I'd

find

surprises under the pillow
my head rests on every
night—an extension of

myself?

Change doesn't come
without invitation.
You won't discover it

in

routine. And you won't
create an all-new and
better you if you wait for

someone else

to give you permission.
Transformation begins—
and ends—inside of you.

Transformation

Isn't easy when most of the people
in your life think you're already
perfect, and want you to stay just
how they see you. Try to begin

a new phase, you'd better expect
push-back. Try to create a whole
new you, your friend list will shrink
considerably. I don't have any friends

left at all, and that's before anyone
knows about Dani and me. I'm so
happy that school is almost over.
Once it is, I'll be free of the pressure

to be someone other than who I am.
Not sure how I'll come out to my
parents, or if that's what I should
even do. Is there a proper time to tell

your relatives that you're a lesbian?
Easier to let them guess than to
stand up on a soapbox, loudly
confess that, hey, guys just don't do it

for me. At least Dad has Conner
to carry on the Sykes family name.
Thank God that was not legitimately
up to me. And speaking of God,

hope he's okay with me being here
at worship on Easter Sunday. One
thing good about Lutherans—most
of them don't ostracize gay people.

Gay. Lesbian. Words. That did not
apply to me until recently. Or did
they? Do you have to admit you're
a lesbian before you are one? Dani

says no. I can't think about her now.
Here. In church. Can I? God, I think
I love her. Is that wrong? Or is that me,
only a footnote to your master plan?

Easter

Is a mad celebration. Imagine
if the story is true. Resurrection.
The ultimate transformation. Son
of man, risen in glory to take his place

at the right hand of God. Okay, that's
the preached-from-the-pulpit version.
But in the historical context, it's even
better. Some guy—a street person

with a resonant message—in turn
wows crowds, then somehow angers
them enough to want him dead.
When the reigning pols agree,

he is crucified. Hung on a cross
to die, while former followers cheer.
Sounds like some modern politicians.
Hope they never have to rely on resurrection.

I Sit With Mom And Dad

Near the front of the church.
Not sure how much of the Easter
story either of them really believes.
Pure light and boundless love

don't seem to relate much to Mom,
who sits straight-backed and ice-cold
in her chair. Dad, at least, sings
the liturgy and semi-tunes in to

>   the pastor's remarks. . . . *He died*
>   *so that we, no matter our lifestyles*
>   *or challenges or histories, might live,*
>   *free from judgment or sorrow, forever.*

No matter our lifestyles. Was that
directed specifically toward me?
Free from judgment. What I find
particularly funny about that is

how judged I felt at the party Friday
night. Hard enough coming to terms
with the label "lesbian," without
somehow having to prove that you

are "lesbian enough." Dani thought
it was funny. *Come on. Don't take
it seriously. They're just jealous.
Easier to call you a fake than to try*

*and wear jeans as well as you do.
Anyway, if you need validation, I think
you're a total lez. You don't need
to look like a boy to prove it. Now*

let's discuss what you do *need to do
to prove it.* We were in her car
and it had started to snow by then.
We drove to a far corner of the Rancho

San Rafael parking lot, and as dime-
size flakes turned to quarter-size,
curtaining the glass, Dani showed me
what it takes to make love to a girl.

It Is Yielding

Flesh, lush and tender as June
peaches. It is giving, gracious,
respectful. And though I lacked
experience, Dani was forgiving,

taught me what I asked to know,
left me to discover what I could.
Her kisses were typhoon, wind,
rain and lightning, storming into

open windows. She blanketed me
with velvet skin, pillowed me with
exotic perfume, lifted me onto a cloud
just one breath away from heaven.

I couldn't say no. Didn't say stop.
I wanted more. Wanted to go on
forever, even after the first burst of rain.
Even then, I begged for downpour.

Afterward

Iced April air touching our heated
skin and lifting, steam, I shattered
beneath the weight of identity.
Shards of uncertainty scattered,

dissipated with each frosty exhale.
Tears too long held inside dropped,
crystals encasing half-truths. Secrets.
Candor would not be denied, and

I told her everything—how I had kept
my virginity until I needed to be sure.
How I teased Sean. Challenged him,
even, only to change my mind. How I

pleaded with him to stop, the end result.
I thought she would chastise me,
say I deserved what I got. Instead
anger billowed up in her eyes.

> *Oh, baby, I'm so sorry. Goddamn*
> *him to hell. Guys like that deserve*
> *a noncommutable sentence of*
> *castration. But why didn't you tell?*

I have to think about it. "The last
few months have been so hard,
with my brother and all. I didn't
want more upheaval, you know?"

You mean external upheaval.
But what about the craziness inside?
Promise, no matter what, you'll
never shut yourself off from me.

And what's going on with your
brother? I had never mentioned
Conner to her either. The subject
just hadn't ever come up. It has now.

Despite only spilling to one person
before, I told Dani everything about
my twin and why he ended up where
he did. Well, she asked for it. I even

proposed my guilt. "I knew he was
messing around with his teacher.
If I would have told, maybe . . . he . . ."
Confessing that encouraged a new

round of tears. By then maybe, just
maybe, I was feeling sorry for
myself. But then again, why? Hadn't
Dani just allowed me to put to one side

the people in my life who I don't have
the power to save? Which brings me
back to church. Back to Pastor's words.
I'm not a savior. And even he, who so

many believe was the Savior, was strung
up to die. Maybe it's time to save myself.
On my left, my mother continues to pray
only for herself. On my right, Dad is still

impossible to read. How do I confess
to either this momentous revelation?
All the strength I felt just moments ago,
every iota of elation, deflates. I am zero.

They Don't Have To Know

Right now. Or maybe ever. Pretty sure
Mom couldn't care less if I marry.
And if I have kids, it will make her old.
Not the way to impress her friend flock.

I drop my head for the benediction—
the final prayer that says we can go
home. When I lift it again, I notice
Dad has turned to stare at someone

sitting in the foyer, Easter Sunday
overflow. It's Conner. Escaped from
Aspen Springs, hungry for communion?
No, he's flanked by some burly bruiser

and a cute, dark-haired guy who
looks very at ease here. More so than
Conner, who looks close to panic,
especially as Dad nears the door.

Mom hangs back, her motive
unclear. Is it out of respect for
Conner's space? Or is it because
of fear? If so, what is she afraid of?

Not Sure, In Fact

Who looks more afraid, Conner
or Mom. The sanctuary empties,
and everyone crowds the food table.
I see Dad shake Conner's hand, say

something that makes Conner nod.
If I can make my way through
the meadow of people, I should
probably say something too. Not

that I know exactly what. "You look
great, for a crazy person?" Maybe
not. I turn to Mom, who hangs back
behind me. "Aren't you going to say hi?"

She straightens, draws herself up as
tall as she can, elevates her chin,
lifts her nose into the lily-scented
air. *I suppose it is expected of me.*

Expectations. Again. Wonder who
she'll be more disappointed in—
her suicidal, no-longer-perfect son.
Or his twin, the not-quite-out lesbian.

Kendra
Disappointment

Can do a couple of things.
It can drop you into a giant
sucking sinkhole of

depression,

a place you have to fight
to climb out of. Or it
can trigger an epic

mania

to overcome the odds
and transform failure
into success. Say you

swing

as high as the chains will
take you because you seek
the thrill of flight, and on the

up-

kick, you lose your seat.
Injury is likely. But if you
worry about falling

down,

and never chance "up,"
the sky will remain
forever out of reach.

Reaching For The Sky

Is not such a hard thing to do, not
        when everyone around you keeps

promising you have what it takes
        to touch it someday. I've always believed

I can. But I've known for a long time
        that it's a long way up to that patch of blue,

and sometimes it takes extraordinary
        measures to reach the stratosphere. Today

                I'm going for broke. Mom drives me to
        the hospital. *Are you nervous, honey?*

"Uh, let's see. She's going to make an
        incision in that flap that divides my nostrils.

Then she's going to pull my nose skin
        up between my eyes, exposing the bone

and cartilage. Two hours restructuring
        those, and hopefully when she returns the skin

to its normal position, all will be well.
        What could go wrong, right?" I watched

an animation of the entire procedure.
        It should have made me feel more secure

about everything. Instead I almost puked.
        God, I hope she doesn't have a problem

reattaching my skin. I almost went and
        read horror stories about rhinoplasty.

Decided that wasn't such a great idea,
        considering I am not going to change

my mind. So I just swallowed megadoses
        of vitamins C and E, which should help

the swelling and bruising. Asked (as opposed
        to Jenna's "borrowing" method) Mom for one

of her Xanax so I could sleep last night.
        No food or water after midnight. (No problem.)

And here we are, pulling into a parking
        space, headed toward a surgical suite and

my skin-peeled-from-my-face adventure.
        Am I nervous? Not at all! Just hope I don't

actually haul off and vomit all over
        myself. That might turn the old doc off.

        Okay, then. Here we go. How exciting!
        Yeah, that's one way of putting it.

Through the big glass doors, into
        the elevator, and up six floors. My legs

are a little shaky, but whether that's from
        nerves or lack of food, I can't say for sure.

I didn't eat anything at all yesterday.
        It's getting easier. Practice makes perfect.

I Don't Have To Wait Long

A nurse comes to get me, hands Mom
        some papers to sign. "See you on the other

side." I follow the chubby nurse,
        wondering how a health-care professional

could let herself go like that. Doesn't
        she know it's unhealthy to be overweight?

                Oh well. She's nice enough. *Put these on.*
        You can change in there. And you can

                leave your panties on, if it makes you more
        comfortable. Under a hospital gown, lacking

anything that resembles a back? The panties
        will definitely remain on. Everything else

comes off. The gown is actually designer,
        by hospital standards. Blue and pink swirls,

instead of the usual white. The hairnet
        and booties are white, however. Nondesigner.

When I come out of the bathroom, Dr.
Kane is waiting. *How are you feeling?*

Do you have any questions for me?
When I say no, she points to a wheel-

chair. *Your chariot awaits. We'll take
you down to the OR and introduce*

*you to Cheryl, your anesthesiologist.
She'll give you a local at the IV*

*site, so you shouldn't feel the needle,
which can be a bit uncomfortable.*

I expect an orderly to be my driver.
But Dr. Kane does the steering herself.

*Here we are. Get in the chair and I'll be
back when you're asleep. See you after.*

No table for this operation. It's a state-
of-the-art recliner. I climb up into it. Wait.

Unlike The Nurse

The anesthesiologist is built like a praying
        mantis—tall, slender, and strong-armed.

                Hello, Kendra. I'm Cheryl. She comes
over, shakes my hand. *I want you to . . .*

                She looks at me. Looks at my chart.
I thought you'd be shorter. Weight,

                *one hundred nine pounds. Says here
you're five foot ten. That can't be right.*

"That's right. I know, I've still got
        a few pounds to drop. But I'll get there."

                Her eyes hold concern. *Honey, you
do not need to drop an ounce.*

She rolls back the baggy sleeves, checks
        out my arms. Ditto the hem of the gown,

running her fingers along my legs.
        Then she studies the backs of my hands.

My wrists. The inside curves of my elbows.
She tsks. *Hang tight. I'll be right back.*

Sweat pops out on my forehead in hot
little beads. I don't think I like the direction

that just went. It's a long several minutes
before Cheryl returns, towing Dr. Kane.

She stomps over to me. *Would you please
take a look at this? You have to have*

noticed! Cheryl pulls at the hospital gown.
You're a doctor, for Christ's sake.

Dr. Kane bristles. *What are you talking a—*
But when she sees my shoulders, she gasps.

Suddenly, exposed, I'm freezing.
I start to shiver. My entire body shakes.

*Get her a blanket, Cheryl. Kendra, are
you eating at all? You are skin and bones.*

Shame And Anger

Collide inside me, roil together.
"Of course I eat. I need to be thin,

though. Xavier says I'm almost there,
too. The big contracts are coming."

Cheryl wraps a thermal blanket
around my shoulders. Blessed warmth.

Whoever this Xavier fellow is, she says,
you'd better quit listening to him.

Dr. Kane butts in. *Kendra, I know
you want to model. But what's going*

*on here isn't about modeling. You are
seriously emaciated. If you keep this up,*

*you're at risk for anemia, arrhythmia,
and osteopenia. And have you had*

*a period lately? Unfortunately, we will
have to postpone the rhinoplasty. . . .*

"No! Why? Look, I promise to eat,
        okay?" Why are they on me like this?

                Honey, there's no way I will administer
        anesthesia to you, says Cheryl. *You must*

                be at a healthy weight or there could
        be serious consequences. . . .

"Are you saying if some skinny person
        needed an operation to save his life

you wouldn't administer anesthesia
        until he plumped up first? That's stupid."

                She looks at me with gentle eyes.
        A rhinoplasty isn't necessary

                to save your life. But maybe coming
        in for one today did. I hope so.

Save My Life?

What is she talking about? I'm fine.
        Okay, maybe I haven't had a period

in a few months. It did scare me
        for a while, right after Conner and I . . .

But the pregnancy tests were
        negative. And anyway, what's so

bad about skipping a few monthly
        bloodlettings? "Look. I'm really okay."

                Dr. Kane shakes her head. *Get dressed.*
        Then we can discuss how to proceed.

                Cheryl, when she's ready, please
        bring her back to my office. Kendra,

                can I get you something? Some cocoa,
        maybe? It might warm you up.

It's a test. "Sure. Hot chocolate would
        be great." Three hundred calories great.

Cheryl Escorts Me

To Dr. Kane's office, where the good
        doctor is in deep conversation with Mom.

Wonderful. Come in for a nose job.
        Walk out with a confirmed eating disorder.

                        Sit down, please. Dr. Kane hands me
                a steaming Styrofoam cup. *Enjoy.*

Chocolate. God. I haven't tasted it
        in months. One sip, I'm totally buzzed.

                Mom keeps checking me out. *Kendra,
        Dr. Kane is extremely worried about you.*

                *She is recommending inpatient treatment.
        I told her we can handle it at home. Am I right?*

Good old Mom. "Of course. I tried
        to tell her I'm fine." To prove it, I take

a long, loud slurp of cocoa. I hope it
        doesn't make me sick. "Can we go now?"

Sean
Sick

how

much

you

can

want

someone.

To your stomach—gas churning
in an empty well. That's

it feels with her gone. Sick
in the head, much too

cerebral carnage. Brain cells
shredded and nothing

can do to put them back
together again. Nothing you

do to stop bleeding anger,
and even if you could, you don't

to because anger feels better
than the pain of losing

Been Asking Around

About Conner. Not sure why
         I feel the need to know, but
                     seeing him at the movies
                made me wonder what
the hell is up with him.

He looked healthy enough,
            as fit as I've ever seen him,
                        in fact. And considering
                he was always an ace running
back, that's saying a lot.

                        Nobody seems to know
                much for certain, but Bobby
            Duvall had an opinion.
                I think he tried to off himself.
                            He's probably been under

                        lock and key, you know?
                Conner Sykes, loose in
            the head? Yep, that makes
                sense. But even if it's true,
                        why should I give a shit?

I Guess I Don't

Unless it means Cara shares
       whatever craziness gene
              he's carrying. I mean,
       maybe she's just a little
confused. Maybe she could

get help for that, and then
       there's still hope for us.
              But how do I find out
       for sure? And even if I do,
how could I ever suggest

to her that her brain chemistry
       might be in need of adjustment?
              Lots to consider. But not today.
       Spring break. No school.
No game until Friday. Fresh

powder on the mountain,
       I'm skiing. I've avoided it
              all season, worried about
       injuries. But what the fuck.
Can't live in fear of a fall.

I Don't Want To Ski Alone

I called Kendra, but she's busy
        having an operation. Fixing
                the little bump in her nose
        that makes her face unique.
What's with girls, always

trying to fix stuff that doesn't
        need fixing? Anyway, since
                she's unavailable, I did
        the unthinkable and invited
Duvall to come along. He's

annoying as hell, but a fair skier,
        and for some lame reason, girls
                are attracted to him. Can't hurt
        to have him with me. Ski resorts
are babe magnets. Maybe I'll

hook up with a Cara stand-in.
        Just something to play with
                until I win her back. Still have
        Viagra left. Hate to let those
little blue pills go to waste.

Rose Has Been Invaded

"Shit. Check out the crowd. Lift
              lines are going to be impossible.
                            We should ski the singles line."
              I watch three curvy pairs of Lycra
ski pants walk by as we put on

                            our boots in the top parking
              lot. *Uh, yeah,* agrees Duvall.
              *Easter week and all. Which
                  means after next weekend
                            this place is closing up shop.*

Spring break is traditionally
              the last week for Mt. Rose, no
                            matter how much snow is left
              on the slopes. "Too bad. Skiing
will be great for a month yet."

                            *Yeah, well, it is baseball
              season. You ready or what?*
              We clomp down a slippery
                  road, skis over one shoulder.
                            Wait in a forever line just to

buy our lift tickets. Glad
          I'm not here for actual
                    exercise, although
          standing in five-year-old
ski boots is kind of a workout.

Finally we're good to go.
          "I haven't skied all season.
                    Lakeview good? I need
          to warm up." Duvall gives me
one of those *whatever* looks.

                    Sure, dude. I'd rather ski with
          a girl anyway. He laughs, slips
into his bindings, and trucks
          off toward the chair. And it takes
                    until I'm snapped into my own

skis to realize he just called
          me a girl. The little (literally)
                    prick. Under my collar, a warm
          seep of irritation crawls
up my neck, toward my face.

From Here

I can choose to go after him,
> show him how this particular
>> "girl" could mess up a certain
> guy's face. Or I can forget it.

Try to remember how to ski.

>>> I push off down a gentle slope
>> toward the high-speed chair
> where Duvall stands, looking
>> put out. *Do I have to wait for*
>>> *you all day, or will you pick this*

>>> *up eventually?* He's smiling.
>> Kidding. But I want to smash
> his freaking dopey smirk right
>> through the back of his skull.
>>> Deep breath. And another.

My blood pressure lifts like
> mercury in a thermometer.
>> Time to take a break from
> the 'roids. When this cycle is

over, or I die of a heart attack.

Even The Singles Line

Is slow. By the time I slide
        my butt onto a chair beside
                three kids kicking snowboards,
        the bottoms of my feet hurt.
Time for new boots. At least

this is a fast chair. It sweeps up
        the mountain until . . . *thud* . . .
                it stops because of a problem
        above or below. To my right,
the old, slow chair keeps on

moving at a forty-five-degree
        angle toward a lower disembark
                point on the same run this one goes
        to. It crosses beneath us, and my
ears catch the sound of familiar

laughter. I scan the line of chairs.
        Cara? I think it's her, buddied
                up with some girl. With a bump,
        the chair starts up again. Before
I know it, I'm at the top, where

Duvall stands off to one side.
   I ski right past him. "Coming?
      Or will I have to wait for you all
   day?" Down the short, semi-steep
face, onto the flat trail that circles

         the resort, I reach for whatever
     speed I can, hoping to catch up
   to Cara. Duvall is right on my
    heels. *Hey, man! What's the hurry?*
      Thought you wanted to warm up.

I don't even know why I want
   to see Cara. She'll only piss
     me off. I've stopped by her
   house maybe a dozen times,
but she won't talk to me, except

      to keep repeating, *It's over, Sean.*
    Just let it go. I can't let it go.
Can't let her go. Sometimes
   I drive by her house, just to see
     if there is anyone there. Anyone else

in her life but me. Sometimes
        I follow her, but the only place
                she ever goes is to rehearsals.
        I know she still loves me, even
if she hasn't forgiven me. Time.

There she is, up ahead. God,
        she's sleek as a dolphin,
                surfing snow. Who *is* that
        she's boarding with? The two
turn down the mountain, and

by the time we reach the trail
        they took, the girls are out of
                sight. I stop at the cornice's edge,
        breathing hard. Not sure I want
to drop over *this.* It's damn steep.

                        Duvall, of course, is up for it.
                What are you waiting for?
        Banzai! I pause for a second
                or two. But what can I really do,
                        but tail the guy through the trees?

I'm Sure It Isn't Pretty

But I manage to stay on my
        feet and avoid running into
                any obstacles. There are lots.
        Trees. Stumps. Rocks. A few
bushes, even, thinking it might

be spring. Turn. Turn. Pause.
        Turn. Turn. Pause. I think
                I used to be better at this.
        Where the hell did Duvall
go? He can't be more talented

at something than I am, can he?
        Because that just isn't right.
                Of course, if I didn't have
        to be so cautious, I could kick
his ass, on or off skis. Since

I don't want broken bones
        right now, however, I'll pick
                my way to the bottom of
        this pine tree slalom course.
Finally it intersects a long

beginner run where I can pick
   up enough speed to catch Duvall.
     It isn't hard, considering he's
   waiting for me at the fringe of
a small stand of cedars. He waves

      rather frantically for me to join
    him. *Check it out,* he says,
   pointing into the trees. *Jesus,*
    O'Connell, you turned her, like,
      gay. What's he talking about?

I lift my goggles, look hard
   at where his finger is aimed.
     Two girls on snowboards . . .
   wait. What the fuck? It's Cara,
for sure. She's with that girl, the one

with spiky hair, now frosted
   blue. They are chest to chest,
     and they are kissing. Not just
   kissing like friends do. Kissing
like people who are in love do.

Andre
People Who Are In Love

Expect certain things.
Time together, to learn
all there is to know about
each other. Falling in

          love

can happen to complete
strangers. Staying in love
requires being best friends

          and

that means accepting the person
beneath the veneer. What
complicates things is

          sex.

Loveless, it's easy. Insert
Tab A into Slot B. Enjoy what
happens naturally. But under
love's influence, the directions

          aren't

quite so straightforward.
It is then, striving for perfection,
you realize that all Slot Bs are not

          interchangeable.

When It Comes To Sex

I was kind of a late bloomer. Not that
I didn't know what it
was, or think about maybe having it one

day. At eleven or twelve, I started having
all the problems young
guys do, waking up sticky and sometimes

turning into walking wood, wrong place,
wrong time. Embarrassing
stuff. My first actual encounter was with

an Oakland girl—one of Gramps's neighbors.
She was a couple of years
older than me. Every guy should have an older

woman for his first. She taught me every
move in the Big Book
of Sex. Guess she liked playing teacher.

I was fifteen. After that, I kind of got a taste
for it, and let me just say,
private school girls aren't exactly all prudes.

But none of them can come close to Jenna
when it comes to
doing the dirty. Part of it is because I love

her, and love really does put a whole
different spin on getting
naked together. But Jenna knows more

than that Oakland girl and my preppie
lays all rolled up into one.
Without carrying a single iota of shame.

I have no idea where she learned what
she knows. To tell
the truth, I really don't want the details.

Enough to have her for my own, doing
those things to me.
Hopefully, we'll be doing them tonight.

This Afternoon, Though

I'm helping Liana teach a dance workshop
for a bunch of underprivileged
kids. Some of them are really young—like four.

> *First, I want you to see how the body*
> *is meant to move,*
> Liana tells the group, who are sitting

> on the floor beneath the barre. *Andre,*
> *will you please dance*
> *the jazz routine—the one to Coltrane.*

She fires up "While My Lady Sleeps," superb
classic sax from one
of the greatest jazz musicians of all time.

Beat comes first, and it remains steady under
the sad song of the saxophone.
The music closes around me, and I draw

it inside, a flowing current that my muscles
float upon. Contract. Release.
I am the music, and the music is my body.

And when it stops, I come out of the trance
that is jazz dance. If there
is a God, he listens to John Coltrane.

The sound of clapping hands pulls me back
into the studio. Lots of
little hands. And some bigger ones too.

Shantell has appeared, like a backlit cloud
reflected on still
water. The look on her face is hard to read.

But then she smiles as Liana says, *Okay,*
kids. Let's break up into
groups. Shantell, Andre, help divide them

up, and each of you take a group of ten or so.
Today is all about movement.
Let the music tell you what to do, like Andre did.

Awesome Day

The kids are amazing, so eager to learn.
I never thought about
teaching before, but I really love working

with them. It makes me feel like I've got
something to give, and
I'm sorry it has to end. Guess we all have

places to go, though. There's a chorus of
thank yous as they leave,
and when the studio has emptied, Shantell

comes over. *I really hate to say this, and
have it go to your head
and all, but you are an incredible dancer.*

How long have you been training? She
waits for an answer
she probably doesn't want to hear.

"A little over a year. I started after we
moved here to Reno."
As I suspected, she reacts with a scowl.

That's it? What made you decide to take
lessons, then? Did you,
like, wake up from a dream, doing pliés?

God she's funny. "Not exactly. Actually,
it was that TV show—
So You Think You Can Dance. I've always

liked street dancing. Used to do it some
when we lived in the Bay
Area. I saw this b-boy picking up ballroom

and thought maybe if he could, I could.
I found Liana online,
and that was straight from heaven.

She tapped something inside me I might
not ever have found
without her. That's my story. The end."

But She's Not Quite Finished

With me. *So what are you going to do*
with all that talent?
Go pro? You could, you know. There are—

I stop her with a shake of my head. "No
way my parents are
going to let their only son make a living

onstage some place. It was always just for
fun. Dancers don't make
the kind of money I need to be comfortable."

Now she looks totally disgusted. *Money?*
You can't be serious.
Dance isn't about money. It's about heart.

If it isn't, you damn well don't deserve
the gift God gave you.
I can't believe you'd let it go to waste!

She jumps up, stomps across the hardwood
floor. "Lots of talent goes
to waste." My voice is lost in her footsteps.

Every Time

I'm around her, I like her more. Not
sure she could say
the same thing about me. In fact, pretty

sure not. Oh well. She doesn't know
my parents, or that I'm
already a major disappointment to them.

Wonder how they'd feel about me teaching.
Other than the money thing.
Because teaching isn't about money either.

> As I start to head out, Liana gestures to
> me to come closer.
> *Uh . . . I happened to overhear your*
>
> *conversation. Shantell is right, you know.*
> *You were destined to*
> *dance. If you try to ignore that, you'll be*
>
> *completely miserable. A new TV dance show*
> *is holding auditions in L.A.*
> *next month. I hope you'll consider trying out.*

Me? On TV?

On the *Jeopardy! College Championship,*
maybe. If I go to college,
that is. But on a dance show? That would

require letting the world know I dance. Which
means letting my parents
know I dance. Putting all that aside, however,

that kind of competition is for *real* dancers,
not a novice like me.
I tell Liana, "I'll think about it, okay?"

> *Not for too long. We'll want to come up*
> *with something really*
> *special for your audition. Call me tomorrow.*

Tomorrow? No problem. I already know
what I'm going to say.
The Quattro takes me home. It must, because

I'm not thinking much about where to turn it.
I'm thinking about Shantell.
Dance isn't about money. It's about heart.

Is Dance My Heart?

I can't say that it is. The only thing
that feels that way
right now is Jenna. She is an obsession,

really. Not sure why. She says she's not
in love with me. Can never
be. Does soul-splitting love have to be

returned to make it real? If I had to give
her up, it would open
a black hole inside of me. But what about

dance? If I had to give it up . . . what? I park
my car, go inside to shower.
Run the water hot, make the bathroom steam.

Soap. Shampoo. Routine. Dance, I realize,
is my escape from ordinary.
If I had to give it up, I would lose something

integral. Why am I afraid to confess that?
I dance. Train. Work hard
to improve. Doesn't that mean I'm a dancer?

431

Believing I Am

Should mean being proud that I am, which
means telling the world.
I'll start with Jenna, work my way up.

We're going to a party tonight. Always
an adventure with Jenna.
When she gets in the car, it's obvious

her personal party has begun. "You drinking
already?" I think her condition
must be due to more than alcohol. But I'm not

> stupid enough to say so. *Only a little.*
> *I don't want to pass*
> *out before we even get there, you know?*

I won't comment on that. "So, hey. I want
to tell you something. . . ."
Tell her, quick, before the fire goes out.

> *Okay, but I have to tell you something first.*
> *Your mom thinks Kendra*
> *is anorexic. . . .* The flame extinguishes.

Cara

Fire

Some people say love is fire—
flame fanned into inferno. A

raging

that all too predictably burns
through the years, fades into

smoldering,

burns down into ash, soot
that cannot be rekindled.
I say that soot is

dust,

swept up by gravity to fly,
untouched by time, with

ice,

a comet. Bright in the vast
azure deep of night, a

flare in

the frozen emptiness of space.
A hot, cold candle, magnified
beneath the glare of

solar wind.

Falling In Love

Was not something I ever expected.
I have no role models for love.
I always thought friendship would
do—that my heart couldn't hold

more. But it can, and that presents
an incredible dilemma. Because if I
truly love Dani as much as I think
I do, how can I deny it? Her? Us?

At Stanford, no one worth mentioning
would care. The Bay Area is a liberal
stronghold. But Stanford presents
another problem. Will I still go there?

It's not so far from here. I could come
home on weekends. Not to see
my family, who I just want away
from. But how can I live without Dani?

Everything is so new, and moving
bullet train speed, we haven't even
talked about next year. It's all
been about how, when, and where

we can see each other again. God,
I want it to be every day. So strange.
Never, ever before did having sex
mean anything to me. But now

I think about it all the time. Is that
sick? I have no idea what normal
is. Has she turned me into a perv?
Maybe the trick is just having lots

and lots of sex until you get tired
of it? Does everyone eventually
get tired of it? Do really old people
still like having "fun" after decades

together? Does being in love influence
any of that? Does love fade with
time? And which fades faster—love
or lust? Too many questions.

That's what comes of sitting here
alone when all I want is to be with her.
Wonder if she feels the same way.
Suddenly the phone rings. Am I psychic?

But It Isn't Dani

Caller ID says it's Sean. I let it go
to voice mail, though I've got a good
idea what he's going to say. He's sorry.
He loves me, and he's sure I love him, too.

> But no. This message is different.
> *Hello, Cara. You might want to*
> *pick up, unless you want your parents*
> *to hear about you and your girlfriend.*

I feel like I just stepped off a high
dive. He waits, and I can almost hear
the *zzzzzz* of his anger. I don't know
what to do. Pretend I'm not here?

> *I know you're there. I can see*
> *your car.* My car? Is he outside?
> *You've got five seconds. Answer*
> *the goddamn phone! Four. Three . . .*

I yank the receiver out of its cradle.
"What is wrong with you, Sean? Why
can't you just leave me alone?"
I am not the type to cry, but this is getting

creepy. Scary, even. "What do you
want from me?" Hope he can't hear
the crack in my voice. And I pray
he can't see me crying. He isn't

> looking through my window
> with binoculars or something,
> is he? *I want to know when you
> went all gay. Not only a whore,*
>
> *but a lezbo whore? Just when
> the fuck did that happen? No
> wonder you didn't want dick.
> Then again, some lezs like dildos.*
>
> *Do you and your little butch girl
> use those? Because I'd pay to
> watch. In fact, I bet I could round
> up a few friends. What do you think?*

Deny. Deny. Deny. He can't know
anything for sure. He has to be
guessing. "Sean, I have no clue
what you're talking about."

His Laugh Is Cruel

Really? And now you're a liar,
too. I saw you with her at Mt. Rose,
off in the trees making out. You
wanna tell me that isn't true?

Oh my God. So, fine, change tactics.
"You *are* stalking me, aren't you?
You realize that's crazy, right?
Sean, can't you see you need help?"

First of all, I didn't even know
you'd be at Rose. Pure coincidence.
And second, considering everything,
I'd say you're *the one who needs help.*

I could tell him that Dani *is* my help.
But arguing with him is useless.
And no matter how much he thinks
he knows, I won't confess anything.

How can I de-escalate the war he so
wants to wage? "You're right. I do
need help. See? You're better off without
me." I expect a fresh barrage of rage.

No, Cara. His voice is unusually
gentle. *I am nothing without you.
Look, I can understand wanting
to experiment. Lots of girls play*

*with other girls. What if I let you
be with her, too? Just give me
another chance to show you
how much I love you. Please?*

What if he *lets* me? Is he serious?
Dumb question. Of course he is.
"Look. I don't have to ask your
permission for anything. Love

isn't about ownership. It's about
respect—something I don't have
for you. Find somebody who does.
Direct your affection toward her."

I hang up before he can respond.
Oh God, what will he do next?
I've got to get out of here. But
first, I have to talk to Dani.

Her Cell Goes Straight

Through to voice mail. Turned
off. Or dead. Should I call her house?
Why not? It's not like *I'm* the stalker.
I can always fall back on the old

"I'm just a good friend" explanation.
Three rings and her dad picks up.
"Uh, hello. Is Dani there? This is Cara."
Surprisingly, he acknowledges me.

> *Oh, Cara. Yes, hello. One second,*
> *please.* The phone moves away from
> his mouth while he yells, *Dani! Phone!*
> Then he's back. *Okay, when am I going*

> *to meet you? I've heard so much*
> *about you.* He reminds me of a Jewish
> mother, talking to a prospective in-law.
> At least, like the Jewish moms on TV.

I had no idea he knew about me.
"Um, any time. Would be great
to meet you, too." How much,
exactly, *does* he know? The next

voice I hear is Dani's. *Hey, girl.*
What's up? Oh, hold on . . . now
she and her dad are talking. *Okay,*
he's gone now. What's going on?

"It's Sean. He called. He saw us
kissing and he got all weird and went
off on me. I hung up on him and now
I'm afraid he'll tell everyone." She

goes off on me too. *So? God, Cara,*
why do you want to hide? What are
you afraid of? That people will know
who you really are? You take pride in

the way you look. The clothes you
wear. Excelling at everything.
But you're embarrassed by loving
me? That is totally messed up.

"I know. I'm sorry. Don't be mad.
Please? Can I see you? I need you."
Need a megadose of courage.
I grab my keys, run to my car.

What Am I Afraid Of?

Good question, one I've asked myself
before. Mostly, I am afraid of failing.
But why? Everyone falls down from
time to time. Why must I always stay

on my feet? I am afraid of not
meeting expectations. But whose?
The answer to that is easy. Suppose
I choose a far different future

than the one my parents require
of me. Will I have made a mistake?
Done something regrettable? Or
will I have set myself free? Am I

afraid of freedom? Of being cut
loose from my family, such as it
is? Would they sever the tie, and
if they did, what do I really have

to lose, especially considering
how much I have gained with Dani.
If I have to be honest, though, I am
afraid of being stained by the lesbian

label. Some girls wear it proudly,
a giant "this is who I am" tattoo.
And much of mainstream society
now accepts the idea of two people

in love, whatever their genders.
My challenge is to accept it myself.
And, a bigger one, to embrace it.
I'll try. And I'll start right now.

This is the first time I've actually
been to Dani's house, a small brick
beauty in an old southwest Reno
neighborhood. Tall, naked trees line

the street like big-boned skeletons.
Dani's dad opens the door. *Come in!*
He grabs my hand, pulls me inside
and across the blemished oak floor

to the living room. *Make yourself at
home. Dani! Your girlfriend is here.
I hope you'll excuse me. I've got
a golf score that needs improvement.*

Dani Comes, Smiling

Into the room. After a few minutes
of three-way small talk, she leads me
back to her bedroom, which is mauve
and sage green. I fall into her arms,

strangely not worried about her dad
suspecting what we're up to. We are
kissing, and there is strength in that,
power in the "two" of us, deepening

> connection. In the truth of our love.
> She lays me back on her bed, lifts
> my sweater over my face so it covers
> my eyes. *Don't be afraid. Trust me.*

Traffic hisses by on the street beyond
the window. And here, on this side
of the glass, in the darkness behind
closed eyes, I put away my fear, place

my faith in Dani. She makes love
to me with borderline ferocity, awakens
something inside. Something completely
new, and at the same time, primordial.

Kendra
Borderline

It's the latest, greatest
twenty-first-century buzzword,
tossed around freely in
certain circles. Oddly, it

                            means

different things to
different lexicologists.
It is defined as the line
separating two

                            almost

identical qualities, i.e.,
between frankness and
rudeness. Definition two:

                            not

clearly belonging to one
or the other of two
categories, i.e., neither

                            here

nor there. Finally, it means
emotionally unstable, self-
destructive, and erratic.
Maybe, like me.

Food Is Not My Friend

My stomach wants nothing to do
        with it. But if I don't at least pretend

to eat, Patrick's talking lockdown
        rehab. In fact, Mom had to argue him

out of taking me straight to Aspen
        Springs. They had a pretty big fight.

                She's my daughter. I'll handle it, okay?
        You just worry about orthodontia.

Mom made me promise to consume
        at least one thousand calories per day.

                Meat. Vegetables. Whole grains. You can
        skip dairy, but have to take a calcium

                supplement. You're begging for brittle
        bones, not to mention bad teeth.

Okay, she got me on that one. I should
        have been taking calcium all along.

No calories there. And a perfect
>   smile is a necessity in the industry.

Meat? I've sworn off anything red.
>   One boneless, skinless chicken breast,

broiled. Two hundred calories. One-half
>   cup steamed broccoli. Fifteen. One slice

whole wheat bread, seventy. There. Two
>   eighty-five. That's as good as I've done

in six months. A thousand calories?
>   Not going to happen in one day. Thank

God she's not standing over my shoulder
>   watching. If she decides to, I'll eat plenty

of veggies. Then I won't have to rely
>   on laxatives, my last-resort backup plan.

I Really Don't Get

Why everyone's so worried anyway.
        God, until that stupid anesthesiologist saw

me without my clothes on, no one had
        ever noticed a problem. And I still don't see

one. When we got home (me, still wearing
        an ugly nose bump), I went into the bathroom,

stood naked in front of the full-length mirror
        I've avoided for months. I guess my arms *are*

pretty thin, and my legs look just about right.
        But my stomach still bulges, and my waist

poofs out on each side. I'll try some
        extra crunches and sit-ups. And, since Patrick

seems deadly serious about the rehab
        threat, I'll run more. Exercise is healthy, right?

And I'll call Sean. See about the Clen.
        Something to make my muscles lean. Strong.

Can't Do That Right Now

Xavier is on his way to pick me up
for an audition. *This one is important,*

he said. *Dress sexy as hell, but we're going
for the modest look with the makeup.*

*This client is developing a new younger
teen line, so the work will reflect that.*

I go for a micro skirt, tights to sheath
my legs. Tank top, no bra. Short, zipped

hoodie. Gentle with the makeup. Hair
smoothed into a ponytail. The mirror says

Young. (Baby fat.) Fresh. (Early crow's-
feet.) Pretty. (Bump, still there.) Teen.

So why do I feel tired? Worried?
Stressed? Anxious? Why do I feel old?

Guess I Don't Look

As old as I feel. When I get into Xavier's
Caddie, he nods. *Perfect. You've got*

exactly the look this guy's going to want.
He punches the gas pedal like he's mad

at the car. Cadillacs sure are smooth.
So what happened with the nose job?

*Not that I'm unhappy. You couldn't even
try out for this job if your face was all*

*bruised and swollen. I've seen a few
girls post-op. It's not a pretty sight.*

Not sure how much to tell him, although
Xavier almost always takes my side.

Might as well fess up. "The anesthesiologist
decided I was too thin to risk knocking me out."

He turns toward me, seriously taking
his eyes off the road. *Really. I think you*

look positively the way you should.
Did he know you're a model?

"It was a she. And yes, she knew.
        She and Dr. Kane tried to convince

Mom that I'm anorexic. Patrick even
        threatened to have me locked up unless

I start eating more. But don't worry.
        I'm okay. Everything's under control."

        I'm not worried about you, doll.
        But play the game. The last thing

        we want for you is treatment. They'll
        plump you up like a little piglet.

"I'll have to wait for summer to do
        the rhinoplasty now." And I might have to

find a different plastic surgeon. Maybe
        I'll get my boobs done at the same time.

Apparently, This Audition

Is happening in a concierge suite
        at the Atlantis, one of the most upscale

hotel casinos in Reno. As Xavier parks,
        he reminds me to use my attributes to our

                advantage. *Like your sister. You know,*
fifteen, going on thirty. Look sweet.

                Talk dirty, and let him talk dirty if he feels
like it. In fact, I want you to do anything—

                everything—he asks of you. Even if it makes
you uncomfortable. Are you up for that?

Uncomfortable? That's what I am right
        now. "I'm not sure exactly what you're asking."

                Okay, here's the deal. This gig can set us
up in a big way. It could take your career

                to a whole new level. We're talking high-
fashion runway, and not just buyers' shows.

*You've worked really hard to attain
the right look. But lots of girls do.*

*Now, you need an edge, something to
guarantee that Gilles will choose you.*

*I want you to be very, very nice to him.
Understand? The sacrifice is minuscule.*

Oh my God. I *do* understand. "You're
saying I should have sex with him?"

Xavier grins. *Only if he asks you to.
Look, it's not unheard-of in this business.*

Oh, I've heard of it, and not only
in the colorful world of modeling, but

also behind the scenes at pageants,
big and small. But I've never once

thought about using my body
to win a crown. Or a runway gig.

I'm Thinking About It Now

Thinking about it all the way across
        the parking lot, through the big glass

doors, along the marble floors, into
        the elevator. Sex in exchange for cash

makes you a whore. What does sex
        in exchange for a shortcut to your dreams

make you? Is there any difference?
        Then again, what about sex in exchange

for love? Some people fall in lust well
        before they ever fall in love, but it isn't

impossible for love to trail sex.
        My little sister, as Xavier noticed, uses

her body to get what she wants.
        Is my moral compass any truer?

Why even worry about it? This Gilles
        guy might be gay for all I know, more

interested in Xavier than me. Ha.
        Wonder if Xavier would give the guy

head if it meant landing the gig. He knocks,
        and I can't tell from the first glance if the guy

                who comes to the door is gay or not.
                Come in. Come in. His obvious appraisal

                (of me, not Xavier) makes my stomach
lurch. *You must be Kendra. Xavier, you were*

                so right. She is a knockout. Come in.
(If he says that again, I am so leaving.)

                Let's talk. He slips an arm around
my waist, herds me toward a big sofa.

I glance over my shoulder at Xavier, who
        gives an A-OK sign. I do not feel A-OK.

                I feel halfway nauseous. And totally
set up. Gilles sits me on the sofa. *Let me*

show you my new line, Teen In-Style. He opens
a big photo album, flips through the pages.

Tell me what you think. Do you like this one?
He is very close. His leg pushes against mine.

One hand lights on my knee. The fashion
he shows me is smart. *The idea is to market*

to teens who don't have unlimited budgets,
who want clothing that makes a statement.

His hand makes a statement, starting a slow
crawl up my leg. *Teens who are innocent, yet*

bold. It reaches my inner thigh. *Girls who*
want to look exactly like you. . . .

I could protest. *Should* protest. Xavier
should protest. But when I glance at him,

he is smiling. Fingers play at the thin strip
of fabric between my legs. And I let them.

Sean

A Thin Strip

Divides a healthy dose
of self-esteem from
a fatal overdose of conceit.

Vanity.

It's a high-wire act
requiring exceptional balance.
Complete control.
Straddling that tightrope

invites

a bone-smashing fall,
death the preferable outcome.
Irreversible brain damage

incites

force-feeding pity parties,
everyone wondering if you sleep
in paradise or fight for
stability in a maelstrom of

insanity.

Caught In A Maelstrom

Of jealousy and anger. That's me.
            It's a static in my brain. A crimson
                        lens I'm looking through, and it
            all makes my head pound like meat
getting tenderized with a mallet.

Why did the bitch lead me on?
            I watch her come out of her house,
                        walk quickly to her car. Does she
            suspect I'm here? If she drives by,
she'll know for sure. But she turns

                        the other way, taking the back
            road toward town. *To her. She's*
going to her, says a voice. *Follow*

            her. I don't look for the source.
                        No matter how many times

I've searched, I can't seem to
            find him. But for the past
                        week or two, he's been
            talking a lot. I've learned to
do what he says. Or my head

hurts even worse. Cara's
little red Saab is easy to
spot. I maintain a decent
distance so she doesn't
see my truck in her mirrors.

*Yeah, but don't let her get too
far ahead, or you'll lose her.*

I turn up the radio. *That won't
work, idiot. I'm louder than
the music and you know it.*

He was practically shouting that
time. I turn the radio back down.
Open the window. A sharp stab
of air attacks my cheek, but it feels
good. Great. My skin is fevered.

"You have to stop distracting
me," I tell the voice. Some
people would say it's crazy,
talking to someone you can't see.
But mostly he's decent company.

Cara Weaves

Through an asphalt maze. Right.
> Left. Left. Into an old southwest
>> Reno neighborhood, where houses
> are brick and river rock, with
covered porches and splintered

>> sidewalks. She drives slowly,
> as if looking for an address.
Maybe I'm wrong. Surely she

> knows where the blue-haired
>> girl lives. *You're not wrong.*

She pulls against the curb
> a couple of blocks ahead.
>> I find a place to park, watch
> her go to the door of a small
house. Some man answers,

>> steps back to let her in. A man?
> She's here to see a man? *No.*
It's the girl's father. Duh.

Maybe the voice is the voice
of reason. *Oh yes, I'm reasonable.*

I sit, waiting. Not sure what for.
Hope the people who live in
the house I'm parked in front
of don't think I'm scoping out
the place. Last thing I need in

my life are cops. After a little
while, blue-haired-girl's front
door opens again. The man
comes out, lugging a set of golf
clubs. He carries them to an aged

SUV parked in the circular
driveway. And off he goes.
Golf, huh? He'll be gone for

a while. Think he knows
what the girls will be up to?

What Will The Girls Be Up To?

I really, really want to know.
Guesswork and imagination
are so unfulfilling. Frustrating.

*Come on. You know what girls
do. You've seen it in magazines.*

*Movies, too. Remember that night
with Cara. It was a girl-on-girl*

*scene that got her all turned on.
Hey, maybe it's your fault. Maybe
you helped flip her gay. How ironic.*

No. Not me, and not the movie.
Gayness comes built in, right?
That's what everyone says.

*Yeah, everyone who's gay. You
don't really believe that, right?*

"Goddamn! Would you just shut
            the fuck up? I can't think straight."

                    Nope. All you can think is homo.
            God. Cara might be in there,
with that girl, doing . . . what?

                    Are they naked right now?
                    Playing naked lez games?

            No way to know for sure.
                    Ever heard of windows? You
                            know, those glass things you

can look through to see what's
            on the other side? Just be careful

                    in case Mrs. Golf Dude is at
            home. And you might not want
to let any of the neighbors see.

Windows Are Made To Look Through

Other than the cars zipping by
        faster than they probably should,
                the street seems quiet enough.
        I get out of the truck, don't lock
the doors, in case I need to leave

in a hurry. What is that noise?
        High power lines? My ears
                don't like the thrumming.
        I try to look like I belong on
this sidewalk, like I have a legit

purpose for walking along it.
        But the winter-bared trees
                seem to be the only things
        that know I'm here. Not too
worried about fooling them.

I slow as I approach the house.
        Glance around, trying not to
                look like I'm glancing around.
        The front door is flanked by
windows, shades drawn.

Shouldn't peek in the front
　　　　　windows, anyway. I veer
　　　　　　　　　into the unfenced side yard.
　　　　　It's screened from the neighbors'
view by a tall evergreen hedge.

　　　　　　　　　Two white-framed windows
　　　　　break up the red brick. I draw
back, against the wall. Listen.

　　　　Yeah, listen to that. Lord, what
　　　　　　　　are those two doing to each other?

From behind the first window
　　　　　come the sounds of nasty girls.

　　　　　　　　Check it out. Come on. Hurry,
　　　　would you? Don't worry. They're
looking at each other, not at you.

I duck under the window, then
            cautiously lift my face to the glass.
                        The voice was right. They are way
            too into each other—literally—
to notice me. The head of the bed

is toward the wall opposite me.
            Blue Hair is on top (of course),
                        which has Cara's feet pointed
            toward me. But even if she wanted
to look at the window, she couldn't.

Her sweater is pulled up over
            her face. The rest of her
                        beautiful body is bared,
            and opened to Blue Hair's
mouth. Tongue. Fingers.

No fair! That should be me!
            Watching is torture. But I can't
                        turn away. Cara moans, and
            I want her to moan for me.
Me! And then she screams.

I Love You

That's what she screams, only
              not for me. The thrumming
                        swells into the sound of a billion
              crickets rubbing their legs.
And, Viagra or no, I am hard.

                    Quick! Your cell. Come on!
              I don't get it until he says,
The camera. A picture is worth

              a thousand words, remember?
                        And two thousand screams.

My cell. Right. I locate it,
              fumble to find the camera setting.

                    No flash. Hold it right up against
              the glass so it doesn't glare. Zoom
it in. Perfect. Now get out of here.

I Don't Bother With Stealth

On the way back to the truck.
        In my pocket, the camera bumps
                against my groin. The boner
        is gone, a sticky glaze left
as a reminder inside my boxers.

                Sick. I am sick, right? I start
        for home, in a fairly straight
line on well-traveled roads.

        *A picture is worth two thousand
                screams. It's her turn to squirm.*

I see Cara squirming. Building.
        Hear Blue Hair tell her yes, now.
                I am seeing through red lenses again.

        Don't get mad, dude. Get even.
You can wreck her. Simple upload.

Yes, now.
        Wreck her.
                Get even.

Andre
Even Now

After so much time nearly
inseparable, connected by
experiences and emotion,

she

can shut me out. Turn
away, as if our investment
in each other

doesn't

carry weight beyond
the moment. Is it possible
that she doesn't really

know

how much I need her?
Can't hear truth when I tell
her how much she means to

me,

that she has changed the way
I look at life, at the future?
Does she even care

at all?

Some Things You Can't Fix

For someone you love, no matter how
much you want to.
I can't make Jenna's sister stop being a star.

I can't change last quarter's report card
so her parents will let
her get her driver's license. I can't insist

her father stop being a racist jerk. And there
is absolutely nothing I can
do about his upcoming wedding. All I can

do is be available to listen, and maybe offer
comments to help her process
the disappointments in her life. Not that she

would call them that. She thinks she's handling
them just fine, rising above
them, as it were. But I seriously disagree.

She's Disintegrating

The fracture occurred a while ago. I noticed
the fissure last week,
after her sister landed a major modeling job.

> *I can't believe it. The guy loved her. He made*
> *her a spokesmodel for this*
> *major new teen fashion line. Not that most of*
>
> *us are skinny enough to wear it and look half*
> *decent. God. It's big bucks.*
> *National exposure. It's all Kendra can talk*
>
> *about, and it's making me sick. Then there's*
> *Mom, who keeps saying,*
> *"All our hard work is finally paying off."*
>
> *Our hard work? She hasn't even noticed*
> *that Kendra isn't eating*
> *again. Or maybe she's just overlooking it.*

She went on longer. And all I could say was,
"The eating thing is a problem.
But as far as the job, you should be happy

for her. It's her dream, and she's worked hard
to accomplish it, right?"
I still hadn't—haven't—mentioned my own

dream, and my decision to pursue it. I started
to do that one time, but when
she cut me off to talk about Kendra's probable

anorexia, somehow the subject of dance just
didn't seem important.
It wouldn't have been to her, anyway.

My supporting her sister pissed Jenna off.
I'm sick of her always
getting the stuff she wants. All because of

her looks? She hasn't worked hard. All she
does is starve herself. And
my mom doesn't even care about that. That's

messed up. No one notices me. Not even when
I got good grades. That was
"expected." But get bad ones, everyone freaks.

Still trying to be the voice of reason,
I dared say, "You know
insurance rates go down when you get

good grades. If your parents are paying
for your insurance, isn't
it fair to expect you to step up and get them?"

Mistake. *Why are you taking everyone
else's side?* It came
out a whine. *I thought you'd understand.*

"Jenna, I do understand. I just think
you're standing a little
too close to have a clear perspective."

Bigger mistake. *You are just like my dad.
Always saying you love
me, but not meaning it enough to prove it.*

"Me? Like your dad?" I snorted. "Yeah, right.
You mean I'm an overt bigot,
semi-misogynistic, and an overbearing prick?"

Biggest Mistake Of All

To my complete surprise, she jumped
straight to his defense.
I don't even know what half that stuff means.

Okay, that one time you met him, he wasn't
very nice. But before Mom
left him, he was my daddy. Sometimes he

was kind of mean, but never to me. After
we moved in with Patrick,
that was when he got nasty. I don't know

why he decided to take it out on Kendra and
me. Not like we told Mom to go.
But he acted like it was our fault. Then, even

more to my surprise, she hauled off and
started to cry. Which shifted
everything back on me, and somehow elicited

my apology. "I'm sorry, sweetheart. Please
don't cry. Everything will
be all right." But I'm wondering if it will.

I'm Also Wondering

If the reason she can't accept the idea
of her dad's wedding
is a simple case of jealousy. She wants

his love. He's focusing it all on Shiloh.
Jenna says they're talking
about having a baby before too long, too.

I can see why she feels left behind.
Maybe even discarded.
Is that why she refuses to accept my love

and return it? Afraid that love doesn't
last? Doesn't really exist?
Afraid if her own father can withdraw

his love (or at least the manifestation
of his love), that maybe
she somehow isn't worthy of the emotion?

I've tried so hard to break through
her enamel, reach the clay
beneath, mold it into a viable relationship.

But a relationship needs more than one
person to be involved
in it. My own parents are anything but

perfect. They hold high expectations for
me, and for each other.
But there is nurturing within the boundaries

of our family. I don't know if they are *in* love
anymore. But they love each
other, and I have no doubt that they love me.

So maybe my lesson here is to learn from
my musings and trust
that my family's love will sustain my dream.

I'm not quite ready to out myself as a dancer
yet. But I have to consider
doing it very soon. Because the more I think

about Shantell's tirade, the more I realize that
while dance hasn't always
been my heart, it's starting to feel that way now.

So Today, I Will Tell Jenna

I'm taking her to a big jazz festival
on the Riverwalk. God,
I hope she likes jazz better than she liked

the ballet. At least it's outside, with lots
of places to walk and sit
beside the Truckee River. The weather

is warming, as if it understands that May
is approaching. Jenna,
of course, dresses for the sun-lathered day

in teeny shorts and a tight little T-shirt, which
leaks cleavage from a low
scoop. For the millionth time, I think how

beautiful she really is. Every other guy will
think so too. I really wish
I didn't have to share her with them all.

At least she seems to have forgiven me
for our last time together.
The Riverwalk is crowded, and, locked

thigh to thigh, we worm our way through
the throng. "What kind
of jazz do you like best?" Please have

                         something positive to say. *Is there more*
                                  than one kind? She smiles
                  at some college-age guys who overtly ogle

                  her scoop. All three are slurping beers. *Do*
                        you think they'd buy me
                one? Like she doesn't know the answer.

"I think they'd probably all give you theirs
if you keep flirting like
that." Irritation is obvious in my voice.

                  Really? I'm going to go ask them. As an
                            experiment. Be right back.
                And off she goes, without waiting for me to

tell her no effing way. I can only watch
as she slinks up to them,
acting for all the world like she wants to

join their pack. One of them turns and looks
at me. I shrug, and he smiles.
In under five minutes, she returns, holding

two almost-full cups of beer. *You were*
right. God, you're smart.
Here. One's for you. She offers a beer.

"No, thanks. I'm not much into brew."
I really don't like an alcohol
buzz, something she still hasn't noticed.

But even if I were, I'd want to stay sober.
"You didn't give them
your number, did you?" It's a joke. But

her answer isn't. *No, of course not. But*
one of them gave me
his. "Just in case," he said. She gulps

down one of the beers in three long pulls.
Good stuff. Okay, now
tell me about the different kinds of jazz.

At Least She Remembered The Jazz

I lead her to an open spot on the concrete
stairs. "I'll tell you about
jazz in a minute," I say, watching her start

on the second beer. Thank God she's sipping
this one. She already looks
a little unsteady. "But first, there's something

I've been meaning to tell you for a while
now. . . ." She tenses, and
her eyes go kind of panicky, and I realize

how that might have sounded. "No, no. It has
nothing to do with you.
It's about me, and what I've been doing. . . ."

She slams down half the beer. "It's all good,
Jenna. I just want you
to know. . . ." I talk about Liana. About dance.

> Dreams. She smiles and nods and when
> I finish, she says, *Cool.*
> *Be right back. I'm gonna hustle more beer.*

Cara
Dreams

connect

Has it only been weeks
since we met? How can
such a short span of time

two people so completely?
Before, I would have sworn
new love this deep could
only be hallucinatory

fantasy,

imagination incarnate.
Someone no one else
could see to spend your
heart-weary nights

with.

Then you appear in my life,
full-color illustration, ink
lifted off pages of my *Big
Book of Fairy Tales*, and into

reality.

My Big Book of Fairy Tales

Takes up a wide chunk of bookshelf
on my bedroom wall. It was the first
big book I read on my own. I always
had a thirst for words, though Mom

was not the one who quenched it.
That was Sandra, our *au pair*
when Conner and I were little.
She was a star in those very dark

nights when Mom didn't understand
her postpartum mood swings could
be regulated chemically. She cut us
early from her apron strings. Sandra

was our mommy substitute, and
she was very good at her job. When
she left to get married, I cried. Next
came Sherrie, who went too far

with Dad. And after her, Leona,
who went way beyond all things
proper with Conner, aged twelve.
Her fall from grace led to her early

demise when a fight with her grown-
up boyfriend sent her driving, head-
first, into a wall. No happily ever after
for Leona. We went without a governess.

Mom took over as mother, compelling
us toward the same kind of perfection
her own parents demanded of her.
It came more easily to me. Poor

Conner fielded the brunt of her
rages, along with Dad, who steadily
withdrew. From her. From us. From
time to time, I return to the pages

of *My Big Book of Fairy Tales*, as if
by doing so, I might rediscover
a few short memories of childhood
happiness. A star in the night, perhaps.

Saturday Morning, Late April

Usually the house would be still
as a crypt. But not today. I'm called
downstairs to the dining room, where
Mom and Dad have slipped into

earnest conversation. *Sit down,* says
Mom. *You know Conner is coming
home for a short visit today. There
are a few things to keep in mind,*

*according to Dr. Starr. She asked
that we please not quiz him about
life in Aspen Springs. As you might
imagine, there is a confidentiality*

*issue. No questions about therapy,
or any of the people he knows there.
Above all, we are not to ask why
he chose to attempt suicide.*

Her expression seems to demand
an answer. But what is the question?
Does she believe I'd argue? "Okay."
I look at Dad, but his resolute jaw

and rail-rigid spine reveal zero
emotion. I remember an afternoon
many years ago, when he tried to set
aside his devotion to work long

enough to play with Conner and
me. It was a board game—Risk—
and what I recall most clearly was
how he struggled not to overwhelm

his children with adult strategy.
Not easy for a man whose entire
existence is centered around winning.
Dad has always hated to lose. Yet

Conner won twice that particular
day. Not sure if it was luck, or if
Dad held back, but the look in our
father's eyes was half pride, half fury.

Mom Goes To Get Her Coat

Sweeps past us, down the hall.
I should be back in an hour.
I hear the garage door open. Wait
until I'm pretty sure she's gone.

Dad has immersed himself in the *Wall
Street Journal.* I interrupt him anyway.
"Someone asked about Conner the other
day. She saw him at the movies, I guess,

with some other Aspen Springs kids,
and maybe one of his doctors. I didn't
know how much to tell her. Is there
a particular story I should be giving?"

Dad looks up from his paper. Our
eyes connect, and I find sadness
in his. *I don't suppose you could tell
people to mind their own business,*

*huh? A few weeks, you'll graduate.
Move on. Move away. Then it really
won't matter much what your friends
have to say about Conner, will it?*

He doesn't get it. "She was his
girlfriend, Dad. She's worried about
him, and I don't blame her. It's like
he vanished without an explanation."

>   *Just tell her he's rehabilitating.*
>   *Getting better every day. No one*
>   *knows how badly he was injured,*
>   *so that's all you need to say.*

Better not mention she already
knows a lot more. Let him ramble
in his fantasy forest in total denial.
It's a gamble, but so is chancing

the truth. Kendra will probably
keep her mouth shut. She has so far.
Is it Conner's reputation she doesn't
want to mar? Or is it her own?

Not Much More To Say

I excuse myself, return to my room.
Try not to think about anything or
anyone except Dani. I wish I was
with her instead of waiting for reunion

with someone I barely know anymore.
After a while, the sound of Mom's Lexus
lifts toward my window. She has pulled
around in front of the house, as if

planning a quick getaway. Past the glass
and two stories below, my brother gets
out of the car. I watch as he turns
to look toward where Emily lived.

He won't find her there. Or anywhere
close by. Even from here, I can see
him processing the filtering information.
She. Isn't. There. Downstairs, I hear

Mom hissing for him to please come
inside. *That woman doesn't live there
anymore. Did you think she would?*
Did he believe Mom would forgive her?

Conner responds with rage. *Why
wouldn't she, Mother? What the hell
did you do?* Enough. I turn up my music
so I don't have to hear her tell him

what he doesn't want to know—
that she is, and always will be, in
control of all of our lives. Unless
we get away. Run away. Fly away.

The Loud Exchange

Between Mom and Conner rises
above my music. I start to turn it up
even more, when my cell signals
a new text message. Dani! I rush

      to see what she has to tell me. Only
      it's not from Dani at all. It's from Kendra.
      THOUGHT YOU SHOULD KNOW ABOUT THIS.
      GOT IT FROM AUBREE. SHE GOT IT FROM SEAN.

What? I click on the photo link. Oh God.
No! How? Sean, what have you done?
You bastard! You are stalking me!
In bold letters, the caption says SLUT.

I'm not, and neither is she, despite

      how Dani and I look. On her bed.

      In her mauve and sage room. Me,

with my sweater up over my head.

The rest of me is stripped to skin.

My mouth is in a perfect O, as I give

myself to Dani's lips, below my belly

button and in between my opened

legs. And tiny spot of glare or no,

the camera caught everything. As if that

isn't enough, another text. Another

photo, this when she has pulled my

sweater all the way off, ducked

to kiss the inside of my knee, leaving

my most intimate places, plus my face,

for the camera to see—and capture.

Kendra Got the Pic

From Aubree. That means it has
been passed around. Who knows
how far it's gone? God, it might
be on YouTube by now. I think

about searching it, but how? He
wouldn't use my name, would he?
I guess I should be thankful for "slut."
I text Dani. CHECK THIS OUT. GET BACK

TO ME. I wait. Wait. Where is she?
I need to go downstairs. Should say
hello to Conner. But I need more
to hear back from her. Way more.

> At last, my cell buzzes. *HOLY SHIT.*
> *WHO DID THIS? WAIT, I CAN GUESS.*
> *LOOKS LIKE YOU'RE OUT NOW. JUST*
> *BTW SEXTING IS ILLEGAL, YOU KNOW.*

Kendra
Out

One word.
A single syllable.
Three letters.
Two vowels.
One thin consonant.

                              Weighted

with meaning.
Out.
Exposed.
All secrets revealed.
Absolutely nothing

                              left

concealed.
Out.
Inside out.
Terrified

                              to

show your face.
Out.
Chained to truth.
Swim. Or

                              drown.

Blown Away

By a series of text messages passed
> around through the ether today. Shocked.

I've known Cara since grade school.
> Cheered with her. Performed with her.

Sat elbow to elbow, shared locker room
> showers, did hair and makeup together.

And I never, ever got the feeling that
> she was gay. When did she get that way?

She doesn't look like a dyke. Well,
> except in those pictures, which leave no

room for guessing. No wonder Sean
> was mad at her. Furious is a better word,

and he had a right to be. But wow.
> What an awful way to get revenge.

Don't think I'll be going out with him
> anymore. Breaking up is at your own risk.

Cara's Reputation

Is pretty much trashed. I mean, most
        people at school are fairly tolerant

toward the GLBTQ crowd. But you
        don't vote for them for class presidents

or homecoming princesses. (Let alone
        crowning one of them queen.) Don't ask

me why not. It's just not done. But
        even worse than knowing Cara is one,

is seeing all the dirty details like that.
        If any one of us ever wondered what

lesbians do, we've got the picture
        now. Literally. If I was her, I couldn't

show my face at school again. Oh my
        God. Maybe she'll have to homeschool

or something so she can graduate.
        And I bet she won't be going to prom.

Then Again, Neither Will I

A couple of guys asked, but since
        I don't even like either one of them,

I'd feel, like, fake if I said okay. God.
        When did I get so . . . mature? Old.

That's how I feel. Tired. No energy,
        despite the pills Xavier keeps giving me.

Maybe I *should* eat a little more. But
        I'm really not hungry. Food is still my enemy.

Especially now, representing skinny
        teens everywhere. Especially now, when

I have to keep Gilles happy. He likes
        the way I look. Especially naked. At first,

I hated being with him. Hated how
        that made me feel about myself. But now

it's not so bad. Ten minutes, tops.
        Usually, more like five. Five minutes

of feeling like a Fourth Street hooker,
        my body used and abused in more ways

than I ever knew a body could be used,
        in exchange for everything I've ever

wanted—a runway career. Designer
        clothes. And eventually, lots of money.

Haven't seen any money yet, and
        I haven't walked a runway. But it's coming.

Gilles says so. Xavier keeps saying so
        too. And once my career takes off, I won't

ever have sick, disgusting sex with
        someone like Gilles again. For now,

I'll deal with it. Go hungry for it.
        Run miles and miles for it. Take pills

that help me accomplish it. But I won't
        go to prom. I'm not a kid anymore.

Jenna, On The Other Hand

Is going to prom. I've never seen her
        quite this excited at playing dress-up.

                        God, I love my dress. Don't you love
                my dress? Took me hours to find it,

                        and I had to keep trying stuff on, and
                you know how much I hate shopping. . . .

"Slow down, girl, or you're going
        to hyperventilate. Let me see how

it looks on." She changes into a short,
        strapless sapphire blue number, with

a gathered bodice cut so low she just
        might come popping out. "Uh, wow.

Yeah, that's an amazing dress. It's a little
        tight up top, but we could let it out some. . . ."

It could be a little longer, too, but I know
        she'll fight me on that. One battle at a time.

And anyway, I have to admit her legs
          look great, even if they *are* size nine/ten.

"You did good. Andre will love you
          in this dress. How are you . . . what?

                    I'm not going with Andre. He has
             some dance thing that night.

                    Bobby Duvall is taking me. Andre
             doesn't know. Don't tell him, okay?

She can't be serious. "Bobby Duvall
          is a creep, Jenna. And what if Andre

does find out? You don't want
          to break up with him, do you?"

                    Not really. But I don't know if
             I want to be tied down, either.

"But . . . he really loves you."
          I would have done anything to make

Conner love me like that. Anything.
"You wouldn't throw that away for

someone like Bobby, would you?
Real love shouldn't be disposable."

I'm too young for real love. Anyway,
of course it's disposable. Look at Mom.

She trashed twenty years of real love.
Or maybe she was faking it all along.

A gasp in the doorway jerks us
both around. Mom is standing there,

close to tears. Angry tears. *How dare
you talk about me like that! How dare*

*you judge me! I loved your father more
than anything on this earth, except you.*

Jenna shakes her head. *Oh, really?
Why did you leave him, then?*

Mom Draws Farther

Into the room. She is trembling as she
sits on my bed. *Look. I tried to keep*

*most of this from you because I didn't
want to damage your relationship*

*with your father. The truth is, he was
sleeping with Shiloh while we were*

*still together. His drinking was out of
hand, and things were sliding downhill*

*before I ever met Patrick. You have
to remember the fighting. . . .*

I do. Yelling and screaming in
the middle of the night. The muffled

sound of Mom crying. "You should
have told us. We thought . . . you . . ."

*I know. I should have. I wanted to
protect you, but that was a mistake.*

Jenna looks ready to cry too. *So I was right about this wedding. It's bullshit.*

No, says Mom. *It's for the best. Your father hasn't exactly quit drinking, but*

he's doing better, because of Shiloh. Look. Do you know why I push you so

hard to reach for your dreams? Because I don't want you to ever have to rely on

someone else to take care of you. I stayed with your dad long after it was clear that

he didn't love me anymore, mostly to keep a roof over our heads. Patrick was

an unexpected gift. I married him right away so I knew we'd be okay. Safe.

Provided for. And loved. He does love us, even if it doesn't always seem that way.

I Have No Clue What To Say

Neither, it seems, does Jenna. Mom
    saves us trying to figure it out. She gets

        up off the bed. Starts toward the door.
Pauses. Turns, says to Jenna, *You look*

        beautiful, by the way. But your skirt
is a little too short. She leaves us in

        stunned silence. Finally Jenna says,
Unzip me, okay? She shimmies out of

the dress. I have pills that would help
    her fit into it better, but don't mention it.

We are both quiet as she changes
    back into sweats, hangs the dress

on a satin-covered hanger,
    carefully, as if it might fall to pieces.

Fall To Pieces

Like her. Like me. Like how we thought
        of our family, until just a minute ago.

I break the silence. "The skirt *is* a little
        too short. Good thing you've got legs

that can wear it. But I still think it's
        wrong that you're going with Bobby."

            I'm only going with him so I can go.
          I know he's kind of a creep. And I know

            it would hurt Andre if he found out.
          And I know he loves me. But I'm not

            good enough for him. I don't get why
          he loves me, but even if I did, I wouldn't

            let myself love him back because love
          is like summer. It only lasts so long.

Only so long. Then it's gone, fallen
        to pieces. Fallen like autumn leaves.

Sean
Pieces

That's all that's left of
my carefully created dreams.
Shards. Slivers. Splinters,
driven into what remains of

my heart.

What's really bad is,
it doesn't hurt anymore.
At least, when I was still
in pain, I knew

my brain

was working. No one lived
inside my head but me.
But now I have a roommate
in there, and I really

don't

like the guy. He talks way
too much. And the words
that keep coming out
of my mouth don't

belong to me.

Growing Things

Are trying very hard to make
        a spring appearance. It *is* spring
                now, though sometimes it's hard
       to tell in northern Nevada. Still
a lot of snow on the mountain.

If I were playing pro ball, I'd
        be off in Arizona or Southern
                California or someplace really
       warm, working toward new
goals. New records. New.

As it is, I'm here, where it's still
        relatively cool, playing regular
                season games, working toward
       the Nevada state championship
at the end of the month. May.

Championships. Prom. Senior
        week. And then, graduation.
                Not so excited about any of it
       anymore. My baseball record
doesn't really matter, unless you

count mattering to my ego. Prom?
        Kendra turned me down, so I'm
                taking Aubree. Don't have a clue
      why I'm going at all. It will only
remind me that I should be there

with Cara. My neck prickles.
        If I had hackles, they'd be
                rising. I've got to stop thinking
      about her, or risk blowing up
again. Risk doing something

                stupid. Something mean.
        Something the bitch damn
well deserved. Talk about

                revenge, baby. Brilliant move.
                  She never saw it coming.

You leave me alone, fucker.
        Chad says you're not here,
                that you're all in my head.
        But he's never heard you
blabbing at me. Go away.

That Guy

The one now living behind
        my eyes, keeps trying to tell
                me what to do, and it's getting
        really annoying. I did what he
said—posted those pics of

Cara and her girlfriend. He said
        they'd go viral, and boy, did
                they! People clear across
        the country, and probably
around the world, have had

the chance to gawk at Cara's
        pussy. I see her at school,
                and I'm pretty sure she
        knows. If looks could kill,
I'd be skinned and left for

the bone pickers. But she
        hasn't said a word. Of course,

                what is there, really, to say?
        She can't even prove that you're
the one who posted them.

I Hope The Guy Behind My Eyes

Doesn't talk all the way through
        prom tonight. It's late this year,
                rescheduled from an early April
        weekend with too much snow
coming down. Duvall and I hired

a limo (with a lot of help from
        his parents and Uncle Jeff).
                Might as well do it right.
        Aubree is wearing purple,
so I got a lavender tux. Hope

                it doesn't make me look gay.
        Gay. Hmm. Wonder if that
bitch is coming with Blue Hair.

       Of course she's coming with
       Blue Hair. Just not to prom.

Shut up, asshole! Oh my
        God! Does she come? And
                just when did she know
        she wanted to come with
girls? And was it my fault?

Think I'd Better Lift

A little before it's time to "shit,
        shower, and shave," as my dad
                used to say. Damn, I wish he
        was here. Remembering him
opens a big sinkhole in me.

Why does everyone important
        have to desert me? I'm almost
                to the basement door when
        the doorbell rings. I look out
the peephole. It's a uniform.

"Aunt Mo," I yell. "You'd better
        come here. It's a cop." I don't
                wait for her to open the door.
        "Can I help you?" Aunt Mo's
footsteps approach quickly,

                and I'm glad she's here when
            the big deputy says, *I'm looking
for Sean O'Connell. Is that you?*
            My head sort of bobs, and he
                goes on. *I need to ask you some*

questions. Do you want to
let me in? He looks at Aunt
Mo, who pulls the door the rest
of the way open, allowing
him to step through. Damn,

the man is tall. He makes me
feel like a dwarf. "Uh, did I,
like, *do* something? Jaywalk?
Run a red light? What?" Does
he know about the steroids?

Do you mind if I ask the
questions? Do you know
a girl named Cara Sykes?

"Uh, yeah. We used to go out."
But now she's a lesbian and . . .
Oh, shit. This can't be about that.

And do you know anything
about posting pornographic
photos of her on the Internet?

Before I Can Answer

Aunt Mo puts the brakes on.
Excuse me, but is Sean in some
sort of trouble? Sean, do you
have any idea what Deputy . . .
uh . . . Rossiter is talking about?

The guy obviously knows
something. Lying would
be stupid. I'll try avoidance.
"I did see some pictures of
her. They were pretty bad."

Rumor has it that you took
them. Which would mean
criminal trespass. And Ms.
Sykes is alleging stalking.
Does that sound accurate?

Guy Behind My Eyes: *Deny!*
"Well, no, I . . . not exactly."
GBME: *That is not denial.*
"I wouldn't call it stalking."
GBME: *I think we're in trouble.*

Being Eighteen

Has a lot of advantages.
        You can vote. You can
                go where you want. Do
        what you want without
a parent or guardian's approval.

One major disadvantage:
        If you're arrested, you go
                straight to jail. Do not stop
        at juvenile hall. Do not take
a parent or guardian with you.

The good deputy reminded
        me that I have the right to
                an attorney and to keep
        my big mouth shut. GBME
agreed. So did Aunt Mo.

                I'll call Jeff and we'll get
            you an attorney. Don't worry.
        We'll have you out of there
            before you know it. She didn't
                even ask about the pictures.

GBME: *Ha! Maybe she's
already seen them.*

"No way. Don't be ridiculous."

GBME: *You never know.*

Deputy Rossiter: *Who in the hell
are you talking to back there?*

"No one. Sorry. Just processing."

GBME: *Maybe Aunt Mo is a lezbo
too. Maybe she'd like them.*

"Aunt Mo is so not a lezbo."

GBME: *You never know.*

Deputy Rossiter: *Did you know
crazy people talk to themselves?*

"I am not crazy."

GBME: *You never know.*

The Booking Process

Takes a lot of time. Retinal
              scan: check. Personal info:
                            check. Photographing,
              face forward, right, left:
check. Fingerprinting:

check. Every step, all new
              to me, just another day
                            at jail for the intake
              officer. Now a nurse
comes to take some blood

and ask a lot of questions
              about my medical history.
                            "What's the blood for?"
              The question seems fair,
but the mastiff-faced nurse

                            seems totally put out by it.
                     She rolls her big bug eyes.
              To identify certain diseases,
                     of course. She squints at my
                            pupils. *Screen for substances . . .*

515

The familiar nervous prickling
        begins at the base of my skull,
                creeps upward. "Like what?"

                Mastiff Nurse: *Why, you worried
        about something in particular?*

                GBME: *You really need to learn
        when to keep your mouth shut.*

"Uh, no. Just curious is all."
        My face flushes embers.
                It must be cranberry red.

                Mastiff Nurse: *Are you currently
        taking any medications?*

                GBME: *A simple "no" will do.*

"Would you please shut up?"

                Mastiff Nurse: *Excuse me?*

                GBME: *I'll shut up if you will.*

Andre
If You Will

Only

pause, as you hurry
through your days,
take a minute to

look

at passersby, beyond
cursory skin-deep
analysis, all the way

into

their eyes, what beauty
you might find woven
from the life threads there.
If you will only look past

my

clumsy attempts at love,
sound the depths of
emotion in my

heart,

what haven you might
find in the soft surf
of my harbor.

Birthdays

Have never really felt like such a big
thing. Certain ones stand
out—my fifth, when my gramps took me

to Disneyland and Cinderella kissed
me. I thought she was
the most beautiful lady in the universe.

My eleventh, when we went to San Francisco
and watched a street dance
competition in Golden Gate Park. I'd been

practicing on the sly, but wasn't nearly as
good as I thought I was.
Seeing those b-boys do one-armed handstands

made me believe I could do one too. I tried,
landed on my head. Never
knew a tiny head wound could bleed so much.

My sixteenth, when I got my driver's license
and the Quattro on the same
day. Mom wanted my first car to be a safe one.

Today is my eighteenth birthday. Jenna
and I are celebrating
tonight. It's someone else's party we're going

to, but that's okay. I haven't seen her in over
a week, and I can't believe
how much I've missed her. Don't know if

absence actually makes the heart grow
fonder, but it definitely
makes it ache. Should love be painful?

I'm getting ready when someone knocks
on my bedroom door.
Mom. *May I come in?* Birthday present?

I'm shirtless, but she's seen me that way
a time or two.
"Of course." I step back and she brushes by.

Your father had to fly to Oakland. Your
grandmother has been ill.
She's out of danger for now, but they

are moving her into a nursing home.
I thought you might
try and get down to see her as soon as

school is out. Your grandfather would
like that too. He's asking
about you and your plans for next year.

Gramps, too? "Why didn't anyone tell
me that Grandma Grace
was sick? Is she going to be okay?"

When people get older, their bodies
deteriorate. You can
make the outside look better, but you

can't always control what's going on
inside. She has brain
cancer. Inoperable. But she's not in pain.

Guilt smacks me in the face. How long
since I've even called to
say hello? "How long does she have?"

A Few Months

That's it. The truth of death grabs me
by the shoulders. Shakes.
Mom comes over, puts her arms around

>   me. She hasn't held me like this since
>   I was little. *I'm sorry.*
>   *I know you were close. And I'm sorry I*
>
>   *had to give you the news on your birthday.*
>   *She would want you to*
>   *go to your party, though. For Grace, death*
>
>   *is a beginning. She's a woman of strong*
>   *faith. I wish I was. It*
>   *would make the day-to-day living easier.*

Easier? How much easier could it be
for her? What is she
afraid of? "Are you afraid of dying?"

>   Her arms fall away, as if they have been
>   around me too long.
>   She smiles. *Only when I think about it.*

She has always seemed ageless to me,
like time has no way
of touching her. I understand now that

> no one is immune to time's embrace. One
> day I will lose her. She
> goes to the door, hesitates. *Happy birthday.*

> *Before he left, your father made a deposit*
> *into your savings account.*
> *Use some of it for a mad splurge, okay?*

"Okay." One day I will lose them both.
"Hey, Mom? I love you."
I think I need to tell her that more often.

> *I love you, too, Andre. Very much. Now,*
> *go have fun. Just be*
> *smart about it. I want you to make nineteen.*

The Party

Is up Jumbo Grade. The pavement ends
at the first cattle guard,
and the Quattro bumps along the packed

dirt. *Why are you driving so slow?*
complains Jenna.
This is a four-wheel drive, isn't it?

"It's all-wheel drive, but that doesn't
mean it was built for
off-roading. I don't want to tear it up."

*You should get a Hummer. That would
be fun.* As usual, she has
already been drinking. Tequila, tonight.

"Where do you come up with all your
alcohol? You can't
just keep taking it from your parents."

She laughs. *No, I only take a few sips
from theirs. Patrick
is a tightwad. He'd definitely miss it.*

It's not that hard to get guys to buy
it for me, though.
I wait outside a grocery store and ask.

"Oh." I can picture the scene clearly.
"And what do you offer
them in return for helping you out?"

Nothing! Hey, are you jealous? I might
flirt, but I wouldn't
follow through. Once they hand it over,

I say thanks. That's it. What do you
think I am, anyway?
She unscrews the Cuervo, takes a long

pull off the bottle, and I'm tempted to tell
her too much. "How much do
you drink every day?" I want her to say it's

not every day. She doesn't. *I don't know.*
Enough to relax me, help
me sleep. Don't worry. It's under control.

Obviously

It's under control enough that she has
finished a pint before
we even get to the party. By the time

we spot the bonfire, up on a little mesa,
she is starting to slur.
There it is. Hey. D'you think it's sh-safe

having a fire up here? Well, she's clear
enough to think about
that, she's probably not too drunk. Yet.

"Considering this place was under
snow not long ago,
I think we'll be fine. I'll turn around

and park downhill just in case, though."
Some twenty cars are
already lined up along the escape route.

I park below them, so it's a long uphill
walk to join the people
gathered around the fire. Most have plastic

cups in their hands, filled with Budweiser
from the keg someone
supplied. Heavy smoke, not campfire-scented,

hangs in the air. I haven't smelled weed since
we moved here. Plenty
of it in Oakland, though I never indulged.

                    Jenna, big surprise, goes straight for
                              the group passing
                    the blunt. *Hey, Bobby. Hey, Aubree.*

               She sucks in a lungful of green-smelling
                         weed. Tries not to cough
                    as she says, *Did you hear about Sean?*

          *His lawyer says they have enough evidence
                    for a trial.* She offers me
               the J. I decline, and she passes it on to

          the Bobby person. *Yeah, I know. He thought
                         Coach was gonna
          kick him off the team, but they're letting him*

*stay, at least until he gets convicted, if he
does. You don't think
Cara will actually testify against him?*

I have no idea what they're talking about,
and I'm starting to feel
like scenery. "Going for beer. Want one?"

Jenna rolls her eyes, meaning, "Duh."
I start through the sage
toward the keg. As I go, I hear Bobby

say, *So that's the dancer? What do
you see in him?
Aren't all guy dancers, like, gay?*

Everyone laughs, and I'm glad I'm
gone, though I might
like to be a mosquito on Bobby's arm.

A big mosquito, proboscis jammed
deeply into an artery.
Except, wait. That sounds vaguely gay.

Suddenly It Occurs To Me

That not only has Jenna talked about
me, she considers me
a dancer. Have I been labeled? Branded?

I fill two cups, return to the group, hand
Jenna her beer.
Don't think she needs it. Between the dope

and the tequila, she is weaving. I put
an arm around her
shoulders to steady her. "You okay?"

She nods, but doesn't look so hot. I pull
her closer, put my mouth
against her ear. "We can leave if you want."

> Bobby shoots me with a jealous glare.
> *So . . . dancer. Thanks*
> *for loaning me your girl the other night.*

"The other night? Wha . . ." Before he can
clarify, Jenna jerks forward
and in one gigantic heave, up comes dinner.

Cara
One Gigantic Heave

Of planet, one massive
yank of gravity, one
magmatic tidal wave.

The ground
shakes.

A silent passing,
moon bold in rotation,
a shadowy eclipse.

The sun
disappears.

Kiss meets kiss, a mist
of eloquence, a gathering
of storm clouds.

The rain
begins to fall.

A lift of hips, upwelling
in the belly. A torrent
in the V of opened thighs.

The earth
moves.

Other People

Have always seen me as strong.
That was a lie. A charade. A disguise
I wore to keep me safe in public.
The truth is, I've always been afraid

of letting anyone get too close. I
built a wall around me, a barricade
to hide behind those few times
someone wanted entry to my heart.

Love, I thought, was the biggest
fraud of all. Sleight of hand,
designed to hold you, cage you,
when flight suited you well.

But my wings are unfolding, and
I'm learning to fly beyond the barrier
of fear. There is freedom in love.
But not if you have to hide it.

Not Much Chance

Of that anymore. I even had to
come out to my parents. Because
of the mess with Sean, there wasn't
much else I could do. Not if I wanted

him stopped. Dani and I talked it
over, and I saw that she was right
when she told me the best way
to fight all the ugly gossip was to

admit it happened. And that took
the power away from Sean. Once
I accepted that, I knew the only
way to keep him out of my life

forever was to file a police report.
To manage that, I had to involve my
mom and dad. It took more than
one try to break down and do it.

First I had to find a time when
they were home, together, and in
relatively passive moods. Then
I had to tether doubt and fear.

The Day The Stars Aligned

I found them in Dad's study, writing
a letter. Together. Totally weird.
Dad looked nervous. Mom, focused.
"May I come in? What are you doing?"

> *We're composing a letter to Conner,*
> said Dad. *He's supposed to head out*
> *on a wilderness challenge. Personally,*
> *I doubt it will do much good, but*
>
> *the letter is for when he has almost*
> *made it through. Incentive to conquer*
> *the mountain, so to speak. Now,*
> *what can your mother and I do for you?*

I almost lost my nerve. Conquering
my own mountain was looking less
and less likely. But if I would have
blown that chance, I might never have

even tried to get a handle on my life, so
I reached way down deep into my small
stash of courage and said, "This is
important, and I can't keep it to myself

anymore." Mom didn't even glance
up from the letter. I plunged ahead
anyway. "I've struggled for years
to come clean about this, first to

myself, and now, to you. Mother,
could you please look at me?" Had
she *ever* really looked at me? Dad
at least pretended like he cared.

Mom finally drew her eyes up level
with mine. "I know this is not on your
Top Ten Qualities In A Daughter list.
But I am a lesbian." It didn't sink in for

a good long time, and when it did, it
only sank so far. *Are you saying you're
attracted to women?* asked Mom.
I wouldn't worry too much. Lots of

*adolescents experiment with same-
sex play. That doesn't make you
homosexual. But please don't let it
get in the way of a normal relationship.*

It Was The "Normal"

That got to me. "For your information,
Mother, I am way above 'normal,'
which means average. And this
is not experimentation. This is love.

I've fought the 'who' of me for years.
I wanted you to know the truth, but
if you're not mature enough to handle
it, I don't care. This is who I am—

Straight-A, top of my class, Stanford-
bound *lesbian*. There's something else
I really need to tell you, but if you can't
handle this yet, I'll wait to bring it up."

> Mom just sat there staring with
> blue diamond eyes. It was Dad
> who said, *Of course we want to*
> *know what you need to tell us.*

The part about Sean and the pictures
wasn't quite as hard to admit. Guess
the worst part was over by then.
"Dani said I should press charges. . . ."

Mom's eyes grew steadily more
severe. *I think it best to let it drop.*
If this becomes public knowledge,
the media will smear it all over

the headlines. Our reputation will
be ruined. Bad enough we had to
deal with all the flak about Conner.
She straightened her blouse, as if it

had been wrinkled by the very idea
of her children disgracing *her* name.
The resistance only made my resolution
stronger. "Very sorry to shame you,

Mother. But he's stalking me, and
it has to stop. To tell you the truth,
I'm afraid of him. I don't know
what else to do but file a report."

Dad stepped in. *If the boy is stalking*
you, of course you must go to
the authorities. These things can end
badly. I have a friend on the force. . . .

He Made A Call

His friend agreed my decision was
the right one. It was the first time
in a long time that I can remember
one of my parents supporting me.

Mom went back to composing her
letter without another word. Later,
she and Dad had a knock-down,
drag-out argument. About Conner.

About me. About cops on the doorstep
and Mom's reputation and if safety was
an even trade-off for what the neighbors
might think. About sexual orientation.

What it means to me. Whether I am.
How I could know. Who the hell is this
Dani? What my coming out will mean
to them. To coworkers. The bridge club.

When things quieted, Mom took two
Valium and went to bed, while Dad hit
the scotch and watched TV. And
because that letter was stuck in my head,

I sneaked into Dad's study and found
it, finished, on his desk. What struck
me first was Mom's perfect cursive
and how she cut right to the chase:

Conner: Hope all is going
well for you, and that your
time in the outback has kept
you fit. You must excel at your

football tryouts. They expect
you to fail. I'm sure, however,
you'll prove them very wrong.
One small detail, which I'll mention

here: You have some makeup work
to do to keep you on track
for your graduation. If you
pursue it diligently this summer,

you won't have to play catch-up
in the fall. By the way, your father
and I have sent applications
to all the colleges on our list.

All you have to do is maintain
your GPA and, of course, score
well on your entrance exams.
Not really much more to say

except to let you know Cara
has already been accepted
at Stanford. You can do as well.
After all, you're her twin. Mom.

No Pressure There, Mom

None at all. Why can't she just be
glad he survived and let him live
the rest of his life on his own terms?
Can't she see how much he wants

her approval? That 4.0 GPA never
did come easily to Conner. Sports,
yes. Schoolwork, no. But God
forbid he excel at one and not

the other. Mom still expects him to
start college on time and keep scoring
touchdowns, too? Perfection carries
a steep price tag, at least it has for

Conner. I hope he finds his way
out sooner rather than later. I'm
thrilled I've found mine, even if it has
its own consequences to worry about.

I'm struggling to take ownership
of this new person I call me. But
every day brings me closer. And
I'm glad I got to know her at all.

Who Knows Who I'd Be

If I hadn't met Dani. Probably
still a Conner clone—striving too
hard to please someone who can't
be satisfied. I'm blown away by

how fate intervened when it did.
Makes me wonder what else I have
to look forward to, once I'm out
from under my parents' control.

> My cell buzzes. Incoming text from
> *Private Number*. Who could that be?
> Little teeth of suspicion gnaw at
> my stomach. He wouldn't dare.

> It's not from him. At least, I don't
> think so. *PLEASE STOP MESSING UP*
> *SEAN'S LIFE. GRADUATION IS ONLY*
> *A MONTH AWAY. THEN HE'S ALL SET*

> *FOR STANFORD. DROP CHARGES AND*
> *HE WON'T BOTHER YOU ANYMORE.*
> Whoever it was wrote the one
> word I didn't want to see: Stanford.

Kendra
I Didn't Want To See

The truth of things. That you
never embraced me the same
way that I embraced

                        you.

That when we lay laced
together, satin yarn and leather
cord, it was you who untied
the knots. That when you

                        told

bedtime stories of love
come unraveled, you were
always warning

                        me

of impending unraveling.
That the promises you wove
into the fabric of us
were nothing more than

                        lies.

Are All Relationships

Destined to unravel? I hear stories about
          people who have been married for fifty or sixty

years. But I've never met any. And if they
          do exist, what are they made of? The cliché

answer is friendship. If that's accurate,
          Mom and Patrick just might last a while.

But Dad and Shiloh will come unwoven
          eventually. Jenna and Andre already have.

That makes me a little sad, although if
          I am honest, I have to admit I was a lot jealous.

Not because of his car or his house or
          his money, but because he really loved her.

               He called me the day after they broke up.
          I don't know how much influence

               you have on your sister, but she needs help.
          She drinks every day. Not just a little.

She doesn't think she has a problem, but
she does. And she won't listen to me.

He said that isn't why he had to stop
seeing her. And I believe that. You can't

stay with someone you love when they
don't care enough about you. Jenna doesn't

care much about anything. Not even
herself. And I really don't get that. On

the surface, she is pure confidence.
What is she hiding? What is she trying to

prove? What is she trying to forget?
How can I ask her any of those questions?

She'd probably ask me the same
questions. And I don't have any answers.

The Only Person

Who has asked them is Shiloh. Like she
        has any right to. Like she really gives a damn.

Today we are shopping for bridesmaid
        dresses. Jenna is supposed to be here too.

                Guess something better came up. *It's okay,*
        says Shiloh. *We can choose the dress,*

                then find one in the right size for Jenna.
        I was thinking burgundy. What do think?

I shrug. "Kind of dark for afternoon,
        especially in June. What about teal?"

Nothing like flipping her entire color
        scheme. But hey, she asked my opinion.

                Hmm. Not big on teal. But you're right
        about burgundy being dark. Maybe . . .

                black? She laughs. *Just kidding. Unless*
        you think it would work. Let's look around.

The first one that we both agree on
        is a strapless sheath in a floral design.

"*Très* tropical," I say. "Not even close
        to burgundy, though." I pull a size two.

Shiloh raises an eyebrow, but keeps
        her opinion to herself. Until I come out

                of the dressing room. *Come over here*
        to the mirror. Tell me what you see.

"Uh . . . the dress is a little big
        in the bust, but the ruche helps that,

and length is good. . . ." It falls just
        above my knee, with a slit up the back.

                She puts one hand on each of my
        shoulders. *Tell me about the girl*

                inside the dress. What does she look
        like? How do you think I see her?

Ambushed

And just when I thought it was going
        so well. "Don't tell me. She's too thin.

You might even call her 'emaciated.'
        Obviously, she has an eating disorder.

Auschwitz survivors look better
        than her. What's wrong with her? Right?"

        Shiloh rubs my shoulders, and that feels
good. She drops her voice very low. *Not*

        exactly. I see a girl who wants to present
someone special to the world. Someone

        beautiful. The pinnacle of beauty. But
she has lost her hold on reality. Real

        beauty isn't thin. It isn't size two, unless
you happen to be four foot ten. What

        the world sees when they look at you
is someone who believes self-worth

is all about how she looks, and that
very often means what she's missing

is love. Not someone else's love. But
love and respect for herself. Why

don't you love yourself, Kendra? You
should. You are perfect, just as you are.

"Shut up! What are you, a psychologist?
I don't need *you* to analyze me! Anyway,

you aren't exactly all innocent and
everything. THIS IS YOUR FAULT."

Which isn't totally true, but it does
shut her up for a minute or two. Her head

tilts sideways as if she can't comprehend
English. *I'm sorry. What do you mean?*

"I mean you took Dad away from Jenna
and me. Have a thing for married men?"

Her Hands Fall Away

From my shoulders. How can I want
      those hands back? The girl in the mirror

looks drawn. Gaunt. Outside and in.
      Shiloh's right about what the world must see

            when it looks at me. *Oh, Kendra. I didn't*
take him away. Please, understand

            that. I didn't even know he was married
until after your mom walked out, and

            she had every right to. By then, I was in
love with him. Believed I could save him.

            I still believe that. But salvation will come
easier if you and Jenna can find the strength

            to forgive him. He never meant to hurt you.
You girls mean everything to him.

"He never . . . ? Oh yeah, he meant to hurt
      me. In fact, he used to fucking wail on me."

Ha! Said It

And it had the exact effect I wanted.
        Disbelief. Shock. Dawning realization

that the guy she fell in love with—
        my father—is so not the man she thinks

he is. "Oh yeah. He'd come home
        drunk. Angry. Didn't matter at what.

Mom was good at disappearing.
        Not me. Jenna was too little. Too cute.

Too much the daughter he really
        wanted. I was chubby. More butt to belt

without doing real damage. *That's*
        who you fell in love with. That's what

the world would have seen had
        it ever actually bothered to look."

For once, the mirror tells me that
        the girl looking back at me is skinny.

The Skinny Girl Crumbles

Tries to fall, but the woman behind
      her—only a moment ago her rival—

             gathers up the pieces of her, attempts to
      squash them back together. *Oh, honey.*

             I'm so sorry. Please try to believe
      your father is not that man anymore.

             I can't tell you that he's sober. He's
      trying, but he backslides. Alcohol can

             be a monster. It's an addiction, but it
      starts as learned behavior. He learned

             it as a boy, from the man who beat him.
      Abuse is a learned behavior too.

"Sounds like an excuse to me." On the far
      side of the mirror glass, the skinny girl

stares back at me. And, safe in the refuge
      of a stranger's arms, she disintegrates.

People Are Starting To Gawk

Not in a good way. I pull myself together.
           "I'm okay." Not. My makeup is smeared

and my hair's a mess. "I like the dress."
           Much cooler than I feel. "Not sure how

it would look on Jenna." They do have it
           in a ten, though. And where is she, anyway?

I go back to change, and am still only half-
           way into my jeans when Shiloh knocks.

           Urgently. *Hurry, honey, okay? We have
to go. Right now. Leave the dress.*

The tone of her voice hustles me into
           my shoes. "What is it?" As soon as I unlatch

           the door, she takes my arm, rushes me
toward the exit. *Your mom tried to get*

           *hold of you, but couldn't. Your cell
must be dead. It's Jenna. . . .*

The Hospital Is Five Minutes Away

Mom and Patrick meet us there. Mom
is freaking out. *I don't understand.*

How could this happen? Oh, Patrick. She
reminds me of the skinny girl falling

to pieces. "What happened?" Neither
of them will look at me. "Please. Tell me."

Patrick draws me to one side of the waiting
room. *We don't have all the details yet.*

He sucks in a big breath of antiseptic air.
Your sister was raped. And . . . hurt.

We sit in a stiff row, waiting for details.
Finally a doctor comes to give them. Raped.

Beaten. Cut. Left to bleed out. Some
good Samaritan jogging by saved her life.

Broken bones. Stitches. And all because
she asked the wrong guy to buy her booze.

Sean
Broken Bones

Are preferable to broken
dreams. A broken heart.
A solid future smashed
like porcelain into

dust.

How do you reconcile
love that won't let go
with the overpowering
resentment of being cast

off,

leftovers for scavengers?
How do you scab over
wounds that deep?
Some believe faith can

move

a mountain. I say that's
not possible if it
isn't strong enough
to build tomorrow

on.

You Could Power The World

On anger. All you'd have to do
        is tap into a deep well of it,
                extract it, fill up your tanks.
        It's clean burning, too. All
except for a thin exhaust.

Anger is fueling my days. It gets
        me up. Out the door to school.
                Reminds me that I need to pass
        my approaching finals. Have
to maintain that GPA to stay

on track for my scholarship, and
        I will *not* give that up, Cara or
                no Cara. Restraining order or
        no restraining order. Stanford
is a very big campus. *She* can

figure out how to stay away
        from *me.* She's done a pretty
                good job of it here at Galena.
        I've barely seen her at all
since she got me locked up.

Okay, other than the initial
            arrest and holding cell time,
                        I didn't go to jail. Uncle Jeff's
            lawyer got me out on my own
recognizance. And when I went

to court, the judge gave me
            community service and
                        warned me any behavior
            even vaguely resembling
stalking would immediately

land me in an actual jail cell.
            Some people might say I
                        got lucky, drew the right
            judge. I say Cara deserves
a little comeuppance for

causing me sleepless nights
            and five days picking up
                        trash along the Truckee River.
            But, as they say, revenge
is a dish best tasted cold.

Especially If I Want

To keep playing baseball.
The thing is, anger has also
powered my bat. It's all in
the focus. Uncle Jeff showed
me that. *It's okay to be mad,*

he told me. What you have
to do is gather up all that
anger, hold it right between
your eyes, and when the ball
releases, laser it. Your arms

will follow. It took a time or
two to get what he meant,
but once it clicked, *bam*. I've
put them over the fence
pretty much every game.

The very best part of that is
it keeps Guy Behind My Eyes
mostly quiet. Lately, he only
talks to me when I'm alone,
something I try hard not to be.

The Main Thing

He keeps telling me is that
       I need to lay off the 'roids.

           I'll stop talking if you do.
           You might shut me up forever.

Chad agrees. He says I'm
       borderline schizo and that
           he won't supply me anymore.
       At least, not for a while. Not
until the current cycle is well

               out of my system. *You're lucky*
           you didn't get busted when
       they did all that blood work,
           he said. *You get busted, I get*
               busted. You've got a big mouth.

I figure I'll finish up what I've
       got left and dry out for a while.
           See if lifting alone will keep
       the ol' bat hot. And hopefully
leave GBME kicking in my dust.

As For The Big Mouth

I struggle with that. Right now,
          seeing Cara down the hall at
                    her locker, it's all I can do not
          to shout something obscene.
Don't want to risk a cell,

though. And now I've got
          Aubree to keep me in line.
                    She's a little like taffy—
          all pliable and chewy and
sticky sweet. Except she's

really not sweet at all. She can
          be one shit-talking, backstabbing
                    girl. And in fact, it was she who
          spread those pics of Cara across
the ether. When I asked her why

                        she wanted to ruin a supposed
                  friend's reputation, she told me,
          Cara only acts like she's your
                  friend. She'd never have your back
                      if it meant offering up her own.

I don't know if that's exactly
                accurate, but now that I
                        think about it, Cara doesn't
                really have friends. Lots of
people hang around her, but

I'm not sure how many of them
                liked her, even before they
                        knew she was a dyke. Too bad,
                so sad. I'm not sure how
many people really like Aubree,

either. She's kind of stuck-up.
                But she's a fine little piece
                        of distraction right now.
                And with her being the one
to keep the pressure on Cara,

I don't have to. She texts her
                sometimes, using stolen cell
                        phones, so the messages
                can't be traced back to her.
Or me. Hey, I don't ask her to.

Cara Knows

Aubree and I are kind of a thing.
            Not like we try to hide it. Aubree
                        flaunts it, especially when Cara
            is in clear sight. Like now. We
have to walk right by her to get

to class. I cinch my arm around
            Aubree's waist, and she tucks
                        her head against my shoulder.
            "You're coming to the game
today, right?" I kiss her forehead.

                        You know I wouldn't miss
                  it. I love watching you play.
            Hit a home run, I'll give you a
                        special reward. She runs her
                              hand down over my crotch,

leaving no room for speculation
            about what kind of reward
                        she has in mind. I glance
            at Cara, who quickly turns
her face away. But she saw.

That gives me some strange
                satisfaction. All things
                        considered, Cara shouldn't
                give a damn. So what compels
me to say, loudly enough so

that she (and everyone else
                nearby) can hear, "Blow
                        job for one homer. All
                the way in for two. Deal?"
People are waiting for her

                                answer. And when it comes,
                it's all Aubree. *Deal. As long*
        as it doesn't turn me into
                a Les. Bi. An. Totally directed
                                at Cara, who shoves her face

into her locker. "No worries.
                I happen to know gay. You're
                        not." Laughter echoes down
                the corridor, and I almost feel
sorry for Cara. But not quite.

The Rumor Hits Full Force

By lunchtime. It's passed on
to me by (who else?) Aubree.
Did you hear what happened
to Jenna Mathieson? Some guy
raped her. Cut her up, too.

"Kendra's sister?" Pretty little
thing, all flesh and curves, usually
sneaking out of her clothes.
Can't say it's a total surprise.
"What happened? Is she okay?"

I heard she was hanging outside
of Safeway, bumming beer, and
he forced her into his car.
Guess it was pretty ugly. A jogger
heard her screaming and banged

on the window, or she might be
dead now. God, do you know
what he did? She goes on to
give me a hideous description
of all the ways rape can be done.

See what you missed, whispers
GBME. *You could have tried . . .*

I force myself not to engage
him. Last thing I need is Aubree
thinking I'm a whack job too.

*She won't be back at school
this year,* Aubree finishes.
*Someone said it took over
five hundred stitches to close up
all the wounds. God. The scars!*

That's what rape is. Not what
happened with Cara. She wanted . . .

You mean she asked for it, says
GBME. *But you think Jenna asked
for it too. Just in a different way.*

"Shut the fuck up!" I yell.

What? demands Aubree.

"No. Not you. I'm not talking
            to you. I'm talking to . . . never
                        mind." What have I done now?

            GBME: *You really need to stop
yelling at yourself. People think . . .*

                                    It's obvious what Aubree thinks.
                        Are you nuts or what? But then
            she smiles. *I kind of like crazy
                        guys. They're hot. Come here.*
                        She kisses me, and it's totally

hot, and if that makes her crazy,
            I kind of like it too. I am so
                        hitting a couple of home runs.
            I just hope I can claim my reward
without GBME giving commentary.

Andre
Crazy

To dream of her still.
To wake, shivering desire,
and wonder if she is dreaming
of you, despite all

odds.

Crazy, waiting for her return,
when you were the one who
walked away. Pushed through
the pain. Spring days

are

growing longer, reaching
for summer. What plans
you made for elastic afternoons,
stretched long to lean

against

moon-shadowed evenings.
Crazy, remembering how
her smile thawed your
winter heart, when what

you

must do to salvage
your sanity is forget her.

What Have You Done?

Tempted fate once too often. Tempted
the wrong man. Dangled
your bait in the wrong place, and the wrong

fish took it right off the hook. Oh, Jenna!
Why couldn't I save you?
Why couldn't I make you love me enough?

You lie here, sleeping. The bandages can't
hope to hide all the damage
to your face. But it will heal eventually.

I wish I could be that optimistic about your
heart. I want to touch you,
but I'm afraid even the slightest caress

will cause you pain. I close my eyes, lay
my head on the bed next
to you. The sheets smell of bleach. But lingering

beneath the Clorox is a faint scent of rot.
Is it from your bloated
wounds? Or is it decomposing dreams?

As If Hearing My Thoughts

She stirs. Her fingers test my hair,
recognize it. *Hey.* Her
voice is raspy. *Thanks for coming.*

I lift my head, look into the slits where
her eyes must be. "Welcome.
Just so you know, you look like crap."

Better than how I feel, then. Guess
you know what
happen . . . the rest is swallowed by

a coughing fit. "Stop talking for once
in your life, would you?
Yes, I know what happened. I'm sorry."

I should h-have l-listened . . . and now
she's crying, at least
I'm pretty sure she is. It's hard to tell.

"Doesn't matter now. What's done is
done, as my grandma
Grace always used to say." The thought

of her, overseeing my childhood, sears
my heart almost as much
as seeing Jenna like this does. "Listen, now.

First things first. . . ." Another Grace-ism.
"You heal up. Once all
those stitches come out, my mom wants to

see you. She's a regular wizard, you know.
Making girls beautiful
is what she does best. You can skip the boob

job, though. Yours are perfect, as is." I stand.
"I should probably go now.
Let you rest. I'll come see you again soon."

> *W-wait. You never told me about your*
> *audition. Wha-what*
> *happened? Are you going to Vegas?*

I Sit Back Down

"Okay, I'll tell you the story, but only
if you're positive you
want to hear it, and only if it won't make

you too tired." She gestures for me to go
on. "The show isn't quite
the cattle call that some of them are.

They solicit auditions from some of the best
dance studios in the country.
Which means it's extremely competitive.

Liana choreographed an amazing routine
for Shantell and me.
We aren't going to Vegas—yet. But we have

been called back for a second audition.
Out of five thousand
dancers, we are in the top one hundred.

Our next audition is in Los Angeles in
three weeks. Liana thinks
both Shantell and I have a decent shot."

Jenna does her best to touch my hand. *I'm*
re-really happy for you.
Know what I think? That you're going to

Vegas. Kn-know wh-what else? I'm glad
you have the guts to go
for your dream. All the talking is tiring her.

"Tell you what. If I make the top ten, I'll
make sure you have tickets."
I whisper-kiss her forehead. "And don't worry.

Jazz isn't nearly as boring as ballet." Her
eyes close, and I think
she must be asleep again, so I start to leave.

Psst, she says, eyes still closed. *Know what's*
bad here? No alcohol.
But know what's good? Killer drugs.

What I Didn't Tell Her

Is that I still haven't decided whether
or not I'm going down
for that second audition. One of the judges,

this brilliant Broadway choreographer,
totally loved me, at least it
seemed that way. He gushed about technique,

and when he found out I've only been training
for a relatively short while,
called me one of the greatest natural talents

he's ever seen. Not sure if that was meant
for the camera or for real,
but I may have a very good chance of finishing

in the top twenty. Which means they'd want
me to do the TV show.
Just appearing on *Now This Is Dance* almost

guarantees work, and I'm just not sure that
dance can take me where
I want to go. Liana says don't even worry

about all that yet. *You're awfully full of*
yourself, aren't you?
was actually what she said. *You haven't*

even made it past the second audition,
and you're already
worrying about how to spend your prize

money and organize your tour schedule?
One step at a time,
Andre. Now, let's work on that solo.

Prize money wasn't even on my radar.
Maybe because I never
expected to get this close. Shantell, however,

was not surprised. *God, Andre. What did*
I tell you? When some
snooty choreographer says you've got an

incredible natural talent, you get all excited,
but when I told you the same
thing, you thought I was blowing smoke?

You have to do this. It's a once-in-a
lifetime opportunity,
and if you don't, I swear you will be

sorry. You can always go to college,
but if you decide to
leave dance behind in favor of school,

you may never come back to it. You'll
end up in some dull
career, with a bucket full of regrets.

Shantell wouldn't dream of *not* going
for it, whatever
the outcome on the far end. Maybe that's

what I'm *really* worried about. *Not* winning.
Not succeeding. I've
never failed at anything. Except Jenna.

She's Sleeping Now

Off someplace too deep to dream in, thanks
to the morphine drip
fed into one of her veins. Good drugs, indeed.

I wonder if this girl can be saved, and why
she won't save herself.
"I love you, Jenna." I know she can't hear

me, and maybe that's for the best. "Bye, baby."
One thing I do know
is that I can't watch her self-destruct anymore.

I glance at the big clock on the wall. Almost
two. I've got a lesson
at three. With Shantell, who will be after

me to make a decision. God, hospitals stink.
All the cleaning they do
can't erase the dirt of sickness and death.

I don't look into open doors as I head for
the elevator. Don't want
to consider what's on the other side. Instead

I look down, counting tiles until I reach
the bank of elevators.
Just as I get there, a set of doors opens,

and who walks out of them but Kendra.
And her father. Oh shit.
"Hello, sir," I say, hoping for civility.

His face goes all red, and hatred feeds
his ugly glare. *You.*
This is because of you, you goddamn—

No! Kendra stops him cold. *This is* not
because of him, Dad.
It's because of you! It's your *attention*

she wanted, just like when she was little.
You left her, Dad. Me
too. Left us for . . . She shatters. Sobs.

Her knees buckle, and I move forward
as she starts to fall.
But it is her father who catches her.

His eyes, wild just a few seconds ago,
soften. *I'm sorry.*
Then, to me, *Go get someone. Please.*

I turn toward the nurse's station, but
someone is already coming.
Can't make a scene like this without

being noticed. By the time the nurse
gets to us, though,
Kendra has reached into some reservoir

of inner strength. She is on her feet,
pushing her father
off. *I'm okay. Let go. Sorry, Andre.*

"It's all ri—," I start to say, but she is
already on her way
to Jenna's room. Mr. Mathieson follows

without a good-bye. The pretty nurse
looks at me and
I shrug. "Just another day in paradise."

Cara

Paradise

A concept embraced by almost
every culture. A land of peace
and harmony. Some say it

doesn't

belong to the earth, that there
is no Shangri-la, no utopian
wilderness for the living.

Only

heaven. Elysian fields. A House
of Song. Afterworlds where
the righteous dead

exist

forever in a state of pure
bliss. But I wonder if there
isn't some blessed place

for

souls in search of the sacred
path. Hungry souls, and lost.
The souls of those who aren't

believers

yet reach for redemption,
in ways small and large.
Those who love and ask for love.

Love Is Chocolate

The unprocessed kind. Dark. Bitter.
But always with the promise of sweet
perfection. All it takes is sugar—
that certain someone's kiss, flavored

with possibility. If Dani has taught
me anything, it's that life is brimming
with possibilities. Every single day
brings choices. Make a bad one,

you deal with the consequences.
Make a good one, you get a reward
of one kind or another. Bad choices
or good, if you never take chances,

someone else will build your life
for you. What if you decide you don't
like their vision? What if they put you
up on a pedestal and you hate the view?

I've never been much of a thrill seeker,
mostly because I'm afraid of falling.
I'm eyeing the mountain. But I'll never
climb it with my parents calling the shots.

Possibilities. Choices. Decisions.
Influencing my own fate scares me.
But it's better than the alternative.
I think. Right now, the future stares

back at me, posturing. Challenging.
Graduation is two weeks away. June
was supposed to be my escape, but I
wish I could hold on to May just a little

longer. Can't say that I want to hang
on to my childhood, because I can't
remember having one, at least not
the kind a kid should have. But am I

really ready to be out on my own?
Ready or not, here I come, I guess.
Just not sure where I'm going.
Or if I'll ever want to come home.

The Phone Rings

And caller ID says it's Aspen Springs.
They don't call here often. Three rings,
no one else answers, so I do. "Hello?"
It's Dr. Starr, and she sounds shaky

when she asks to talk to one of my
parents. What's Conner done now?
"Mom? Dad? Pick up the phone."
Dad's just coming in from a run.

> He goes into the kitchen, and I'm
> about to hang up when I hear Dr.
> Starr through the receiver. *I . . . uh . . .*
> *I don't know how to tell you this*

> *but . . . uh . . . there was an accident.*
> *Uh . . . it's Conner. I'm afraid . . . he . . .*
> *didn't make it.* Didn't make what?
> What is she saying? Dad asks the same

> question, and she answers bluntly,
> *He's dead.* Dead. Dead? He can't be
> dead. My stomach swells with bile.
> Dread. No. Not Conner. Not my brother!

I drop the phone. Don't want to
listen to the details. I run downstairs,
find Dad collapsed on the cool
kitchen tile. One of the chairs is

overturned, like he missed it. "Dad!"
Daddy?" Tears streak his face,
and his hands shake so hard he can
barely hold the phone, let alone speak

> into it. But he won't let me take
> it from him. *No,* he says. *Go find*
> *your mother.* I turn around, run
> blindly into the living room. Not

here. Upstairs, to her bedroom,
don't bother to knock. She's asleep,
and I don't want to wake her. "Mo . . ."
Now it's me that can't talk. "Mom!"

She comes up out of her dreams,
and it's all I can do to say, "Dad
needs you. Now," before I crack
into a million pieces. Not Conner.

But Conner Is Dead

It wasn't an accident. He stepped
over the edge of a very tall cliff.
Brought our world crashing down.
Smashing us into the rocks, right

along with him. We are zombies.
The living remains of the dead.
They flew him out of the wilderness.
Already cold. Almost as cold as Mom.

She is frozen. All emotion ice dammed
inside. She never even cried. *Someone
has to stay calm,* she said. *Someone has
to handle the details.* Will she ever cry?

Kendra

The Details

Of death are the fabric
nightmares are sewn from.

They weave

daylight grieving with
deep-of-night memory.

They chase

hope into the shadows,
leave it trembling there.

They menace

summer's green dawning
with winter's gray shroud.

They strike

like lightning. Electric,
unstoppable.

They stab

like wooden spears, drive
splinters into the heart.

Irredeemable

That's what Mom called Conner when
       I told her the news. No way to save him.

I don't believe that. Everyone can be
       saved, if they just have the right person

trying to save them. Right? How could
       he want to die so badly? He looked okay

when I saw him that day at the movies.
       Almost like his regular self. I didn't see death

in his eyes. Didn't see the desire
       to leave this world behind. Leave us behind.

Goddamn you, Conner. You always
       were a selfish prick. You got us this time.

Nailed us right to the wall. And
       some of us will never heal completely.

I Got The News

From Cara, the day after they brought
    Conner's body back. Laid him on a chilled

slab to poke and prod and probably
    dig around in his brain for some tumor

or other abnormality that might make
    a perfect kid like Conner choose to die.

I was sitting by Jenna's bedside,
    watching her pick at her hospital food,

        when Cara's call came. *Um, Kendra?*
    I knew something was wrong from

        the way her voice quivered. *I wanted you*
    to hear this from me. She drew two

        long raspy breaths. *Conner died*
    yesterday. He, um . . . committed.

My first thought was bullshit. Why
    would you make up something like this?

Then I realized immediately that no
        way would she. "Oh my God. Are you . . ."

I almost said "sure," but of course
        she was, so I finished it with, "all right?"

                        Not really. I have to go. The wake
                is Saturday. Will you let people know?

"Definitely. Cara, if I can do anything . . .
        help . . . anything . . . please call me, okay?"

I felt like someone had just smashed
        into me with a semi truck. And I must

                        have looked like it too. *What?* asked
                Jenna, eyes wide. *What's wrong?*

I couldn't tell her. Repeating it would
        make it real. The dam failed, and I cried.

The Wake Is This Evening

Mom's taking me because I don't
        want to go by myself. We drive into

Reno, on the same highway as always,
        passing the same trees. Same billboards.

Same buildings. But nothing
        will ever be exactly the same again.

"Did you ever lose someone you loved?
        I mean, did someone you loved ever die?"

                Mom is quiet, remembering. *My first*
        boyfriend died in a car accident.

                A drunk driver ran a red light, hit
        him going sixty. It was horrible.

"Does it still hurt, thinking about
        him? Does the pain ever go away?"

                The pain diminishes over time.
        But it still hurts thinking about him.

The pain is sawing me in two.
I can barely breathe, and part of me

doesn't want to. "Did you ever want
to die enough to think about suicide?"

*I think everyone considers it at some
point. But I never would have done it.*

*Too many people rely on me. Too
many people love me, and I would*

*never want to make them feel the way
you're feeling right now. You know?*

*Life is precious, Kendra. Never throw
away a single second. And never*

*forget about the people who love you.
There is tremendous value in that.*

Sean
Never

Again. Never again.
Few things create never again
like death. Biting the big

one,

and not talking burgers.
Kicking the bucket.
Taking a one-way trip

to

who-knows-where.
Is there a heaven? Hell?
I mean, who can really

say

what happens after
the lights go out? Is there
a "hello" after the final

good-bye?

Word Travels Fast

Along the "someone died"
       grapevine. It might not
            always be accurate, so
       you have to do some
double checking to make

sure what you heard is
       something close to true.
            I heard about Conner
       from Duvall, not exactly
the most reliable source.

But this time, it seems, he
       was right. Conner fell off
            a cliff, somewhere out
       in the Black Rock Desert.
He was on a wilderness

challenge. Still not clear why.
       Not like Conner couldn't hack
            a challenge course. But why
       was he there? And did he fall
by accident? On purpose?

Hell, maybe someone pushed
        him over. Some pretty rough
                kids go on those challenges.
        Rougher than Conner, who was
a total prep, if a jock prep.

Was. Hard to use the past tense
        when talking about someone
                you know. Someone your age.
        Someone who could be you,
if things were a little different.

Aubree and I are going to
        the wake. I didn't want
                to. Not like Conner and
        I were tight or anything.
Plus, dead people give me

                the creeps. Too many bad
        memories. Ghosts, walking.
But Aubree says we have to.
        *It's expected. Everyone will be
                there. They'll talk if we aren't.*

Not Going To Argue

Dad would expect me to go.
        Conner and I were teammates,
                if not friends. The team will
        all be there, for sure. The least
you can do when a teammate

dies is go to his wake.
        They're having it at
                the biggest funeral home
        in Reno. Aubree was right.
Everyone is here, to judge

by the parking lot. "We have to
        park on the street and walk."
                It's a long few blocks, made
        easier by sneaking peeks
at Aubree's legs, mostly

exposed by the very short
        skirt of her black dress.
                Everyone is in black except
        me. I wore navy blue, just
to shake things up. Oops.

Okay. Cara is not in black.
　　　　She's in a dark red dress
　　　　　　　　that fits her like skin and
　　　　she is beautiful, even in
her obvious grief. Or maybe

　　　　　　　　　　　　because of it. She looks like
　　　　　　　　a child. Vulnerable. Easy
　　　　to hurt. Aubree notices who
　　　　　　　　I'm staring at. She elbows
　　　　　　　　　　　　me. *Kind of inappropriate.*

Maybe. But I still want to
　　　　go to her, hold her, despite
　　　　　　　　her girlfriend (hair no longer
　　　　blue) standing so close
there can be no doubt that

they are an item. I turn away,
　　　　take Aubree's hand, and we
　　　　　　　　go down a far aisle to find
　　　　two seats way in the back.
Who sits up front at a wake?

I Watch Who Goes Up Front

Conner's family. His father,
        who walks all bound up,
                like if he lets himself sway
        at all he might stumble and
fall. Conner's mother, who

looks straight ahead, no
        hint of expression on her
                beautiful, sculpted face.
        Cara, her own face a carbon
copy. Except hers is sorrow

streaked. Her girlfriend, who
        scaffolds Cara. Kendra and
                her mother. Shantell, with
        some guy I've never seen
before. And just in front of

them, a young couple. Maybe
        my age. Also strangers, but
                apparently not strangers to
        Conner. They hold tight to each
other, struggle not to fall apart.

Andre
Strangers

Death gives strangers
common ground
to walk on.
Encounter
obstacles on.

To fall

down and cry on until
it sponges their tears.
Muddied,
they struggle

to pick
themselves up,

clean off the dirt,
stitch their wounds,
and together fight,
no longer strangers,

to get on
with living.

I Never Knew

Conner Sykes or anyone in his family,
I'm only here because
Shantell didn't want to come alone.

She brought me up front, close to Cara,
who I did meet that one
time. She seems different. Older, touched

by death. Sitting next to her mother, I can
see what she will
look like one day, when she is older still.

It's an open casket. From here, the boy
inside appears to be
sleeping. Only his mostly colorless face

gives his lifelessness away. He is—was—
younger than I when
he left this earth. He will never marry.

Never have children. Never find his way
back from wherever
it was that he lost himself. He will never

live his dreams, whatever they were.
Did he have them? Lose
them? Can you lose sight of a dream

that you don't have time to discover?
I think of Grandma Grace,
who will leave this planet soon. Did

she have dreams she never realized?
I will ask her when I go
visit her. I don't want to see her sick,

but I have to tell her I love her. That
I will miss her. That she
helped make me what I am today.

A dancer. That's what I am. Only a few
people know it
at this moment. But that's going to change.

One of Those People

Is sitting next to me right now. A year
ago, I wouldn't have
given her a second glance. Wouldn't have

gotten to know her because she isn't a classic
beauty. Doesn't have curves
like Jenna. Isn't model thin like Kendra.

But she is pretty, and perfect in her own
way, because she knows
who she is and doesn't pretend to be

anyone else. Doesn't care who she pleases,
as long as she is good
with herself, and what else really matters?

Shantell has her eyes firmly on her dream.
Is reaching hard for it,
and encouraging me to reach for mine.

Tentatively, I slide my hand over hers.
The Vs between her fingers
notch into mine, and she squeezes.

The Service Starts

With recorded music. Pink singing "Amazing
Grace." Beautiful and kind
of weird at the same time. Like the singer.

Shantell glances at me, and we share
a smile. She must be
reading my mind. The priest gets up and

spends much too long talking about God's
plan and how to recognize
it in our own lives. And now the eulogies

begin. Conner's football coach outlines
his many and varied
records, then laments about talent

the world will never see. Kendra stands,
tries desperately
to put her love for Conner into words.

She only manages a couple before they are
swallowed by sobs.
More than a few people join her in tears.

A half-dozen schoolmates of Conner's
say how much they'll
miss him. Finally the priest calls a young

                        couple to the front. They go forward,
                                 hand in hand. *Hi,*
             says the auburn-haired girl. *I'm Vanessa.*

                 You don't know me, but I got to know
                           Conner in Aspen
               Springs. I think Tony and I knew him

               better than most of you. Conner was
                      good at hiding the
             scared little boy inside. . . . At that,

Kendra's crying becomes almost
hysterical. Her mom
does her best to console her as Vanessa

               continues, *Conner couldn't be what*
                     everyone else wanted
            him to be. So he chose the easy way out.

Cara

Death

Is

only

the

easy

way

out

if

you

are

the

one who dies.

At The Red-Haired Girl's Words

Dad gives a little gasp. Mom barely

flinches. Now the dark-haired boy says,

> *I'm Tony. And Conner was my friend.*
> *Maybe the only friend I ever had, except*
>
> *for one other person. Vanessa and I both*
> *loved Conner, and not because he scored*
>
> *touchdowns or got straight As. We loved*
> *who he was when he let his guard down.*
>
> *When he let us see who he wanted to be,*
> *free of expectations. The real Conner.*
>
> *We thought he was stronger than it turned*
> *out he was because he saved us both,*
>
> *more than once, and in different*
> *ways. I will never forget him.*
>
> *What I want to tell you is what*
> *I think he would tell you, if he could.*

Living means taking chances. Risks.
Playing safe all the time is being dead

inside, even if you happen to still be
breathing. People expected Conner

to play it safe all the time. And when
he did, he felt dead inside. I saw him

take risks, and then he was the most
alive person I've ever known. He would

ask you *to take chances. Sometimes*
that means getting hurt. Getting an F.

Losing a game. Losing someone you
love. But if you always play it safe,

you lose anyway. Tony turns, goes
over to the casket, bends and kisses

Conner. *Fuck you, dude. You should*
have hung around. Proved 'em wrong.

He Turns Back, Crying

Which is fine, because everyone here
is crying. Even Mom. She makes no
sound, but her eyes glisten, and I think
Tony has given her permission to break

all the way down later. He gestures to
Vanessa to come say good-bye. Protocol
might dictate Conner's family go forward
first. But I think Tony and Vanessa are

Conner's family. Probably better family
than the rest of us. Dani whispers, *Thanks
for taking a chance with me.* She kisses me,
in front of everybody. And I'm good with it.

Kendra
Chance

Brought us

together.

Tattered us

twisted us

wrenched us

wide apart.

But it wasn't

chance that

ended you

took you

away from

me forever.

People Move Forward

To say their good-byes. But I'm afraid.
> Afraid to see what's left of Conner.

Afraid I'll see too much. Too little.
> Afraid that what I see will convince me

it's not Conner at all. From here,
> the thing in the coffin looks like it's made

of wax. A fake Conner, meant to fool
> us into believing he's dead. Maybe he's not

dead at all. Maybe this is just some
> crazy scheme he came up with so he could

get away. From school. From football.
> From his family. From me. Maybe he's living

large with Emily Sanders somewhere.
> Oh my God. What's the matter with me?

Of course he's dead. Look at his parents.
> At Cara. At those two—Tony and Vanessa.

He has leveled them. Shredded them.
       I would say he got the final laugh, but

would he laugh, knowing what he's done
       to them? Knowing what he's done to me?

              Kendra, says Mom. *Don't you want*
       to say good-bye? She stands, takes

my hand, coaxes me to my feet. I let
       her lead me forward. My head is light.

I haven't eaten a bite since I got
       the news. Death as a weight-loss tool.

Wonder if I could market that.
       The thought makes me laugh. Mom

gives me a sideways glance. But all
       it takes to sober me completely is reaching

the casket. I've never seen Conner
       in a suit. That alone makes him look

a lot like a mannequin. A suit is so not
        Conner. I'd rather remember him naked.

Next to me. Under the trees. On a blanket
        of pine needles. The memory catches in

my throat. Did he ever think about
        that afternoon? Can he think about it now?

"Where are you, Conner?" I whisper.
        "Can you hear me? Can you remember,

wherever you are? Will you remember
        me, the way I will always remember you?"

            I don't want to say good-bye, but Mom puts
her arm around me. *He'll remember you.*

Sean

Good-bye

Watching
　　　　　good-byes.
　　　　　　　　　　Long ones.
Quick ones.
　　　　　Sad ones.
　　　　　　　　　　Angry ones.
People say
　　　　　good-bye in
　　　　　　　　　　many ways.
How will
　　　　　people say
　　　　　　　　　　good-bye to me?
How will
　　　　　people
　　　　　　　　　　remember me?

I Didn't Hang Out

With Conner. Didn't miss him
　　　　when he wasn't at school
　　　　　　　　after his so-called accident
　　　　with the gun. That must
have been on purpose too.

But I have to admit, seeing
　　　　him dead, no more chances,
　　　　　　　　no more choices, no more
　　　　ways to make things better,
is making me think. Rethink.

That Tony guy wasn't totally
　　　　right. I mean, yeah, he was
　　　　　　　　spot-on about other people's
　　　　expectations, and how trying
to live up to them can take

a guy out. But fact is, I
　　　　don't always play it safe.
　　　　　　　　I take calculated risks,
　　　　always with a focused goal
in sight. But sometimes

I feel dead inside anyway.
        Cara made me feel alive.
                Maybe that's why I can't
        let her go. I don't want
to feel dead anymore.

What I think is, I need to
        find a way to feel alive
                that doesn't require
        someone else to make
it happen. I mean, putting

a ball over the fence, and
        hearing people cheer for
                me, well, that's a solo
        effort, and a definite rush.
Dead people don't get rushes.

Getting into Stanford,
        mostly on my own
                willpower, that came
        close. It's the "mostly"
that bothers me. Am I really

good enough to play Cardinal
        ball? I think the time has
                come to find out. To dry
        out. They're going to pee
test us first thing anyway.

                        Up in front, Cara's girlfriend
                kisses her. Jealousy pierces
        me, but when Aubree comments,
                Oh my God. Isn't that, like,
                        disgusting? Especially here.

I say, "Yeah, gross," but on
        some level, I think it's not
                so bad, really. And maybe
        the way it was always
supposed to be. Cara was

never meant for me. Pretty
        sure Aubree isn't either.
                But I'm swearing off girls.
        For a while. Long enough
to know I don't need one.

Andre
Enough

Mourning.

Enough.

Crying.

Enough.

Lamenting
what can
never be.

Enough.

Eulogizing.

Enough.

Second guessing.

Enough.

Apologizing
for what you
cannot change.

Play It Safe?

That's my middle name. Wait. Okay,
my other middle name.
Andre Marcus Play-It-Safe Kane.

Can't in good faith add the III to that.
Gramps never played
it safe. And neither did my father. So where

did I get it from? Maybe from observing
how taking chances
sometimes leads to failure. Neither Gramps

nor Dad hit the jackpot every time. Win some,
lose some. The concept
is integral both to innovation and speculation.

I mostly choose the path of least resistance.
Not because I'm lazy.
But because I hate to lose. Probably why

I hung on to Jenna for so long, even though
I knew our relationship
was doomed. Not because of her father.

But because I tried to put her up on such
a high pedestal. Obviously,
Jenna is afraid of heights. I hope she finds

the courage to stand on the pinnacle one day.
She deserves to be there.
But she has to learn to make the climb solo.

Speaking of solos, I have some rehearsing
to do. Shantell and I rocked
it as a couple. But the second audition is all

solos. If I don't want to fail, I'd better put
in some hours with
Liana. I'll need my parents to help me pay

for those lessons, so it's confession time.
I have to quit playing
it safe eventually. Might as well be today.

The Wake

Is officially over, except for the food part.
Death and hors d'oeuvres
never did make much sense to me as a pairing.

Still, I ask Shantell, "Hungry? Looks like
a pretty nice spread."
A long line has formed for the food tables.

> *Think I can skip it,* she says. *But we should*
> *go say good-bye to Cara.*
> The family stands at the far end of the hall.

Shantell and I join the receiving line, which
rivals the food line.
"Did everybody in town know him or what?"

> *Apparently, nobody* really *knew him. Except*
> *maybe those two.* She points
> at Tony and Vanessa, who comfort each

other as only two people very much in love
can. I hope to know love
like that one day. Love you can't help but notice.

Cara

Love

Is

a curious thing. Sometimes
it barrels into you, leaves you
breathless. Other times, it comes

in-

to your life, a tentative beam
of morning sun sneaking
through the blinds, and you think

this

light isn't possible. The shutters
are drawn. Night should linger
on. I don't feel like waking. Yet the

room

comes slowly lit. Sleep slithers
away, and at last you can no
longer deny the dawning.

The Funeral Mass

Is tomorrow. Mom allowed Dad to reclaim
his Catholicism long enough to bury his
son. One hour at the church. Fifteen minutes
at the cemetery, and Conner will be left

to the will of the earth—and God. The wake
is winding down. The food is mostly gone,
and so, mostly, are the mourners. More than
I expected came to pay their last respects.

A few stragglers come late to talk to me
privately. Kendra looks horrible, like she's
forgotten food. She leaves her mother's side
just long enough to say, *I can't believe*

he's gone. I always kind of thought
we'd have another chance. But deep
down I guess I knew that was wishful
thinking. Just . . . not . . . like this.

We hug, as we're supposed to do.
I watch her go, leaning on her mother,
wonder if she'll be around next year, or
if she might wind up starved, in a coffin.

Sean walks by with Aubree. I expect
a smirk. Instead he offers a genuine
smile, and I don't see anger in his eyes.
More something like . . . regret.

Finally, as the room empties almost
completely, Vanessa and Tony approach.
"Thank you so much for coming, and for
your words. I think we all took them to

heart." Meaningless banter. But they
are strangers. What else can I say? That
I am sad they knew my brother better
than I did? Better than our parents did?

Vanessa looks ready to turn away, but
Tony stops her. *We have something to
tell you. Something you might want
to know. We were on the challenge*

with Conner. He was okay at first.
I mean, as usual, he was far out
in front of us most of the way. But
then he stopped taking his meds.

Things started going downhill.
He was edgy. Then, the last night
before the climb, they gave us letters
from home. After he . . . uh . . .

Vanessa and I found this, out in
the desert. I think it drove him over.
He hands me the letter my mother
wrote that night. And it is folded into . . .

. . . a perfect paper airplane.

Author's Note

Daily, we are bombarded with messages telling us we aren't good enough. We're too fat. Too thin. Too stupid. Too ugly. Our body parts are too little. Too big. Too bumpy. Too hairy. (Or if you're a middle-aged man, not hairy enough.) It's important to understand that those messages come from all the wrong places. From companies who want money to make us "better." From people who want to take advantage of us; who are jealous of us; who feel better about themselves by making others feel unworthy.

Perfection is a ridiculous goal because there is no such thing. The definition of the word is subjective—it means different things to different people. The same person who is ugly in one estimation is beautiful in another. You've heard it before, but I want you to believe that real beauty is what you are inside. If you were my child, I would counsel you to invest your energy crafting inner beauty, because your outside will never please everyone anyway.

I was the chubby kid who suffered peer abuse. I had a bump on my nose (still do) and thought it made me ugly. I spent too many years hurting because I believed the mean things other kids said about me. But I refused to let their words make me become something I wasn't. And I blossomed inside. Finally one day I looked in the mirror and thought, Wow, I'm kind of pretty. My high school friends will tell you I was kind of pretty. I had lost the "chubby," but that isn't why. It was because I learned to let my inner light shine through. And so can you.

If someone only likes you because of the way you look, that someone isn't a friend, and definitely shouldn't be someone you want a relationship with. (Do you really want a guy to like you only because you've got big breasts? Or flip that. Do you really want a girl to like you only because you've got big muscles—I won't say what kind!?) There is a certain power in outer beauty. But if you possess great outer beauty and use it in the wrong way, it can come back to haunt you. Witness Jenna, in this book.

What we all strive for, ultimately, is love. You won't find real love because you're beautiful on the outside. It is drawn to inner beauty. Spend your energy crafting that, and you will know true love.

Some Statistics

- Anorexia and bulimia affect nearly ten million women and one million men (primarily teens and young adults) in reported cases in the United States, and both can be fatal.

- Anorexia nervosa has the highest premature fatality rate of any mental illness. At least one thousand people die every year from anorexia.

- The average age of sufferers is dropping rapidly (as young as elementary school), with peak onset among girls ages eleven to thirteen.

- It's estimated that another twenty-five million people suffer from binge eating disorder.

- Although teens make up just two percent of cosmetic surgery patients in the United States, these numbers are increasing. According to the American Society of Plastic Surgeons, the number of procedures performed on kids aged thirteen to nineteen nearly doubled to 244,124 between 2002 and 2006.